BANGALORE CALLING

Brinda S. Narayan has worked for fifteen years in the corporate sector. She holds a BA in Economics from Wellesley College and an MA in Communication from Stanford University. She currently lives in Bangalore.

Bangalore Calling

BRINDA S. NARAYAN

First published in 2011 by Hachette India
An Hachette UK company
www.hachetteindia.com

SRD

ISBN 978-93-5009-219-4

Hachette Book Publishing India Pvt. Ltd
4th and 5th Floors, Corporate Centre,
Plot No. 94, Sector 44, Gurgaon - 122003, India

Typeset in Nebraska 11/13.5
by InoSoft Systems

Printed and bound in India by
Manipal Technologies Limited, Manipal

MIX
Paper from
responsible sources
FSC™ C043100

For
Amma and Appa

More than once, a society has been seen to give way before the wind which is let loose upon mankind; history is full of the shipwrecks of nations and empires; manners, customs, laws, religions – and some fine day that unknown force, the hurricane, passes by and bears them all away.

- Victor Hugo, *Les Miserables*

Contents

Contents

Over Curry Dinner

The cafeteria jibber-jabber dwindled into a classroom hush when agents streamed in after a tea break. Yvette Pereira leaned on the trainer's desk in Room #3 and scanned a list of names to link with the approaching faces. When she looked up, they were shuffling to the desk chairs.

It was only the second session but she could spot them already – the two or three likely to cross over, adopt tedious Americanisms shrugged off even by emigrants to the US. The Bengali chap for sure, the one with the annoying bangs, the pockmarked Tamil boy, and that woman – she couldn't tell if she was Malayali or Tamilian – yes, the rabbity woman would soon acquire the talons of a bald eagle.

Yvette was in some ways spawning this falseness, this abject wanting to be *them*, but she tried to check excesses.

At least this group was on time. The rest retained a disregard for trainer instructions and class times, an Indian trait she'd gladly stamp out. She launched into the American idioms session without waiting for stragglers. Her voice, like her appearance – starched salwar, tightly braided hair, carefully centred bindi – was stiff: 'Class, I've told you this earlier. You guys have to be on time, always. Remember, for Americans, time is money. This afternoon we'll work with American idioms. I'll call out some expressions and I'd like you to guess the meanings. Let's start with *off and on*.'

Many hands shot up amidst cocksure 'Me, Ma'am's. Yvette picked the rabbity woman, her hand uncertainly angled behind another agent. Thrust into the spotlight, the campus recruit lurched forward. Yvette hoped she had the right answer.

'That's like when a switch is turned off and on?'

'No, that's not right. The whole point of an idiom is you don't interpret the words literally. *Off and on* means *now and then*. Next, *read between the lines*?'

This time, Yvette chose the pushy Bengali know-it-all in the last bench. In distinct Bong tones, his hair flopping over his face in uncombed waves, he surprised Yvette with his response.

'To understand what is not said?'

'Yes, that's excellent. It means to grasp what is not directly stated. Class, you must learn these idioms or you'll mess up on calls. With one of our earlier agents, a customer said, *"I'll take a rain check on that"* when an agent offered a new package. You know what that means, right? The American wanted to postpone the decision. And the agent responded, *"Great, can I go ahead and sign you up*

2

now?" I need a volunteer to read out this paragraph with italicized American expressions.'

The Tamil boy, eager and unaware of native cadences in his speech, pitched into the passage. 'I just *got canned* from my job so I really need *to cut corners*. I think I just *got carried away*, you know with the internet, cable TV, etc. Then, I bought myself *some new wheels* last year. I guess I just *got in over my head* and tried to *bite off more than I can chew.*'

'Good. Now I'd like all of you to start using these phrases. Will two of you volunteer to role-play using *out of the question* and *come through*?'

Two agents, both boys, shaving nicks visible on their thrust-out chins, moved to the white board.

First agent: 'I don't want to join the call centre.'

Second agent: 'Why are you simply *out of the question*?'

First agent: 'Call centre job doesn't *come through* for me anyway.'

Yvette sighed. She had miles to cross with this group. But syntax could be taught. She was more worried about the Bengali-English and Tamil-English. Accents were harder to reform. She knew: this was her twelfth training batch and it hadn't become any easier.

Recruits, recruits, recruits thronged the centre. It was a busy training season. Large numbers of young men and women, propelled into sudden and awkward adulthood, moved in and out of four Callus training rooms. And the trainers, all four submerged in session after session – accent modulations, linguistic switches, cultural briefs, condensed histories – were wizards who transformed raw material from Indian metropolises and small towns into a savvy global workforce. Despite the large numbers and unremitting work, Yvette could pick out the tiresome wannabes from the ones who'd hardly change.

It was the same batch, the twelfth batch during their last session. After fourteen days of training it was hard to recognize the group. The diffident woman now flaunted a false brashness. The Tamilian flung his American *r*'s with the spunk of a novice soldier. Only the Bengali belied her good judgment and remained staunchly, almost obstinately, Bengali.

The last session was always boisterous. The session that triggered their chameleon colours, mutations from Ashok-to-Ashley, Seema-to-Samantha, Jaswant-to-Joshua. In spite of eight months at the centre, the trainer felt a vague unease at the agents' eagerness to adopt American names. She expected or even hoped for a redeeming timidity, a tremulous shedding of 5,000-year-old baggage. But the new generation, impatient go-getters, reached for new selves with a gusto that didn't seem right somehow.

Someone called it a christening. 'Aye, this is fundoo, dah, I'm going to be Tom Crooz.'

'Ramanathan can be Ramone,' smirked another.

'What about Sanathanalakshmi, man? Santa? And her last name, Claus?'

'Good one, imagine saying this is Santa Claus speaking, how can I help you?'

'Hey, Krishnan Kutty can be Christopher Kutty. Awesome no, Kris to Chris?'

'Dude, where's your frontier spirit, dah? You should adopt a wild west name.'

'Yah, what is that country singer called? John something?'

'Denwer, man.'

'Not Denwer, Denver.'

Yvette's voice, raised like a school teacher's to reinstate order, was drowned by shrill hoots and whistles. When the sounds finally subsided, she asked trainees to confirm their name choices for Callus ID badges. It was the CEO's brainwave to print American names below Indian ones on laminated cards. 'This will reinforce their belonging to the customers' world,' Sashwath had said in a meeting with trainers. Yvette wasn't so sure.

It was disturbing in food lines, amidst the clatter of steel trays, to collide with ex-trainees: people who once sported modest braids and regular clothes greeting her with punk hair colours, studded belly buttons and an unnatural fondness for *their* food. 'Hate this cafeteria food, ma'am. Like only pizzas and burgers now.' More than anything else, it was their affected use of American phrases:

'No class tomorrow?'

'No way.'

'Awesome, man. Let's horse around.'

'Don't be a bummer.'

As agents continued to baptize themselves, Yvette's eyes roamed across the Bangalore classroom, across laminated pictures of the Golden Gate Bridge and Washington Monument, across mounted maps of the United States and clocks set to Atlantic, Mountain and Pacific times. Rollicking squawks emerged from other training rooms. 'I will be Sally, ma'am.' Sally was a hot pick with women as was Joshua with men.

She heard Akriti, a fellow-trainer, endorse Pamela: 'Call yourself Pamela Anderson – wouldn't that be wild? Guys will go ballistic.'

Fellow-trainers didn't share Yvette's concerns. To them this was just a job. In fact, Akriti was exalted by the training mission. 'It feels like a great service to transform vernacular types. These kids, especially South Indian ones, lack polish. They're lucky to get trained like this. And think of the big picture, Yvette. With accents like this, they'll make it to Bodmas.'

That was the other thing that bothered Yvette. There was no loyalty or commitment. Agents at Callus yearned for one thing only: to springboard from the smaller company into Bodmas, the largest Indian call centre, with a dazzling city campus and offices in twenty countries. Each week, talk about the other centre grew more fanciful: 'Bodmas is the ultimate, twenty percent hikes, guru. Year on year.' 'Massage parlour, dude. At any time, for free.' Everyone agreed getting in was tough. 'Need a bloody good accent. Perfect English, super Maths scores. Easier to get an American visa.'

Scrub, fuss, scrub, fuss. Yvette hadn't ever seen her mother do anything else.

'OCD. Obsessive Compulsive Disorder,' said the psychologist. 'She's obsessed with cleanliness and is compelled to clean and clean. It's not rational, she cannot stop herself.' He suggested therapy first, pills later.

Earlier Yvette had wished for many things: she wished

for a more Indian name, something Hindu like Kavita or Asha. She wished her mother wore saris like other mothers, not absurd knee-length dresses. And wore her hair straight, long and black rather than in cropped, grey curls. She wished they went to Gujarati garbas, not waltzes at the Anglo-Indian Railway club. But now she'd put up with anything if Maureen stopped scrubbing again and again at the germs, the muck and 'all that Indian filth' in their sterile Anglo home. OCD, Yvette wanted to tell the psychologist, in sanitized, western countries was one thing. In a city overwhelmed by piles of dirt and the mess of new construction sites, it was intolerable.

Her aunt thought it was her father's death at the station – there were rumours he'd jumped onto the tracks – that did it. Yvette, who had inherited her father's pinched face and beetle eyes, suspected her mother's compulsions had driven him below those grinding wheels.

The trainer herself was careful not to tread on her mother's obsessions. Adopting an unmistakably Indian custom, she removed her shoes at the shoe rack outside the threshold. 'Don't you dare bring that Cantonment mud in,' her mother exclaimed each time. Even when Yvette stripped her sweaty socks and slunk in on smelly toes across the recently mopped living room, it was difficult to elude an ever-watchful Maureen who leapt up for the umpteenth time with a wet mop and plastic bucket: 'See your toe-marks on the floor? Filthy.'

Since her spouse's death, Maureen had become more finicky. Puckering her soft, pudding cheeks, she said the sink was dirty: 'Germs in the water, so disgusting.' Other days, the floor: 'Grimy footpath dirt.' One day the maid's hand-washing: 'Low-caste Hindu doesn't know how to wash.' Yvette bought a machine, a Samsung washing machine, but when the clothes came out twisted and wrung, her mother said the detergent wasn't strong enough. 'Doesn't smell right.' Her dresses and stringy stockings spun through four heavy-duty cycles.

Despite Maureen's efforts, dust mites swirled into their rooms and settled in spidery whorls on the bead curtain separating the living room from the kitchen, on the low altar with framed pictures of Jesus and the Virgin Mary, on the cane show-case with a plastic Big Ben, on a 1976 desk-top calendar with British cattle breeds – their Railways flat mimicking unseen English cottages. 'Even cows there,' said Maureen knowingly, 'give clean milk.'

Outside the house, plain-faced Yvette merged with the city's muck. People rarely stared at her rat face the way they did at lighter-complexioned Maureen, who scurried on stocky legs and dimpled knees to the Nandini milk booth behind their flat, her powdery curls bobbing, her button nose and button lips muzzled by a small pink hand. Instead of dresses, the trainer wore salwar kameezes or churidars, and sometimes jeans. Her hair, long like a traditional Hindu girl's, was plaited. She was rarely seen without a bindi.

The cane show-case, Maureen decreed, was not 'good enough' to display Yvette's American souvenirs. The trainers had travelled to Springfield, Illinois, to be trained by real Americans. After a three-week orientation they were to teach American culture with the assurance of those who'd seen the real thing: life, liberty, happiness in the original setting.

The city they visited was the same one Lincoln had lived in. Then they had log homes, iron stoves; now they had Lincoln tours. The five Indians pored over brochures in the hotel foyer. *'To this place, and the kindness of these people, I owe everything'* – Lincoln's words inspired a plethora of tour choices to revisit his Springfield life. 'I'm sure we don't do any such thing for Gandhi,' said Mani Muthanna, a stout, middle-aged Team Leader who accompanied the four youngish trainers. 'We have to give it to these Americans, they can market, package anything.'

Lincoln tours were pushed to future weekends. They were expected to be ready at 8:45 a.m. the next day for their first training session. Akriti, who wasn't jet-lagged like the others, rented a cab to an outlet mall. The rest explored the hotel carefully picked out by Callus. Not too far from the historic centre and close enough to the training site, it was, by American standards, cheap. They didn't know that then, not on the first day when they explored every nook and corner with an enthusiasm reminiscent of school picnics: the grim lobby with faux-wooden steps and white potted ferns, the breakfast room with tiled floors, cane chairs and wooden tables thrown together as if the mix-up was intentional.

The five Indians shared two rooms: the two women, Yvette and Akriti, in a single with an extra cot, the three men in a double with an extra cot. Optimal room rents with extra cots were diligently computed by Callus accountants on the premise that 'Indians can squeeze into any space.' Akriti, who claimed to be a 'trainer-cum-counsellor' was miffed at sharing her room. 'Can't believe they're so cheap. At Bodmas, all levels get singles.' Returning late at night with five shopping bags, her pixie face was unmoved by thick quilts on poster beds, fresh flowers – hyacinths, dahlias – and spotless baths with scented towels. Taller than Yvette, she quickly claimed the plastic shelf under the bathroom mirror where she laid out an expansive makeup kit. This was her second trip to America, she said. 'Guess this place would impress people who haven't seen better stuff.' She waved her eyeliner absently at Yvette. 'When we came to Florida, we stayed in this really, really awesome place. America is an awesome country, but this is not *real* America. Look at the wallpaper – so tacky.'

The breakfast spread the next morning – three kinds of juices, five kinds of cereal, boiled and scrambled eggs, breads and pastries, make-it-yourself waffles – overwhelmed the greenhorn travellers. Stuffing plates with a 'little bit of everything' they paid scant attention to time. Their American trainer had been waiting in the foyer since 8:40 a.m., vexed and very impatient.

'Welcome to America,' said Natalie when they straggled to the front desk by 9:15 a.m. 'You guys are *late.*'

'We're so sorry,' replied Akriti, startling Yvette with her sudden American accent.

'I can see we already have a cultural difference here,' said Natalie, much older than Yvette had imagined. She had too many freckles on her white-pink skin, her hair frizzled and untidy. 'Did you know we were starting at a quarter to nine?' she asked.

'Yes, they said 8:45ish,' said Akriti, the self-appointed team spokesperson.

'Did they? Well, in American parlance, we would never meet at 8:45*ish*. We're very precise about timings here. And that's one of the first things you guys need to learn. You are going to, after all, train others to be American.' Delicate lines above her cheekbones didn't quite crease when she laughed.

While Natalie pulled up in a wagon to transport them to the training site, Akriti unsnapped her crocodile leather bag and yanked out a Springfield scarf and lip gloss. Pouting her lips in a pocket-mirror, she glossed them shell-pink. On the way, Natalie earnestly pointed out Springfield landmarks, rapidly recovering from her earlier petulance. She pointed out the Lincoln-Herndon Law office – a red brick building with several white windows and doors.

'You do know who Abraham Lincoln is, don't you?' asked Natalie.

'Yes, yes,' replied Akriti, eager to make an impression on the American trainer, 'the first black President.'

'Well, not exactly,' said Natalie.

'No, man, he freed slaves,' said Yvette quickly.

'But he was black, wasn't he?' persisted Akriti.

'America hasn't had an African-American President yet,' said Natalie, rattling the wagon over a sudden kerb.

'You have someone contesting the Democratic ticket, don't you?' said Yvette.

'America is a democracy,' said Natalie. 'Anyone can contest anything. So, I guess, you don't know too much about Lincoln, do you?'

Yvette remembered a play at school and the lead actor's line: *You can fool all the people some of the time, and*

11

some of the people all the time, but you cannot fool all the people all the time – he said that, didn't he?' The rest of the play eluded recall.

'Really? I haven't heard that one,' said Natalie. 'Anyway, you guys are going to get a dose of American history this morning and over the next couple of weeks.'

The trainers were excited, anxious, jet-lagged on their drive through downtown Springfield – cobbled pavements, baronial buildings – everything scoured and spring-cleaned as if a monster Maureen had been at work here.

The objective of the training, said Michael, the head-trainer, was to impart condensed versions of American history and culture. And highlight accent issues with Indian agents. Trainers would be taught modules they would impart in Bangalore. Michael himself was distractingly handsome, a blond Shah Rukh Khan with a floppy grin and arresting dimples. Akriti rapidly shifted her smitten eyes and tiresome parroting to the more compelling head-trainer.

Pictures of bone-weary Europeans alighting from ships flashed on the screen while Michael described the arrival of the first English colonists during the late 1500s and the growth of the Anglo population to more than 275,000 by 1700. The colonists, said Michael, were characterized by their ethic of hard work, their zeal for education and their disdain for class differences. Mani whispered: 'Obviously angrez who came to India were a different sort.'

'Weren't there people here already before the Europeans arrived? Red Indians?' asked Mani loudly.

'Er... yes,' said Michael, his face suddenly flushed. 'We call them Native Americans.'

'People with long hair and feathers on their heads? Where have they gone? We hardly see them on TV?'

'Many died,' said Michael. 'The few that remain are confined to reservations. I believe the current Native American population is about 2.8 million.'

'How much was it earlier?' asked Akriti, riveted by her own intonations and the effect of her curly, American 'r's on the 'he's-so-cute-yaar, just-like-an-actor' trainer.

'Good question,' said Michael, beaming kindly at Akriti. 'There are debates about the original number and I'm not sure if there's a consensus. But we do know large numbers of Native Americans have been killed in conflicts with Europeans as well as by Old World diseases. The majority live today in California, Arizona and Oklahoma.'

'Good thing we were so many people, if not saale angrez would have finished us off as well,' muttered Mani.

Michael objected to the use of non-English speech inside the classroom. 'You have to dissuade agents as well from speaking in Indian languages. Remember they can't do it on the phone. So, we were talking about the decimation of the Native Americans, weren't we? Of course, there were also issues of miscegenation.'

'What's that?' asked Akriti.

'Intermingling of races that produces mixed-breed children.'

'Oh, like dings?' she asked.

Yvette shuddered; the woman was tactless. Wasn't she aware that her own roommate was Anglo-Indian? Of course, Yvette hadn't declared her origins and neither had Akriti; it wasn't relevant to their Callus work. Perhaps Akriti thought she was Syrian Christian or, more likely, she hadn't thought about her at all.

'What are dings?' asked Michael.

'It's a demeaning word like *nigger*,' said Yvette. 'We don't use it anymore.'

Twelve days later, driving back from the training to the motel, the team was severely homesick, all except Akriti. As they passed spotless suburbs, strictly trimmed hedges, weedless lawns, look-alike front-yards of look-alike houses, Yvette missed the deformities and disfigurements – the gunk and gook and gutters, betel stains, potholed roads, reeking garbage, sooty emissions and more than anything else, the crush of brown faces jostling on Bangalore roads.

In the room that night, Akriti planned more mall visits before their departure. Yvette looked out at the Japanese garden outside their room: overgrown bamboo trees, a bamboo bridge arched unevenly across a dried-up puddle and a large stone lantern, unlit, discoloured by mould. Her thoughts seesawed between her Springfield surroundings and her muddled childhood, her desperate attempts to blot out her mixed-up roots in cosmopolitan Bangalore. As trainers they were expected to purge mother tongue influences in agent speech, soften *t*'s, curl *r*'s and sever *v*'s from *w*'s. Yvette wondered if the changes

14

would stop with sounds. Would she birth a population of half-breeds, counterfeits and shams, who belonged neither here nor there? Natalie had played snippets of *My Fair Lady* in their class and of course, everybody loved Professor Higgins, witty, pompous, endearing. Eliza's guttural sounds, her coarse lower-class speech evoked loud chortles from the group, but what about her angst after the ball? They hadn't watched that scene but Yvette had seen the movie five times back in India. How would agents cope without a messianic Rex Harrison to anchor their new selves?

She pitched her thoughts, half-formed and unsure, to her roommate, who squashed her qualms with a dismissive, 'Yvette, just chill, okay? It's just a job, what's the big deal really? An American accent sounds better anyway. Besides, just think of the *money*.'

'Did you know I'm an Anglo-Indian?' asked Yvette suddenly.

'Really? How sweet! I had this middle-school teacher who was an Anglo. She always had holes in her stockings. We used to crouch below our desks to spot them.'

Sweet was a word Akriti used often; what aggravated Yvette was not the word itself but the patronizing note in her voice. A note more aggravating than Natalie's condescension on their second training day: 'You're on time today. So I guess you are learning our culture.'

When she turned to Akriti now, Yvette's tolerance was worn thin: 'I'm not sweet, Akriti, and I don't care about your middle-school teacher because I'm tired of being stereotyped and linked with the only other Anglo-Indian you've encountered in your life.'

15

Akriti, who had been patting her neck with a powder puff, dropped her shiny compact, and Yvette couldn't read her expression when she scrambled to pick it up. When she emerged from behind the bed, she looked wary. 'Yvette, I didn't mean anything. You take everything too seriously.'

'All my life, I've been fleeing your stereotypes, talking and dressing like everyone else. And now we're asking agents to fake accents and fake their ease with another culture. I know there are salaries, but are they paying for this – for messed-up identities?'

'You know what I think? You're just too serious. You need to relax.' Creasing her forehead in the mirror, she widened her eyes as if she'd just discovered something more significant. 'I hadn't realized that Audrey Hepburn was sooo cute. Even those retro hairstyles, I mean they suit her so much.' Carefully combing her hair into her eyes, she tripped out of the room with a distinctly American 'I gotta go, see you later.'

Twelve months later, the Springfield experience seemed unreal, as if they'd never been there. Their training content, imported on slim DVDs, was identical: they showed the same videos, played the same songs and flashed the same slides. But the original trainers, the real Americans, had it easy. All four trainers had convent accents that adapted easily to American ways. Agents in Callus classrooms, emerging largely from lower-middle-class families, had studied in Indian-English schools. And they'd spoken during lunch-breaks and tea-breaks in Kannada, Tamil, Telugu, Konkani... in one of the many Indian languages whose echoes the trainers had to banish. At her sessions, Yvette toned down Callus requirements: 'Keep your pronunciations neutral, no need to fake American accents.' For some, this was easy, for others, childhood habits still lingered on in voices.

In Yvette's fifteenth batch, there was a joint session: Yvette and Akriti combining to teach a larger group. Michael had recommended co-training to keep agents interested. Yvette was awfully sleepy. The projector beam dotted her vision. Callus training programmes, held at bizarre hours to orient agents for night work, left trainers perpetually fatigued.

Akriti projected 'Key American characteristics' onto the board:

Americans:
Raise kids to leave home
Believe in right to fail
Believe they can recreate themselves
Are religious
Work hard
Believe in good and bad
Believe in continuing education
Believe they are going to get rich
Have love marriages

'Can we discuss these points? Let's start from the last one,' she said. 'In India, do most people have a love marriage?'

'No,' responded a loud boom of voices. 'Yes,' said a few.

17

'These days, mostly yes,' said Akriti. 'In modern Indian families, most people, you know, they find their own partners. Like me and my boyfriend, there's no way we'll have our parents pick someone for us. The whole concept, it's just so, you know, primitive.'

'I had an arranged marriage,' said one of the men. 'And I really like my wife.'

'Really? Doesn't it feel weird?' said Akriti. 'I mean, like…'

Yvette cut her short: 'There are so many good things about arranged marriages. In India, most of us are family-oriented, so it's important for families to feel comfortable with each other. It's also a great support system. In any case, we're not teaching you about American culture in order for you to become Americans. It's only to understand the psychology of callers and help you perform better on the phone. Why are we telling you this about Americans?'

'Because love marriages are better?' ventured an agent. Akriti beamed at the woman.

'No, no, we're not trying to pass judgments here. By the way, class, just because we say this is the American way of doing things, doesn't mean it's better. There are so many positive things about Indian culture.'

'Yvette, we need to move on to the next point,' said Akriti, tapping insistent fingers on the trainers' desk. Trainers couldn't disagree during sessions.

Yvette wasn't done: 'The reason we tell you all Americans have love marriages is to avoid questions when they announce a marriage. If you hear someone's getting married, don't ask if it's "love" or "arranged". They won't know what you're talking about.'

'Let's switch to a history module and come back to this later. Let's do the Baby Boomers,' said Akriti, swapping slides on her laptop. 'Did you know seventy-eight million Americans were born between 1946 and 1964? People born in that period are called baby boomers. Some of these customers will call you and you need to understand their history, their influences. I'll play a few songs for you first. These are *cool.*'

Akriti clicked on the audio content and played in succession *I Want to Hold Your Hand* by the Beatles, *The Sound of Silence* by Simon and Garfunkel and *American Pie* by Don McLean. While notes of 'Bye, Bye, Miss American Pie' wafted above their desks, agents tapped their feet and fingers. 'Aren't these so cool? I *so* dig the American sixties, don't you?' she said.

'I'd love to be a baby boomer. Their music is awesome,' said an agent.

'In India, we're all baby boomers. Each year, we have a baby boom and our music's cool too,' said Yvette, arresting the agent's wistful look.

'Yvette, man, you're one hell of an uptight person,' said Akriti offline when the session ended. 'Here I am, giving them a chance to be happening, learn the lingo, walk the talk and you keep interjecting with moral science lessons. Makes it boring. C'mon, ya, it's a global world, everyone has a choice, and they can be whatever they want to be.'

Next week, the Indian trainers were asked to dress formally for reviews by American mentors visiting from Springfield. Natalie and Michael were to sit in on live sessions and rate trainer performance. Trainer increments, promotions, even their survival in the company would be determined by these scores.

'You have to act as if we're not there. Treat us like a painting on the wall, an object. You mustn't be conscious of our presence,' said Natalie. She seemed more genial, friendlier in India, less brazen about her Americanness. As Yvette's reviewer, she was less unsettling than Michael who was still taken in by Akriti's Americanisms. The trainer-counsellor had, over the last four months, soaked up all the expressions: 'That's cool', 'All-righty', 'What a mess', 'It's a breeze', 'How awful.' She claimed such expressions were 'natural' to her. 'Used them before joining Callus,' she said with an annoying twang.

But review sessions were held back for a day. In an unusual departure from process, trainees were asked to take calls. A bizarre call surge triggered by bad weather in Texas.

'Bloody chaos on the floor, man, we need everyone, anyone who can speak English, to get on the phones. You have to stop training till we tide over this crisis.' Friday training was aborted. Michael and Natalie were taken aback. Americans, they contended, rarely broke rules like that. The operational fiat implied scant respect for training. But, in any case, they welcomed the respite and planned to wander around the city's sandalwood shops.

Yvette, who had moved that weekend to a new apartment, used the unforeseen break to enact a personal coup. She invited for dinner, that Friday, her three fellow-trainers and the two Americans to 'a sort of housewarming' at her new place.

This was the trainer's reward for so many tedious nights: a 1500-square feet penthouse in a red brick seven-storey complex with basement parking and gleaming steel lifts. It mattered little that the living room overlooked crisscrossing, rusting railway tracks or that the bathroom windows rattled every so often as engines rushed by. Maureen's gripes about the city's grime had been muffled by green marble floors.

Before her visitors arrived, Yvette ensured their home was immaculate; she couldn't have unforeseen stains or dirt setting off one of Maureen's cleaning attacks. A new teak showcase showed off her Lincoln memorabilia – she had brought home a Lincoln hat, a Lincoln brooch and an Abraham Lincoln coffee mug.

That night, fumes from the masala steak climbed in spicy whirls towards the warbling exhaust. Yvette's mother was a good cook, but the masala steak, historically toned down for English palates, was her chef-d'oeuvre. The spread included shepherd's pie, Indianized with cumin, ginger, cinnamon and garlic, mulligatawny soup and lemon pudding. The trainer bought two-litre bottles of Coke, Sprite and Mirinda and laid out glasses, knives, spoons and forks in the likeness of a peacock. Most gratifyingly, her mother had worn, at Yvette's urging, a sari. Despite her short grey curls and plumpish body, she appeared at least like other mothers. Maureen suggested they serve wine. 'Like the good old days,' she sighed, but they had only three wine glasses and buying another set for one night seemed extravagant.

The five guests arrived together, directly from work. They'd heard on the way, at traffic lights, Bangalore's popular radio channel, goofy RJ talk punctuated by peppy Bollywood songs. The Americans were impressed by Bangalore radio jockeys: 'Such refined accents, can't believe they've grown up here,' said Natalie, who wore a satiny purple salwar acquired from the shop inside her hotel. 'Indian fabrics are wonderful, your colours are so rich.' Freckles on her neck, fierce, brown dots on pink skin, gleamed under the raindrop chandelier in Yvette's living room. Maureen, dazzled by her white Anglo guests, shimmered in splendorous silk. 'We are very happy to have you over,' she said.

'Should we remove our shoes?' asked Akriti, stopping at the threshold in a small black dress. Yvette's heart skipped a beat. She'd have liked to shrug off the awkward shoe-removal with an American laxity but she was afraid of fresh grime evoking a startling response. 'Yes, yes, if you don't mind,' she said, and the group, already inside, stripped off shoes and sandals near the front door.

Akriti tugged Yvette aside and whispered: 'Yvette, your mother has really nice skin.'

A couple of hours later, the trainer was visibly relieved. The night had gone off without a glitch so far. For the first half-hour, everyone was carefully polite, but after the soup and authentic Anglo-Indian meal, they turned truly gabby. The Americans had brought a bottle of wine that Michael, with his easy grace, handed over to Yvette's mother. 'Thank you so much for having us over. Eating in an Indian home gives us so much insight into your beautiful culture,' he said. A courtesy that endured after the meal. 'That was wonderful curry.' Yvette blushed. She hoped her mother wouldn't expand on differences between Anglo-Indians and Indians, masala steak and curry – after all, to Michael they were uniformly brown and generically spiced. But her mother was tongue-tied. Entranced by his politeness, she arched her neck over his shoulder, preening herself for neighbours who might have sighted her fabulous visitors.

And later, Michael's wine served with dessert, in paper glasses, continued to boost spirits and diffuse cultural divides. Trainers grumbled about operational staff. Such folks, they agreed, were despicable across continents. Companies rarely recognized trainers, the backbone of the industry. They joked too about people. Yvette was startled by Michael's bawdy wit.

'How's that fellow doing?' Michael asked suddenly. 'The Team Leader fellow?'

'Mani Muthanna?' said Yvette, who had befriended the guileless 45-year-old after the Springfield trip. On the call floor, which Yvette sometimes visited, hapless Mani drifted from agent to agent, from the electronic call board to his monitoring screen, floundering in the clamour of voices.

'Yeah, yeah, same guy. All those questions on Native Americans. Natalie and I were like – *where* did he come from?'

At 11:30 p.m., Michael rose. He had a meeting the next morning with the Operations Manager. The Americans, though jetlagged, had adapted quickly to Callus timings. Amidst overlapping goodbyes – effusive American 'Thank you so much'es, 'Very nice of you to have us over's, succinct Indian 'Bye, Yvette's, 'Thanks yaar's – they hunted around absentmindedly for missing shoes and sandals. Perhaps her mother moved them to the cane shoe rack outside? No, they were not there either. The team even walked over to the balcony and peered behind pots and dusted chrysanthemums. This was strange. Yvette did not own a dog that could have stashed six pairs in an unknown hideout. 'We left them inside, I don't think anyone could have carried them off,' said Akriti.

Maureen was wiping moisture off dessert bowls in the kitchen. 'Ma, have you seen their shoes?' asked Yvette. And then she stopped. She heard the banging sounds of rubber thrashing against leather, soles flapping, spinning in sudsy froth. She whirled around towards the washing machine, whirring in the corner of their new kitchen. All six pairs – Michael's Nikes, Natalie's strappy sandals, Akriti's gladiators, Kuldeep's Liberty keds, Hari's kolhapuris – twisted and twirled in Samsung's fizzy Full-Load Extra Rinse. 'They were muddy, you know, and inside the house,' murmured her mother.

On Monday, Natalie was a silent observer at Yvette's session: 'Think of me as wallpaper,' she said, her leafy chiffon blouse reinforcing the image. Yvette began, like always, with caveats about training objectives. She hadn't planned to reprove hyper-Americanisms in Natalie's presence but strangely the Friday dinner and its difficult end had coarsened her senses. She'd steeled herself for all reproach. Of course, that morning, everyone had been exceedingly polite. Inside freshly-laundered shoes, they were professionals again, and did not mention their visit to Yvette's home. Only Akriti gave her commiserative glances.

'Class, we're not trying to make you Americans. That would be a disaster. There are just a few words you may

24

have to say the American way,' said Yvette. 'And this training is not the end of your learning. Tell me, how did you learn about Indian culture?'

'Naturally,' replied an agent.

'We grew up here, we know it,' said another.

'Yes, but you do NOT know everything about Indian culture, do you? Similarly, you have to keep learning about American culture as an ongoing process. And, by the way, America too is changing. Do you know, for the first time in American history, an African-American might become president? To keep up with all this, watch CNN, read blogs, watch Hollywood movies, log on to YouTube. And I'd like to add again, don't step out of this room trying to sound American. You have to watch for cross-over effects. What are cross-over effects?'

'When a person tries to cross over from one culture to another and does not succeed?' volunteered an agent.

'Yeah, kind of. What we're talking about here is "becoming more Catholic than the Pope". You have heard that saying, haven't you? What does it mean?'

'The Pope is the ultimate Catholic. No one can be greater than him,' said an agent.

'No, not exactly, it describes side-effects when one tries to over-imitate. You end up looking ridiculous.'

Yvette turned on a British documentary that depicted the vexations of cross-cultural communication. She glanced at a grim Natalie.

On the screen, an Indian immigrant walked up to a British social worker and tried to tell him about his woeful condition. Although eligible for unemployment benefits, he received none. The British social worker, a crisp communicator, asked the struggling Asian for facts

25

while the latter fumbled in a swirl of emotions, unable to structure his thoughts into brusque, to-the-point responses. Yvette looked at her training notes: *Stop Video. Discuss episode with agents. What should the Asian have done differently?*

Yvette switched off the video and asked the team, 'So what happened there?'

'Miscommunication,' answered an agent, brightly.

'Yes, that's right. But why was there miscommunication?'

'Indian is mumbling and so he can't be trusted,' 'Indian is very emotional,' 'The Indian is not clear in his communication,' agents responded eagerly, all at once, their voices more spirited in Natalie's presence.

'Okay, okay, I hear you. But, class, you have to learn to speak one at a time. This is a very Indian trait. We all speak together and interrupt each other. Anyway, to summarize our video, the Britisher was looking for facts. But Indians come from a low-content and high-context culture and do not go straight to the point. How many of you agree with this?'

All agents agreed. Yvette added, 'What could the British social worker have done differently?'

'Nothing,' replied an agent. 'He was just doing his job, he was rational.'

'Maybe,' said Yvette. 'But, perhaps, he could have been more empathetic to the immigrant's situation? Just think of the man, jobless in a strange country, and the Englishman is rather harsh, isn't he?'

Yvette moved on to the next module: American History, Part 3. 'Show Cowboy Scene,' read Yvette's training notes. She projected pictures of the American Cowboy. Strains

26

of *Home on the Range* evoked breezy Midwestern pastures inside the Indian classroom.

'Cool, man, cowboys are fundoo,' said an agent.

'You can't be one, man, won't get a visa,' retorted another.

'It's no big deal to be a cowboy. If I were you, I'd rather be an Indian cowherd,' said Yvette.

Natalie scrawled something in her notepad. Shortly after, she left the room and signalled for Yvette to meet with her later.

At the terrace canteen she studied Yvette's face before commencing her formal review. 'Yvette, do you like this job?' she asked.

'Yeah, I think so,' said Yvette, 'why do you ask?'

'You were a teacher earlier, weren't you? Did you prefer that?'

'No, not particularly. I mean I like both jobs, but this pays so much better and it's a nice office.'

Natalie nodded. 'In any case, my overall comment on your training performance is that you're capable but you seem to be holding back. Why are you so defensive about the programme?'

'I don't think I am,' said Yvette. 'Can you give me specifics?'

'Well, as a point of comparison, let me tell you how Akriti does it. She excites everyone about the training. She cites the advantage of a global accent in a changing world as well as knowledge about American history, other cultures. She really motivates the class. In your class, I feel agents are confused. You're introducing a coyness, a reserve about acquiring American traits. Why are you doing that?'

Yvette stared back at her mentor, silent. She wasn't dejected or anything. She had after all inured herself to rebuke, to censure of any kind. She excused herself for a minute – she spotted on her hand a small fleck, a mite of cigarette ash. She walked into the Ladies behind the canteen, the one that had washbasins with liquid soap. She turned on the Jaquar tap and washed her hands over and over and over and over again.

The Callus Demon

Waiting, waiting, always waiting, a life described by pauses. Yvette Madam late today, 2:05 a.m. and ten minutes late. Dark forms on the pavement, street dogs with heaving bellies. Bloody curs sound asleep while he struggled to keep his red-veined eyes open. He honked once, goading the dogs into rackety wakefulness. Two minutes later he whipped out his new Reliance mobile from a rexine bag below his seat and cautiously pressed ten digits, Madam's number. If he was late again, the office people would yell at him, not at Madam. But this Madam was all right, not like others – *whores*. She knew his name, spoke in Kannada. 'Pandu, *solpa* wait *maadu, aidhu nimisha.*' Five minutes later, no sight of Madam. Panduranga was anxious: 'Drivers only responsible.' That's what Nanjundappa said, his contractor boss. Rogue. He called again: 'Office scold Madam, fast, fast.'

She was the last pickup that night. A vegetable vendor nudged an empty cart under the plastic awning of the

Iyengar Bakery. On the wall facing an open drain, a man urinated across an election poster. A second honk, a shrill sound that ripped through the street's silence. The squirter, rattled, sprayed his liquid unevenly. A few metres away, a thin boy was perched on a ladder, black paintbrush in hand. Panduranga had seen him before, smudging English words on product billboards with ferocious blots. The night watchman – drunken dog, sleeping on the job – waggled a frail arm. In the Matador van, five riders were already asleep, necks twisted, heads askew, ears and minds plugged into portable players. A boy and a girl, sighted in the rear-view mirror, huddled in the back-row dimness, holding hands.

At last Yvette Madam arrived and Panduranga ignited his Matador to a jerky start. His Telugu bhajans roared from his personal Philips player. An incense cloud swirled above the dashboard, shadows darted on the van's bonnet.

Panduranga had bought the player from the Bangalore Burma bazaar, a market that traded in smuggled goods. Nanjundappa said he could not indulge drivers with car audio systems. 'You will put when engine is off. If you want, you get yourself.' Scoundrel claimed to make 'zero' profit, drove a Ford Ikon, re-painted his three-storey house and admitted his daughter into an English-speaking, pant-wearing college. And he called drivers *rascals*. The rascal himself had been a driver at one time. A driver for the famous Mr Basu, the big boss of the biggest, most famous company, Bodmas. Everyone in that company was made rich by the big boss, including the scoundrel. Who blathered to the Callus Admin Manager about other drivers: 'Sir, all these peoples are good-for-nothing rascals. I am paying 8,000 rupees salary plus overtime but they will still be complain. You don't time waste, sir, with these rascals, I will be manage.' Spat out lies with his drooling paan, his gold chain glittering on a hairless chest showing bare beneath his half-unbuttoned shirt. Villain doled out 5,000 rupees and measly overtime wages. But drivers cloaked their grievances in sullen silence. Varghese and other company insiders would never hear them out. Their lives rested in that rogue's betel-stained fingers.

Two front rows sniffled. Smoke clouds from scooters and night rickshaws seeped into the van. So fragile his van riders, they'd hardly weather the harsh roads he'd surmounted with his Srinivasa lorry.

Fifteen years on the Indian highways. By 35, he'd seen it all. Dogs pulped into stains, men mangled in steel, Amul hoardings uprooted – buttery-yellow, upside-down – instant deaths washed out by new rains. Panduranga was a real man, not wimpy like these coddled pickups. He was short, even by South Indian standards, a pygmy. But in his Andhra country, in his native village, he was a big man, thick-skulled villagers swayed by his Telugu spunk.

As the van careened past the rising steel rods of a new building, he recalled his lorry days. He'd driven on the Grand Trunk Road, scattered goats, thwarted dacoits, ferried sadhus, gathered black and red soils of places so different, almost like other countries. He skipped over the everyday diarrhoea and vomiting when he left rice-eating states. Or sealed bottles of toddy, his deliverance from sleepless days, checkpost bastards. After several road trips, he learned snatches of Hindi. But wilted like a woman at Bihari checkposts where hissing sounds hurled at Madrasis impaired his manliness. He shuddered even now at the memory of moustached bloodsuckers and their lewd Hindi jibes, scoffing, spitting at his permit papers; his pleas in tremulous Hindi, too soft, not guttural enough.

He jammed on the brakes, squashing his cringing shame with his right foot.

The driver's seat in Panduranga's *cab* – the company word for his Matador van – was a holy preserve, a refuge from the carnal ways of its occupants. An embroidered, beaded cushion to raise the seat, a plastic incense stand to the left of the steering wheel, Lord Ayyappan framed in white, a plastic Ayyappan dangler on the rear-view mirror, a mini-temple suffused in holy sounds from his Saregama CD. Godly vibrations to shut out unsettling images in his rear-view mirror, depravity worse than his lorry days.

First few weeks in his cab he'd been astonished by lesser things: young women venturing out at night, unescorted. Surely those houses, much bigger and sturdier than his, weren't desperate for *any* kind of income? If he ever had a home like that, with four rooms or five, he'd keep womenfolk home. Away from vile paws that strayed inside his van. He performed pujas on special weekends to wash out residues. Not just roaming hands, he'd seen more fantastic spectacles: lips smacking lips, sucking sounds blowing into the middle aisle. Rare sights, but he'd seen the hankering for wretched thrills.

Not everyone, not Yvette Madams, not front rows. But poisoned back rows, it wasn't just what they did, but how they dressed.

He used to think, in his lorry days, that the glass towers sprouting at the edges of the city were inhabited by shiny suits and gold-rimmed saris. Panduranga, in his full-pressed uniform and neatly combed hair, outshone raggedy back rows with torn jeans pants and unpolished shoes. He conferred often with other drivers on the *real* business, the bizarre purpose of the Callus company – what did they do with such people?

The driver closely watched his pickups but they rarely regarded him. Except for front rows like Yvette Madam. Only one time when a white woman entered the van, he had been noticed, remarked upon and even spoken to. When they had reached the IT Valley basement, he turned off his player while she dismounted. 'Thank you so much... er, what's your name?' she asked. Panduranga was taken aback. This big Madam talking to him?

'Panduranga,' said the foreigner's escort.

'Jeez, that's a mouthful. Is it Paan-doo-raangah?'

'Yeah – you're right, it's Paan-doo-raangah,' said the escort, alighting at the same time.

'Thank you so much, Paan-doo-raangah. That was a great ride,' the white woman said.

After that, every rider who alighted from the van, echoed the white Madam's words as if it were an everyday routine, 'Thank you so much, Paan-doo-raangah.'

❧

Saranam Ayyappa. Swamiye. Saranam Ayyappa. Harihara
sudhane. Saranam Ayyappa.

The chants reverberated through his gut as the cab skirted an unfinished flyover near the Airport Road junction. On his windshield, his son, unborn but already named, skipped across rubbery wipers, rascally and playful.

The driver had been reclaimed by Ayyappan after the birth of his second child: a daughter again, an unwanted birth. His mother, a strong woman despite her smallness, killed the baby – gently, decisively, with finesse. A few drops of yerakkam paal, the juice of the oleander plant, squeezed into the infant's mouth in place of the mother's milk. They respected her in the village, Chilakamma, a woman of quiet strength and unwavering wisdom.

These were tests, she told him, two daughters, tests of his faith. Look at Chandrababu, three visits to Sabarimala, three sons: the rules absolute, the gods constant.

Panduranga saw him already, his son, unlike the driver, a big-boned child with strong shoulders. A deliverer who resisted his father's transfer from lorry services to call centre transport. 'Less driving, more money,' Nanjundappa had said. He meant more driving, less money. Yes, his valorous boy would stand up to the rogue. Venkateshwara, his reprieve, would be born with Chilakamma's courage.

Each night, while the van wobbled across treacherous Bangalore roads, the driver petitioned Ayyappan, the wonder child of two male gods, with his mother's steadfastness.

Two months into his new job, he wore a garland of tulasi leaves. 'Sabarimala pilgrimage a must,' said Chilakamma. At the Jayanagar Siva temple, in front of two priests and his mother, he committed to ninety-nine days of purity in thought, word and deed: abstinence from meat and fish, from cutting or shaving his hair, and from lusty actions, licentious dreams. And vowed to wear for the next three and a half months, only black, a black lungi on a shirtless body. No beedis, no alcohol, no sex. Small sacrifices for a large payoff. He outdid Chandrababu, who commenced ritual surrenders forty-one days before the taxing Sabarimala pilgrimage in December or January.

The change in Panduranga's appearance – unshaven, long-haired, ash-smeared, shirtless, barefooted – was hardly remarked upon by other drivers. Each year, a few flouted workplace norms to abide by Greater Sanctions. But this year, his transformation, ahead of the Sabarimala season, was caustically seized at by the Callus manager, a piddling Maruti 800 owner and Christian to boot. 'Nanjundappa,' said Varghese, 'I know this is for Sabarimala and all but we keep getting foreign visitors here these days, many Americans. If they see him driving the van half-naked, they might get a wrong impression like we're not paying him enough or that he's a dacoit from the forests. They have stereotypes about Indians. At least tell him to wear a shirt.' Nanjundappa, ever obeisant, relayed the message. Panduranga resisted but a colleague, a regular on the pilgrimage, suggested he wear a black cloth wrapped across his back and shoulders, a compromise that would appease Ayyappan and Varghese. The driver bought another CD, Ayyappan chants by KJ Yesudas, the Christian singer-devotee of the Sabarimala god: a resonating, full-bodied voice that intensified Panduranga's immersion.

A few weeks later, the saboteur of his godly engrossment was a new passenger, an unwelcome entrant in his van. A veteran agent shifted from another van. A wild-haired hunk with long sideburns, frayed, sleeveless jackets and on his upper arm the picture of a fire-breathing beast – a dark purple drawing.

In a few days, Panduranga glimpsed the clod's fingers in the rear-view mirror, straying in repetitive motion along the legs of a permitting woman. Legs that rested on impossibly high wooden heels. To stall his own sinful thoughts, the driver skirted rear-view shows except when traffic conditions demanded attention. He also raised the volume on his CD player, the voice of Yesudas booming, the clangour of cymbals, the thunder of a thousand drums, the scaling notes of feverish devotion, *Swamiye Saranam Ayyappa, Ayyappa Swamiye, Swamiye Saranam Ayyappa,* the chants, faster and faster, louder and louder, drowning out the back-row evil.

The driver's real tribulations started a week later when the woman did not alight at her stop. He honked to urge her decent departure but she ignored the van's summons. Both she and the Rakshasa stayed huddled in unholy union, their hands linked till all departed. When the last rider left and Panduranga had only one stop to go – the Rakshasa's stop – they abandoned control. The woman climbed on the Rakshasa's lap, his hands hungrily groped her body, unbuttoned her shirt. The driver jabbed his van horn thrice, loud shrieks to trumpet his presence but they continued unperturbed, breathing hard, gasping. Panduranga hardly looked but was defiled by foul thoughts. Enraged by his wasted continence, he raised the volume of his Ayyappan chants, his player blaring while the couple fondled each other unabated. The van stopped. The man hurriedly zipped up his pants, the woman buttoned her shirt, patted her hair. They alighted and walked their separate ways.

For two weeks, they continued in the same wicked manner. The driver was no longer aghast when the woman did not dismount at her regular stop. And when all but the two were left, they kicked off their impassioned lovemaking, oblivious always to Panduranga's presence. The van rocked with full volume Ayyappan chants, washing out sullying sounds from the last seat.

The second week, he had the player fixed by a roadside *'All Electrical Items'* repairman to amplify his combative music.

Panduranga asked the other drivers during their nightly halts in the IT Valley basement for ideas to destroy the Rakshasa. 'Send to my van,' said someone. 'Free show better than cinema.' All sixteen drivers had time to kill between shifts; some played cards, some smoked, some rubbed against the latest girls in Kannada magazines. Sometimes they fantasized about magazine girls landing on van bonnets, voluptuous fleshiness to pinch and touch and rub against, plumper and juicier than their skeletal pickups. Other times, they spoke of driver salaries at Bodmas, that biggest, largest, most generous company. And the way drivers were treated there: free canteen lunches, take-home murukkus on festival days. Then someone would say, 'Varghese sir in lift,' bringing them back to the drip-drop of the pipes and the perennial blackness of the basement.

The Callus company rarely heeded their existence. Until the accident, a few days later, between a Callus van and a motorbike on Hosur Road. Another driver's van, not Panduranga's. The bike was headed the wrong way on a one-way street but the police charged Callus, a big company, capable of bigger bribes than a measly biker. Reports seeped into English papers, small columns into Kannada ones, about 'Big companies killing small riders'. Callus launched investigations into 'driver quality'. For the first time, the big bosses paid attention to the 'basement blokes' as Varghese called them.

Nanjundappa staggered into their presence, shirt open, gold chain flapping, betel-juice dribbling from his mouth. In a few minutes, the Admin Manager arrived.

'Does anyone work double shifts?' asked Varghese.

The contractor did not answer. He turned to the drivers instead: 'You be knowing rules no? Nobodies working overtime, correct? See that Rajappa, how he has made accident?' Such 'rules' hadn't been mentioned before. And it was the blackguard contractor who enforced double shifts. When the rogue blew his betel breath into the muggy basement, they could hardly speak up, not with his red eyes fixed on their faces.

'Sir, you don't worry. Nobodies working overtimes, no double shifts. I will take care.' The contractor always spoke in English in the presence of the Callus manager. But as soon as Varghese was swallowed by the basement lift, he retreated into Kannada and drew from his own language succulent curses to fling alternately at the drivers and the Callus manager.

After the accident, stickers printed in English were affixed on the back of each Matador van: 'If I am driving badly, please call 99443-23322' – the scoundrel's number. The drivers, the ones who read English, said the stickers were like cowbells, designed to warn the cowherd about straying animals.

The sticker was not the company's last word.

One night, a Lancer, a Biggest Boss, rode Panduranga's van. Drivers distinguished small, big, bigger and biggest bosses by the cars parked in the basement. Small bosses drove Maruti 800s or Maruti 1000s, big bosses Maruti Zens and these days Hyundai Santros, bigger bosses Maruti Esteems and Ford Ikons, while biggest bosses rode Mitsubishi Lancers and Honda Citys. The Biggest Big Boss travelled in a Mercedes Benz with a white uniformed chauffeur who acted in the basement like he belonged to a superior caste. Those who weren't bosses of any kind rode in vans.

The Lancer's presence in Panduranga's van was a sequel to the accident: surprise inspections of driver behaviour and van routes. Panduranga hoped to expose the tattooed Rakshasa and his corrupt doings, report his vulgar passions to the Biggest Boss but last-row high heels alighted at her own stop.

And more than anything else, the Rakshasa turned his attention to the Lancer. Not with roving fingers but with the same ooze and charm directed at high heels.

Panduranga could barely hear the words (though he turned down the volume on his player) but caught several 'Yes, sirs' and 'Absolutely, sirs' uttered by the lecherous voice. And as he listened more closely, he heard the word 'driver'.

'Can you comment on the driver's behaviour?' asked the Lancer of the filthy character.

'Uh… he's okay… there's only one issue… his music's too loud.'

Music too loud? Because of *him*, because of *his* obscene, foul presence. Unvoiced curses swelled inside Panduranga, almost bounced off his tongue but receded into seething wordlessness. The van shot across a speed-bump, knocking the Rakshasa off his back-bench perch. The Lancer looked up startled and flicked a tattling pen across his paper.

Panduranga expected a call from the rogue: 'Why are you driving badly with the big boss in the van?' But there was no such fallout. There was instead a ceremony. Varghese briefed Nanjundappa in the basement. 'We're using a carrot and stick approach,' he said. 'We plan to give badges to reinforce a sense of belonging to the company.'

A week later, in a rented marriage hall, with steel chairs and a velvet-curtained stage, drivers were invited to a special function with the company's Big Bosses.

At the ceremony, the Mercedes Benz was missing but three Lancers were clustered together in ties and suits, Panduranga's Lancer among them. To fellow-drivers,

Panduranga narrated the Rakshasa's latest doings, loudly so Lancers could hear but Nanjundappa had an eye on him. The contractor didn't like drivers talking near office people.

Varghese, who despite his bluster was a mere Maruti 800, pranced around the hall. Nanjundappa, stiffly buttoned in a safari suit, slapped the drivers' backs when the Lancers were looking. The Callus manager summoned Nanjundappa on stage. Velvet curtains parted to reveal a satin-pink backdrop, *Asha Weds Vijay* woven in dry marigolds, a string of withered mango leaves across the tasselled top. Drivers were called one at a time by Nanjundappa, since Varghese did not know their names, garlanded with a company ID card and ribbon that had *Callus–Callus–Callus–Callus* printed on the strip. Each badge had *Contract Worker – Callus* and the driver's name printed in English. Even Panduranga, taken in by the singular attention, forgot the muscle-man menace.

Shortly, the Lancers vanished and drivers were served samosas and gulab jamuns with tea. 'Need more accidents,' someone remarked. 'Or we'll remain in the basement, forgotten under leaking pipes.'

Panduranga prized the photograph: a Kodak imprint of his stooped head garlanded by a Lancer, framed in ivory-coloured plastic and mounted below the Ayyappan calendar in his mother's village home.

In two weeks, the accident was old news and the van's inhabitants reverted to their normal motions.

Until the 'hurricane' night when the Rakshasa invaded his zone, the cushioning sound of his CD player. When the man boarded that night, he linked lecherous fingers with another woman, a third row with blue lips, while his initial consort stared out of a front-row window, unfeeling on high heels. At first, the driver was gratified – a debauched woman duly punished.

But his head was ready to explode when the Rakshasa walked up from his back seat to the driver's seat before they reached the Callus campus.

'Hey, man, driver, can you please change that CD? We're sick of the same bloody noise every night. Can you put this on?'

'That I not put,' said Panduranga.

'Well, you have to, man, as employees we have rights. What's wrong with this bugger, yaar?' he said, addressing the back rows.

'No, I not put, that's all.'

'I will speak to the manager,' the villain said.

How dare he invade Pandu's personal player with his filthy sound? Panduranga raced at a livid 80 kmph for the rest of the journey, almost scraping buses, autos and two-wheelers on the busy night roads. He expected a major showdown at the workplace, a fierce battle. He had nothing to fear with Ayyappan the tiger-tamer to slay the beast. His wife was pregnant again. By the shape of her stomach, said Chilakamma, you could tell it was a boy.

He pulled into the basement and nothing happened. For the next eight hours, Panduranga waited, ready to strike or hit back but no one appeared, not the manager, not Nanjundappa. His phone did not ring either. He dreamt that night, inside his van, of his son astride a tiger, ripping out the Rakshasa's tongue.

After eight hours, the drivers restarted the engines for the drops and waited. There was always a throng of home-goers by 10:00 a.m. But this morning, even at 10:15 a.m., the drivers shifted between the neutral and first gears, and watched barren lifts go up and down, down and up, with no pickups inside.

At 10:30 a.m., Panduranga and another driver shut off their dawdling engines to investigate the no-shows. At the Callus reception, they asked to speak to the Admin Manager. Moron Nanjundappa had switched off his mobile despite a 24x7 service commitment with Callus. The receptionist, speaking to a friend from the many-buttoned, complex machine on her desk, waved them to cushiony leather seats to wait. Agents rushed in and out of mysterious glass doors. On a side table, English magazines with thin, glossy pages were laid out in a neat fan.

Shortly Varghese emerged from the glass door. 'What's up?' he asked the two drivers. 'Sir, no pickups coming, we are waiting in basement,' they said.

'Shit, you know, in all this confusion, I completely forgot you guys. Everyone's on an extra eight-hour shift so they'll be down only later this morning. You guys go ahead and have lunch,' he said, forking out a generous 500-rupee note. Drivers downstairs grumbled about the unexpected halt. They agreed jointly to demand from Nanjundappa a higher overtime rate. The 500 rupees were spent at a neighbouring dhaba. Panduranga did not like Punjabi food, more ubiquitous these days than sambhar-rice in Bangalore.

The riders finally arrived, with pink-red spangled eyes and high-pitched delirious voices. They flopped into their seats inside the vans. As Panduranga pulled out of the basement, he heard the word 'hurricane' several times. They called homes to confirm their release. They spoke about some 'Ike' who invaded the centre that night; many callers, who spoke these days like the white madam, reverted that night to Kannada. Someone mentioned a storm in America that resulted in a longer shift. In the turmoil the driver almost forgot his fracas with the Rakshasa. As he turned on the Ayyappan CD, he watched furtively in the rear-view mirror for back-row reactions. There was no movement till MG Road, a quarter of the morning's journey.

At the Trinity Circle signal, now weighed down with peak-time evening traffic, the man revived his obnoxious claims. 'Hey, man, driver, I completely forgot, didn't Varghese speak to you? We have the right, in this van, to play our own music.'

'I NOT PUT,' said Panduranga. His response, rehearsed for the last sixteen hours, sputtered like hot oil.

'Hey, dude, what do you mean, I've spoken to Varghese, okay?'

The signal was almost green. The engine rumbled into readiness. The Rakshasa called Varghese from his mobile. Panduranga waited, his breath stopped. 'Okay, that's fine, that's fine,' he heard him say. His opponent slunk into his rear-seat, rebuffed. Varghese had defended the driver's position. For Ayyappan faithfuls, anything was possible.

Panduranga defiantly raised the volume. Three minutes later, as the van skirted the shimmery-clean Ulsoor

Tank – recently dredged and re-filled – his mobile rang. It was Nanjundappa

'Why you are fighting with company peoples?' the contractor scolded him in English. 'Please put music which they want.'

'Sir, this my player. I not put,' said Panduranga. His mastery over English had, in the recent past, overtaken his proficiency in Hindi.

Nanjundappa responded in Kannada. Maybe the driver did not understand. The job or the music, he said. The choice was *his*. Panduranga switched off his mobile. Silence buzzed in his ears, louder than Ayyappan chants.

The CD was inserted. Profane, rocking sounds filled the van. He pointedly drove with one hand on the steering wheel and the other uselessly blocking one ear. Of course, the Rakshasa did not notice, entwined again with his new conquest. It was early evening, a time when surrounding auto-drivers, scooterists, bus drivers, beggars, magazine peddlers, peanut vendors peered into see-through van windows. The two remained in a lusty embrace as if cocooned in darkness. Shameless.

But Panduranga was angry now, angry with the Lord for deserting him, letting him down. When the couple departed he parked the van near the entrance to his lane and walked to the corner Krishna Bar for the first time since his temple pledge. How could Chilakamma tell by a stomach's cast the gender of an unborn child? Maybe it was a girl, a third daughter.

A Knock on the Door

Natalie disliked visitors on Sundays. Not that she had anyone knocking on her door, not on Sundays, not on any day if she were to be honest about it, but Sundays she liked being alone. If this were a hotel, she'd have hung a *'Do Not Disturb'* sign on the knob. As it was, there wasn't anyone to ruin her Sunday plans. But for the occasional domestic spats at 43A across the corridor, she was undisturbed.

She had set her Sunday alarm a half-hour ahead of her Monday alarm. Monday mornings were a blur: her lip-liner ran in with the gloss, her mascara smudged the eyeliner. But Sundays she dawdled near the mirror. As Bob said, for the Lord, no compromises, no second-class acts. It was miraculous the way He changed her Sundays from dreary laments about 'what could have been if Chris hadn't vamoosed with that tart' into a rapturous appointment with His Messenger on earth. Bob himself was modest about his assignment, called himself an agent, an emissary who carried The Word till the Lord returned.

She was careful with her makeup on Sunday mornings. She read *Allure* for tips. She used to read *Glamour* when Chris was around but not anymore. *'Seven Steps to a New You'* – she liked that, a process broken up like the telephone work at the Beam America call centre into easy, deliberate tasks. First the Prep: the moisturizer to open up pores. Like the greeting – 'Be polite,' she told agents – for the opening, after all, could diffuse tempers. And then the concealer: a few quick strokes on the puffy patches that ringed her eyes. She wondered if that woman, the scam artist who stole her man, concealed blotches. She quickly dispelled such thoughts with the foundation stick and Bob's scolding last week: 'Don't dwell on the past. For those of you born again into a New Life, it's over. Think of the future. Of tomorrow and possibilities.' Eyebrows, eyes, cheeks, lips and she was done. Her pearls, her brooch, her shoes, a gulp of coffee, maybe some toast and it was almost 9:50 a.m., almost time for Bob.

Dim morning light, filtered through the blinds, fell on the scant furniture: a futon couch with pink rosebuds, a glass-topped centre table from a Chinese furniture store, a rosewood rack for her TV. The rent was steep – $700 a month – for the tiny one-bedroom. Natalie would have liked period furniture, a Queen Anne table with scalloped shells, pleated curtains with tassels, a flowy feel to the place but her savings, post taxes, had been negative. Her boss muttered something about shrinking economies and tough market conditions but she hadn't seen that tightness cramp his life. She rapped her forearm to blot out the thought. Like Bob said, everything in her life sprung from her thoughts. She shovelled the week's clutter from the wobbly made-in-China table – a sewing kit with needles and buttons, her reading glasses, a nail file, a radio alarm, her paperback Bible, an empty root beer can, a box of half-eaten croissants, a bunch of bills – to the breakfast ledge.

At 9:55 a.m., she was on the couch, upright, not slouched, with the TV on mute – couldn't have some other channel's vulgarities corrupting her spirit. As Bob said, it was obscene and sinful, the stuff that went on in this country. Three more minutes, 9:57 a.m., she was on the right channel, #27 on her new cable, fifteen dollars more each month but a picture so clear she could spot the moles on his neck. She rose to twist the blinds shut and dissolve the triangular glint on the screen's right corner. She fetched the calfskin Bible from her bedside table, a generous reward for twelve monthly contributions. At 9:59 a.m., she was ready. Always on time, every Sunday, for the past two years.

'Greetings, America,' said Bob. 'I thank you again for joining me this morning. And for those of you who are with us the first time, I extend a warm welcome. It's not an accident you're here. It's God's will.'

Natalie inched closer. She was sure he had more grey in his styled bangs, another crease in the wide forehead. She could spot wear-and-tear, the weekly strains of running a ministry. It couldn't be easy to take on the entreaties of a million watchers, to intercede on their behalf with higher powers. Poor man hardly had time to shave. She could, if she looked under his chin, pick out grey stubble. Aaahh, there it was – the sign of an unsupportive wife, an inadequate staff, of too much resting on those wide, stooped shoulders.

His sermon started. He was reading aloud from some man's letter. 'Dear Bob: I have no words to describe what you've done for me. Last time I wrote to you, my wife had left me and I had no job. But after I sent my monthly contribution, God has been kind. Not only do I now have a job that pays me more than my earlier one, I've also found this wonderful woman...'

Natalie wondered when the man first wrote to Bob. Was it around the same time that she sent her letter? Was it earlier? Were prayers being answered in sequence? Did Bob not pray for everyone together?

He was thundering into his wireless microphone. In his black satin suit and red tie, the man was dashing in a way most pastors weren't. 'And he calls God kind? *Kind?* Ladies and gentlemen, God has given him more than he asked for – a glorious job, a higher salary, a beautiful woman, a wonderful woman and he's thankful but he has to be more than thankful – he has to cry out with his whole heart, and his whole soul, with every fibre in his being that God is not just kind, but generous, *too* generous, too magnanimous – remember, folks, when you give to God, God gives back more and more than you can ever imagine with your small minds, more than you can ever see with your small eyes.'

And then he lowered his voice, almost to a soft mumble, like he was letting them in on a secret. Natalie raised the volume. The reason, Bob said, this man was chosen for God's bounty was his unswerving faith in the Lord. The man had been faithful in his monthly payments, foregoing at times a personal expense or indulgence for a higher cause. The TV was at its loudest but he had dropped his voice so much, it was a faint whisper in her ear. She shifted closer. She felt he was talking *to her* – not to the studio audience glimpsed on the screen, not to some dispersed TV crowd but to Natalie and Natalie alone.

Just then her doorbell rang. An annoying buzz. On a Sunday morning? Didn't they know better? She ignored the intrusion, the breach of her Sunday peace, but the caller was relentless. She put the TV on mute and stomped to the peephole. No one there? The buzzer continued to shriek, hysterical like an ambulance siren. Was this Bob's emissary? Flushed, her hand trembling, she twisted the doorknob – and spied the two-feet-something 43A twerp.

'Yes? What is it?'

'Ma'am, would you like to support the Boy Scouts of America? We're selling some special popcorn this month, chocolaty caramel, butter light, gourmet caramel, cheddar cheese, regular butter, three-way...'

'No. And don't knock on my door on Sundays. Your parents should teach you better than that.'

'Yes, ma'am. Shall I come back tomorrow? It's eight dollars for the medium size.'

'No.' She slammed the door. What impertinence to send a pesky kid out on a Sunday morning! And during Bob's time?

She walked back to the TV, seated herself on the couch. He was reading from his Bible now. Fabulous, the way he came across those words, relevant words, key ones that addressed *her* concerns. 'I'm reading now,' said Bob, 'from 2 Corinthians 9:6. He which soweth bountiful shall reap also bountifully. Folks, think about that... He which soweth bountiful shall reap also bountifully.'

Yes, of course that was logical. That's what she loved about his sermon, everything so simple, so logical, the message reached her heart. Not like the fumbling pastor of her childhood, in that fussy Catholic church, an old man doddering behind his pulpit, ushers waddling with plates, the lady beside her drooling, a sermon filled with knotty, high-sounding words – so removed from Bob's transparent cathedral, snazzy chandeliers, neon signs, swirling stage, live band, shiny suits. God deserved to be entertained and more than anything else, explained.

'Folks, unswerving faith – that's what He deserves. To send in your monthly payment to God, please call us at 1-800-233-2323 or write to us at Ministry of Giving, P.O. Box 232312.'

She wondered what she missed when the 43A scout rang her doorbell. Had Bob noted her missing payments, her guilty defaults of October and December? She had her check book in hand to endorse her commitment before she changed her mind and her work-week disbelief crept in. It was hard sometimes to trust the Lord or even Bob when a sea of shouting voices demanded product returns or service discounts.

She stapled a small prayer request form to her check: *Dear Bob, I love your show, I love your sermons. I know you've prayed for me already, but I ask you to pray again. I'm still waiting for a good Christian man, an honest, faithful man. I know there's someone special waiting for me, but I haven't met him yet. Please ask God to bring him into my life and I will be eternally grateful to the Ministry of Giving. Please do not forget my special prayer.*

    P.S. I'm 47 – I trust God already knows that but you might want to mention it in your prayers.

Monday night. Natalie was writing another letter to Bob. She rarely watched weeknight sermons but tonight she needed it. She needed to look at his reassuring face, hear the certainty in his voice – her world, already teetering, had toppled over. The good Christian man, her future life-partner, significant as he would be, was no longer sufficient. Her job, her nearly thirty-year-old job at Beam America was on the line. It was almost like the end of the world was here and she was not ready. Not yet.

    'We're moving the call centre to Bangalore,' her boss had said. 'India,' he added, as if the word explained everything.

    Natalie hadn't been one of those women who expected life to work out. Freckled, brown-haired, dimpled with fat, she wasn't the object of any man's desire. Not at church, not at high school, not at work. 'Frumpy,' an aunt had remarked. Her father, a staunch Catholic, too drunk for church, rarely held a job. Her mother, absent, woolly-headed, relied on Natalie to keep the house humming. Unlike friends who got married right after high school, she gladly joined the telephone company as a call centre rep. The regular salary exceeded her moderate ambitions. In the company, not yet Beam America at that point, she steadily inched her way up. Not, as managers pointed out in frank appraisals, because of quick wits or well-honed skills but merely because of her presence. 'We appreciate your commitment,' they had said. Both above and below her, bosses and subordinates drifted into newer companies, bigger jobs, a shifting world where Natalie was a rare constant. Even the company had been sold, merged, split and sold again.

In such a life, Chris was an unforeseen entrant. After he left, she wondered why he'd singled her out. A fourth marriage for him, perhaps Natalie, a virgin at 43, was a sort he hadn't tried out yet? When that tramp spirited him off she'd have hardly sought a replacement if it hadn't been for Bob. The preacher uncovered everything, her submerged self, her latent desires, unexpressed needs and wants. There wasn't any reason why God shouldn't give everyone everything, no reason at all; limits, if any, were self-imposed. 'Sometimes,' Bob said, 'we're too harsh on ourselves. We stop asking for things. We imagine we should live without them. Why should we when whole wide worlds, the universe, the planets, the stars, the galaxies, all of God's creations are teeming with His Energy?'

Her writing pad on her lap, a glass of gin on the coffee table, Natalie watched Bob chat with a celebrity, some fresh-faced Hollywood actor she didn't recognize. Bob's Monday shows were distinctly different from his Sunday sermons. He knew his flock returned from a tired workday and could hardly deal with biblical abstractions or arcane musings. So he had real people instead, mostly good-looking, always famous, cheery people who described how their lives had been touched by God.

Most Mondays, it was uplifting, but tonight Natalie was sunk in disbelief. Her job in Springfield, unlike her fleeting marriage, was a rock. To retain that, she was willing to offer God an extra fifteen dollars, even thirty. *Dear Bob,* she wrote, *you do not expect another letter from me tonight. You might imagine I've already asked for everything possible yesterday. But a terrible disaster has struck. I cannot believe God has forsaken me in this manner. And I know I should not lose my faith but believe me, this is hard. It's a real test. I've been at this company for twenty-eight years and today they tell me my department will be off-shored to Bangalore, India. In case you haven't been reading the papers this means jobs will be shifted to Bangalore. They haven't said I've been fired yet, but I'm sure that's coming next. In the meantime, they want me to travel to India to meet with potential vendors. A fine assignment indeed, picking my own assassin.*

No, she shouldn't say that. She scratched the line out. Not to a preacher. Then she crumpled the letter, the words weren't right somehow. It read like a journal entry, not a formal Christian letter seeking God's favour. Maybe she should pray. Just then, the actor who was chatting with Bob turned her white swan neck to Natalie. Her blue eyes sparkled: 'You know,' she said, 'I was just like you. Completely lost. Really did not know where to turn next. I wondered if I should just sink to my knees and pray. And then I remembered something else. Bob's number. I called Bob's number at 1-800-233-2323 and poured my heart out to a prayer counsellor. And that was it. A couple of days later there was a knock on my door. It was the mailman carrying God's answer to my prayers, a new contract for a wonderful TV show and a chance to share my light with the world. I had a job again.'

The actor lost her job too? This was incredible, absurd. If Natalie described freakish correlations between her life and Bob's show to folks at work, they'd scoff and sneer. But this woman, this white swan in a black mini just answered her question and she didn't know Natalie was watching. Or did she? Did Bob? Of course, the telephone, why hadn't she thought of that? So much quicker than letters in a crisis. A person to talk to, someone to relay her urgency to the preacher himself.

On her knees, she cradled the cordless and punched the number – 1-800-233-2323 – quickly before the ticker dissolved into a scrolling hymn.

'Good evening, this is the Ministry of Giving, God appreciates your calling us today, can I have your first name and last name please?' The voice was funny, not like Bob's at all, but how could she expect him to man the phones when he was talking to the actor-woman on TV?

'Um, it's Natalie Foster.'

'Thank you, Ms Foster. May I call you Natalie?'

'Yeah, sure.'

'What would you like us to pray for today, Natalie?'

The voice didn't seem Christian somehow but how could *she* tell? Besides, she was letting the Devil in, the Doubting Devil before giving it a chance.

'Oh, it's my job. I mean I'm also looking for a life-partner, but right now, it's my job. I don't want to lose my job. I've been at this place for almost thirty years and now they're sending jobs to India.'

The Ministry was silent. Perhaps the counsellor did not get it? Sounded like an immigrant anyway.

'I want to pray to keep my job. I can't find a new one at this age,' Natalie repeated.

'Sure, we can pray for that. I'm sure God will answer your prayer. Do you have a member account with the Ministry of Giving?'

Yes, she did. 'Can you give me a few minutes while I retrieve it?'

'Sure, I'll hold.' At least they were patient, these prayer counsellors. She retrieved Bob's card from her telephone drawer – a printed card with the words from Matthew 18:19: 'Again I say unto you, that if two of you shall agree on earth as touching anything that they shall ask, it shall be done for them of my Father which is in heaven.'

Two of you, Natalie and the prayer counsellor. It made sense. Why hadn't she used the phone earlier? Maybe she'd have found her man by now.

At Bangalore airport, her senses were overpowered by the spill of colours. And she couldn't take, at this age, such deafening noise: high-pitched yowls at the exit where an excited family reunited with a young man, knocking him over with a large garland; elsewhere, a crowd crashed past customs officers and lunged at a pot-bellied passenger dressed in an all-white Indian suit. Natalie watched in disbelief when the group collapsed in a heap, all twenty at his feet. Was he a local saint or preacher? Meanwhile, a gaggle of drivers near the exit hailed her like a celebrity.

'Madam, taxi, madam.' 'Prepaid taxi, madam, straight drop hotel.' 'I take madam, safe, airport taxi.'

What assaulted her now, attacked her like a sudden storm was the smell, a wild mixture of taxi fumes and sweat and dog breath – she couldn't fathom what the stench was but it was mixed into the heat and drizzled on every patch of exposed skin. The sleeveless cotton shirt wasn't a good idea. She needed to screen herself from this fierce country, from unrelenting vapours that blew in from all sides as she fumbled with her luggage cart on a concrete ramp.

Her boss had said an official from Callus, the service provider pitching for their contract, was meeting her. There were several signs: 'Mr Sharma,' 'Infosys Welcomes Mr John Carrier', 'Mr Abraham, Leela', but she couldn't see a 'Natalie' anywhere. And then she spotted a 'Mrs Foster'.

'Hi, you must be Mr Varghese. I'm Natalie,' she said and extended her hand to the sign-carrier. 'I... I... driver,' said the man, flustered by her action. 'Mr Varghese meeting for you in hotel.'

'Oh, I'm sorry.'

Behind the wheel the driver was pointedly silent. As if he feared another improper action by the clumsy American. She wondered why her company dispatched her, a mere manager not privy to shareholder plans. She suspected her boss, tuned out from his shrinking operation, was preoccupied, engaged in wrapping up his own future. He had been fuzzy about her role on the trip: 'Just meet the fellows, we've made up our minds already but we want a first-hand feel of agent quality.'

As she watched the road, flanked by an assortment of vendors with mobile carts – caps, watermelons, potted plants, ceramic pots, dolls, oranges, mangoes, bananas – she wondered if her makeup was intact. Had Bob ever been here? Poor man, so tangled in his

American problems, no time for the rest of the world. They passed a cemetery with upturned granite slabs, a roadside temple where a motorbike, garlanded and anointed in red and yellow powders, was worshipped like some machine-god, and then a billboard that announced 'Special Services for Seventh-Day Adventists.' Bangalore too, so densely crowded, teemed with Energy. The Lord's ways were inscrutable. Perhaps she'd meet her man in this kaleidoscopic crush.

While she waited for Varghese in the hotel lobby, Natalie surged with a girlish gaiety, induced by the wonders of a new place and the plush surroundings of her five-star hotel. That she had weathered the long flight and made it so far in a foreign country filled her with a newfound impunity. If she could survive this, she could survive anything.

'Wonderful,' said Varghese. 'Wonderful to meet you.' He rapidly escorted her to a sleek, purple car. He had scanty hair slicked back with a thick gel and a wide mouth from which teeth spilled in all directions. From the back seat, she spotted dark stains on his neck. Seated next to the driver, his head turned 180 degrees: 'You are from Springfield? Wonderful. I have been to USA once – is this your first visit to India?'

Just then, their car ploughed into a black-and-yellow three-wheeler. Screeching swiftly into a side-road while the three-wheeler driver flailed his arms, they bumped into a cyclist with a sack of white plaster. Powders billowed from the sack and covered the sidewalk. Unshaken, their driver fled with an imperious honk.

Varghese chattered on as if nothing had happened: 'First I went to Boston, then Chicago, next San Francisco...'.

The car halted at a junction. On the left, there was a broad tree with thick rubber tubes and a sign that read 'Volcanising Tyres'. Around the tree, there were deep trenches. 'They are laying fibre cables for broadband connections,' explained Varghese. The shirtless 'volcaniser' pressed a metallic disc against a large tyre; another man, leaning against a truck, bent over him. Despite the dust, smog and stale heat, the men were animated, unfazed.

'What is he doing?' asked Natalie.

'Hah? Oh, that – I don't know, some tyre repair. Anyway, all this will be removed once roads are widened. Government is already taking action.'

A few metres ahead, the car stopped again. A black van, dressed up in orange flowers, trundled behind a clot of boy-drummers.

'Some celebration?' asked Natalie.

'Dead body,' said Varghese.

Soon they arrived at the IT Valley. Natalie's heart stopped. For many months she had pictures of Bob's community campus in her head, an 'Eternal City' the preacher planned to build for his faithful few, for committed lifetime members. All she had seen were watermark imprints on Ministry brochures. But in her mind the settings were fleshed out: leaf-filled trees, sunshiny skies, wafts of bird-song, a tranquil resting place before the Final Journey. So far, Bangalore had been everything she expected, overflowing, unclean, an emerging metropolis not possessed of First World standards. But this campus, this wretched Callus campus bettered her notion of Bob's world. The city's traffic sounds and smoggy vapours, 'volcanizing' rubbers and pressing metals halted at those gates. Suspended inside an astonishing silence was a sweeping driveway, flanked by bird-shaped hedges and dewy grass. Broad trees, flaming red-orange, carpeted brick-lined pathways with their pulpy blossoms. Four tall glass towers, flat-panelled and burnished like her plasma TV, reflected milk-white clouds. Further down, there was a courtyard, and a row of shops and eateries and outdoor cafés. A self-contained world, a city inside a city. The Lord's artwork could hardly out-dazzle this. The Beam America building was stark and square and boxed like a warehouse. Was this the low-cost service provider her boss described?

'Does Callus own all this?' asked Natalie, in a voice too hoarse to be her own.

'This is the IT Valley, one of our premium technology parks. Callus is on the 8th floor, in the Cupertino Building.'

At the Callus reception, a black board displayed a bold 'Welcome to Ms Natalie Foster, Beam America.' The receptionist greeted her with an excited, 'Welcome, madam, please wait here,' while she buzzed someone on the intercom. 'She's here, she's here.'

Three Callus managers, beaming like Varghese, strode into the reception while a woman in shimmering Indian clothes bounced in with red roses. Natalie blushed. Chris hadn't given her flowers, not once.

Ushered into a meeting room, Natalie was aware of

60

many pairs of eyes trained on her movements as she passed by. Black heads behind cubicles bobbed up and down. Inside the room, an oval table was set up with water glasses, cookies, tea, coffee; on a white screen a PowerPoint slide flashed 'Welcome to Ms Natalie Foster, Beam America.' All three men talked at once. Did she want tea, coffee, Coke or Diet Coke, they asked. 'Water, please,' said Natalie, sinking into a plush, high-backed chair. She had never been treated like this, not at Beam America. Despite rising to Manager, Customer Service, she was dispatched from meetings with the kind condescension doled out to secretaries. 'Can you please dig up that email, the one with the latest data? Thanks so much, Natalie, what would we do without you?' But in this room when a man bent to carefully fill her glass with sparkling water, another one hesitantly asked if she needed ice, she felt like a different person. She glanced around the table with a toasty affection. Did they really believe in *her* influence? The three men gushed in an effacing friendliness and she felt suddenly strong, newly energized. She wasn't just Natalie Foster or a Beam America Manager, she was America the Beautiful, a Super Power and World Leader, a woman entrusted with a Mission.

The tallest of the three men, all shorter than the 5'8" Natalie, launched into a corporate brief. High-sounding words bounced off the double-walled, low-ceilinged conference room – 'Strategic Outsourcing', 'Business Transformation Outsourcing', 'High-Performance Sourcing Models', 'Climbing the Value Chain'. After the long flight, this felt like the murky sermons of her childhood church, ethereal, transcendent and important in some higher realm but what did it have to do with agents answering phones? She was impressed nonetheless by these Indian men. Brazenly upbeat, dapper in ties and suits, they could have been from anywhere in the world. The power of positive thinking, a future looming with hope, it shone through in fierce smiles, cocksure voices and peppy PowerPoints. Their world was expanding, hers shrivelling. She thought of her tiny Springfield flat, and wondered if they lived in sprawling chateaus.

She was escorted to the CEO next, to a corner office with wooden flooring, a terrace garden and a spectacular view of a sprawling golf course beyond. 'I'm Sashwath,' he said, rising behind a large oak desk in a room filled with abstract art, crystal lamps, paperweights and ashtrays, many things that cost money, lots of money, in any currency.

The CEO, in his casual Friday T-shirt and Dockers, was charming, not bashful like his managers. He was a fierce man, Natalie could tell. He had about him, in his bearded face, in his fidgety, small body, a bristling impatience. Steering her to a black leather couch, he launched into a monologue: 'Ms Foster, a pleasure to meet you. You work with Mike, isn't it? I know several people at Beam America. Please pass on my regards to Kevin. Have you been around our centre? Callus is unlike any other call centre in India, you will see the difference in the details, in our people, in our organization structure, in the way we do business, and more than anything else, in the quality of our agents...' After every point about the difference between Callus and other centres he watched her with an unsettling raptness. Did she get *it*? She wouldn't find, he went on in that severe manner, any

62

company in Bangalore with such arresting interiors, such attention to quality. 'Others, you will find, don't share the same outlook. We understand client mindsets.'

She was less worried about other companies in Bangalore, more worried about Beam America in Springfield. How could these Indians start having it all – weren't riches reserved for people who believed in the Right Words, led the Right Lives? Instead of being banished into unchristian hells, these people were staking for themselves personal heavens, plots scaffolded to skyscraping heights. Could Bob justify the Lord's unevenness?

Two days later, Natalie was beginning to lose her earlier geniality. Midweek, she had visited the other centre. If she thought the IT Valley was spectacular, the Bodmas campus exhibited a many-times greater splendour – an ethereal otherworld with buildings of all shapes, trapezoids, hexahedrons, octahedrons erupting among lakes, golf courses, swimming pools and shopping centres. A steel-glass grandeur that mocked Natalie's idea of American dominance. More than anything else, she was struck by her own smallness in the place: when she signed in at the gate, she was one of several overawed foreigners. The tour was flawless. 'We encourage employee self-expression,' said immaculate managers, in immaculate suits who conducted her through a jumble of cubicles. The agent quality, when she listened in to a few calls, was astonishing. She wouldn't have known, if she hadn't seen brown faces, that the voices were Indian.

After four site visits – two to Callus, two to Bodmas – she was positively crabby. The city was hot, streets messy, traffic chaotic, the exuberance stifling – managers too buoyant, agents too vivacious. When she listened to live calls at night, the energy was cloying. She was stung as well that everyone she met had a college degree. So far in Beam America, she hadn't been conscious of anyone's learning. She thought of college kids as somehow spoiled, kids who never had to work for their living. Now in this country, her experience seemed diminished, as if her years at Beam America were propped up on specious grounds.

Of course no one probed her background except Varghese who got nosy during long car rides. One night she toyed with the idea of Varghese as a possibility. A fellow Christian, even Bob might approve? Such thoughts were banished by the sporadic rancour that leaked into his talk. 'West deserves this, colonized us for 200 years.' 'Americans can't retain jobs, don't even go to college.' 'Americans have it easy, no idea what life's like in other parts of the planet.'

She could hardly withstand another late-night re-run at Callus, but the CEO was insistent: 'We have something special lined up tonight, you can't miss it.' When Varghese met her at the Callus lobby, flashing his teeth, she wanted to scold him like her second-grade teacher: 'Wipe that smile off your face.'

'We have a surprise for you,' said Sashwath, who escorted her that night. 'You will be astounded by what my people have done.'

When they entered the call floor, the place buzzed like a farmer's market, with rows and rows of black heads, sitting, standing, strutting with headset-phones, chattering easily to Americans. But there was something else that night, a makeover in scarlet.

'What's this, an Indian festival?' asked Natalie.

'Indian festival? It's Valentine's Day, Ms Foster. Isn't this wonderful?'

Natalie swallowed air to ward off the choking. Everywhere she turned there were hearts, hearts, hearts, paper hearts, cardboard hearts, balloon hearts and heart-shaped cupids, all in ghastly pinks and reds. Like oversweet candy, the hard kind with too much sugar. The CEO gushed: 'We really try to make them feel a part of the culture. Look at this place today! I'm sure Sears or Wal-Mart doesn't look better. And when customers greet them with a "Happy Valentine's Day" they'll share the feeling, not respond with an "Ah? I don't know what you mean."'

He led her inside a cubicle cluster: 'Listen to these agents, live on the phone. They compare with the best in America.'

A woman nodded shyly at the intruders in her cubicle. She spoke on the phone with a distinct Indian accent, slightly covered up by a put-on drawl: 'Sure, sir, can I have your account number please?'

Natalie bent down to pick up the words.

'Thank you. And what would you like us to do today?'

She was not sure why her sing-song inflections sounded familiar. What was the woman saying? She moved right into the cubicle, stifling her quick breaths, while the creature continued to speak. Natalie slipped on the side-jack headset, the one used for barging into calls. 'Sure, we can do that, sir. Just give me a few minutes while I retrieve your account.'

The cursor flashed near an empty box: *Customer Account Number.*

And suddenly it came to Natalie like a thunderbolt. Bob's agents or counsellors or whatever he called those people were in godforsaken India. In another centre, in the same wretched city perhaps. Of course, that explained the strange voice that day: *an Indian accent.*

Sashwath continued to talk while Varghese nodded eagerly. 'These agents go through four-week training programs. Listen to the accents, they're so authentic. You won't find that at other centres.'

Natalie didn't process the CEO's words, the man's eyes flickering like a throw-and-use camera. 'I need to get back to the hotel,' she said. 'I feel unwell.'

Another Sunday in Springfield. Ten more minutes for Bob's show. She had many letters from the preacher, some delivered while she was in India. For two weeks she had stuffed them in the bin. Now she was sorry. The Ministry, Bob announced in a frank note to its members, was in dire straits. In such dire straits, he'd have to halt his shows on several channels. No Sunday services, no Monday talk shows. He was doing his best, he assured them, to keep it going but even the Ministry needed funds. More crucially, member support.

It would be a shame to close the church. She couldn't imagine her Sundays without his booming cheer. She wondered how he kept it up despite his troubles. And more than anything else, in the midst of his hardship, he hadn't forgotten his members' needs. Because Natalie's prayer, the one she communicated to the Ministry's counsellor, had been answered.

Her job was staying, her boss assured her. They needed an old-timer to manage the offshore process at Callus, the centre chosen because of its lower cost. There weren't any plans to let her go. Not just that, they had expanded her role. She'd train Indian trainers – five Indians were scheduled to arrive in two months – and travel to India to monitor trainer quality. As Bob frequently reminded his congregation, there wasn't any way to outdo the Lord.

She started another letter to Bob. *Dear Bob, I'd like to update you on new events in my life. No, I haven't met my man yet, but I'm sure now, it's going to happen soon. I'm feeling positive, everything's falling into place. I'd like to thank you for praying for me. I have my job back or rather I haven't lost my job as I feared I would. The company has been kind to me. And I know this is because of the Lord's goodness and I thank Him with all my heart.*

I've also returned from a recent trip to India and I believe your prayer counsellors are located there. I was initially upset that calls were being answered by unbelieving people but I understand now, you have financial problems and don't have a choice. I'm praying for your recovery and I'm enclosing a 30-dollar check. I hope my small contribution helps in tiding over your crisis.

The show started. Natalie sat up, with the letter pad on her lap and turned the mute off.

'Greetings, America,' said Bob. 'I thank you once more for being with us today. And I do hope we can continue to be with you on Sunday mornings. We so want to continue our special relationship with you but we have certain obligations to the TV networks and unless we can fulfil them we might be off the air in a couple of weeks. Yes, folks, I do not like starting this program on a negative note, but this is what the network guys have told us – a couple of weeks and then...'

Bob had tears in his eyes. Natalie clutched at the couch, choked. Her eyes misted up, she could barely see him. The poor man, all alone in his mission. Here she was rejoicing in her recent victory while he was sinking, drowning. They were zapping him out, the evil network guys – didn't they see the good work he was doing? She'd do anything to buoy him up, keep him appearing in her living room at any cost.

She looked at her unfinished letter and at Bob's eyes on the TV screen. And suddenly it came to her – a flash evoked by the Lord Himself – something her manager had said about the company's move to India. 'Do you know why we're shifting to India?'

'Lower costs?' said Natalie.

'Not just that. India's going to be the biggest market for our products.'

The country doesn't just have voices, English-speaking, telephone-answering voices, no, not just that, she added excitedly in a postscript. *Besides hundreds of telephone agents, India has a billion people. And televisions in every village. Just think, Bob, if a hundred million Indians contribute ten or twenty dollars you can stay on the networks for many years to come.'*

She sank back into the couch and straightened her hat. She wore a new silk scarf that the Indians had gifted her. She shifted the knot to spruce up her boat collar. Blue light from the TV screen shone on the couch. She expected at any moment a knock on her door.

Platinum

At 3:00 a.m., the Callus van stopped near the Shivajinagar Aryavaidya Clinic. Dr Menon Kutty hovered at the storeroom entry and hollered to Bitty: 'Your office van has come.' Unlike the other homes on the street, the Kutty household was lit with a daylight bustle.

In a few minutes, sinking into the van's darkness, Bitty watched her father recede from her tree-lined journey: thick, blackish lips, curly hairs sprouting from his ears, the slight paunch that held up a checked lungi. Her parents had asked her to skip work that day. The Onam lunch with Dr Kutty's extended family, they said, warranted Bitty's presence. They asked her to invite that Akriti friend, the one Bitty always talked about. 'No way,' said Bitty. 'Not Akriti.' Her parents had no idea. She shuddered at the thought of the Callus trainer fluttering manicured hands before avial and payasam slopped out from steamy buckets while Achan, exalted by his yearly charity, strutted between gluttonous relatives.

The van turned into the sari street, where grainy white letters glowed in the neon lights of a large Pepsi signboard: 'Dr Menon Kutty, Ayurvedic Practitioner, Clinic Timings: 9:00 a.m. to 1:00 p.m.; 4:00 p.m. to 7:00 p.m. Sundays Holidays.' For thirty years the same board had been repainted, his timings unvaried, while around the clinic, gaudy polyesters and shrill chiffons were displaced by 'can't believe so cheap' China silks. He was never late. Started on time, ended on time, with a three-hour break in the afternoon. It was only in the last nine months, after Bitty's night job, that Dr. Kutty made morning patients wait a tad longer.

As another convent-type agent settled herself into the cab's dim interiors, Bitty sniggered at another thought: Akriti in her father's clinic, beaming fluorescent teeth at slobbery men who patted the grown-up Bitty with an overly fond '*Endha mole, Bitty*' and burkha-shrouded women who flipped lace-edged veils to behold Dr Kutty's daughter. 'He's a doctor,' she had told the trainer, hoping to evoke, in modulated English, the dapper image of an allopathic physician, a white-coated, UK-educated specialist who prescribed enticing Crocins and Teramycins, not unseemly *Hingvashtaka Churnams* or *Punarnavadi Kwaths*. Akriti climbed on at a later stop, many van stops from Bitty's Shivajinagar home: the Napa Meadows stop in Koramangala, same city but another world entirely.

A difference her parents, tethered to narrow gullies that made up their small world, would never fathom. How could they if they couldn't distinguish CK's Obsession from Chanel No. 5, or Hugo Woman's green apple aroma from DKNY's 'hip New York attitude'? A

70

year ago, an untutored Bitty would have barely sniffed the difference. But after several trips to Shopper's Paradise and the Bangalore Mall, guided by a sharp-nosed Akriti, Bitty had mastered the art of telling apart the scents of cities she'd never visited. 'I mean it's just so... you know what I mean... New York,' said Akriti, her senses as expansive as her cultural knowledge.

The perfumes were invisible traces of Akriti's patient coaching. More striking suggestions lay in the L'Oreal shimmer that dressed up Bitty's cheeks, in the matte-steel Tissot that bound her wrist, in zebra-printed sandals that loped across the Shivajinagar house. She ripped off the barcoded stickers before carrying possessions home. The Kuttys' economics, informed by Shivajinagar trifles, would snap under the costs of Akriti's grooming. Her parents were satisfied, even deplorably appreciative of the 9,000 rupees she handed over each month, oblivious of her 14,000 take-home or 7,000 monthly credit.

It had been Akriti who signed her up for a credit card. 'Makes it easier,' she said. On Bitty's first Shopper's Paradise trip she was taken in by the startling ease with which Akriti shopped. Unconcerned with prices, the trainer lifted stuff off racks, heeding only the style, the cut, and what was 'in' among the city's designers. To Bitty, this was a new and disquieting experience. Each time she'd been shopping with Amma, the budget steered them to low-price shelves. 'What salwar suits you have for 400 rupees? No, no, not higher range,' Amma said firmly. But the price to Akriti was a non-issue, a number to contend with on the final bill and that too on extendable credit.

On that first trip, when Akriti was trying on a fifth pair of khaki Dockers, Bitty tried on her first 501s. She wasn't conscious of the brand then but she had noticed they were an appalling 4,200.

'Oooh, you look so good in that, it really, really suits you, Bitty, the cut is awesome,' chirped Akriti. 'I would take it if I were you, it makes you look so-oh slim.'

Bitty swivelled around in the changing room. The jeans did look good. Her svelte figure, accented at the waist, felt leaner than ever. But it was something else entirely, above the low-waist jeans, above the small black T-shirt that held her attention: under the white changing room light, her large eyes and sloped cheeks glowed orange. The jeans did something to her, something new and terrible and heat-producing. But 4,200? The price of ten Diwali outfits for a pair of trousers? Outside the changing room, she paused.

'It's too expensive,' she said, lingering near the attendant who snatched the rejected pair.

'Expensive? Really? How much?'

'Four thousand two hundred.'

'Rupees?' asked Akriti as if the shop traded in other currencies.

'Yes.'

'Bitty, *honey*, that's a steal. These are Levi's. Original 501s. You have heard of 501s, haven't you?'

'Not really,' admitted Bitty.

Thereafter, in trip after shopping trip, Akriti drilled Bitty on the new economics, on brand value, on fashion, on styles, on what's in and out. 'It's not cost,' she explained. A Levi's at 4,200 rupees was a steal but a Lee was NOT. Chanel No. 5 was NOT a scent and not to be compared with local fragrances; it was 'Parisian vogue distilled in vanilla-musk redolence'. Gucci, she explained, was pronounced 'gooch-ee,' not 'gu-key.' The trainer said knowing how to pronounce brands was as crucial as curling *r*'s.

Of course, Bitty's accent wasn't there – not good enough yet to be recruited by the dream company, Bodmas – but with practice and after several hundred calls, she was getting it. There hadn't been customers that month who asked to 'speak to someone who knows English'. A big climb from the early weeks when after the standard greeting: 'Thank you for calling Columbus Instant Connect, Mr Daniels. My name is Betty,' she had tottered on the first question: 'Can I go ahead and call you by your first name, which is Tom?'

'That sounds crude, Bitty. Don't say "can I go ahead" and "by your first name". Just be casual, "Can I call you Tom?" Keep it simple.'

Such brevity had taken weeks to master. She'd be bumbling still on clunky phrases if she hadn't been marked out on Valentine's Day – among two hundred new recruits – for private coaching and extra sessions by the centre's best trainer.

The call centre that day was like the fairyland Bitty dreamt of in school. 'Cool, man, like movie sets,' someone said. The special Valentine décor, funded by a generous company allowance, surpassed Diwali razzmatazz on the sari street. The glass doors were eclipsed by heart-shaped wreaths, more extravagant than wedding flowers. Walls normally filled with humdrum announcements – 'This Week's Best Agents' or 'Special Incentive for Super Achievers' or 'From the CEO's Desk' – were plastered instead with L-O-V-E garlands, with heart ornaments, with pink arrow-wielding babies that Akriti said were 'sweet Cupids'. The electronic wallboard, which usually flashed irksome warnings about 'Calls in Queue' and 'Disconnects' floated among helium-filled Barbies. And moreover, every cubicle had a box of heart-shaped chocolates with a card from the management saying 'Happy Valentine's Day'. It was 4:00 a.m. in Bangalore on the next day, but that wasn't the point. It was Valentine's Day in America.

Bitty excitedly ripped open her gift-wrapped chocolates. Across the main aisle, the Callus CEO, a handsome, bearded man she sometimes glimpsed from a distance, escorted a prospective American client inside the profusion of pinks: 'We really try to make them feel a part of the culture,' he explained. 'Look at this place today! I'm sure Sears or Wal-Mart doesn't look better. And when customers greet them with a "Happy Valentine's Day", they'll share the feeling, not respond with an "Aah? I don't know what you mean".'

Bitty was assigned that week to an internet service provider's account. 'You have to take down change requests,' the Team Leader had said. 'This is a pilot phase where the client is assessing our capability, so be extra polite.' Bitty wasn't familiar with the script but most calls were easy; internet subscribers merely wanted the job done quickly. Her eyes fixed on the computer screen, where the script flickered at the bottom, Bitty read out the greeting: 'Good evening, this is Columbus Instant Connect, we appreciate your calling us today, can I have your first name and last name please?'

She heard footsteps in the adjoining aisle. 'Listen to these agents, live on the phone. They compare with the best in America,' said the CEO, and before the agent had registered his words, he ushered the American lady into Bitty's cubicle. She could hardly attend to the headset voice. She fumbled while confirming the caller's first and last name.

'Really?' said the American lady, lowering her fuzzy, brown head to listen in to Bitty's call.

The agent tried to hide the tremor in her voice. They hadn't warned her, yesterday or earlier tonight, about intrusions into live calls. It was one thing to have a foreign voice at the other end but another thing entirely to have a foreign face watching your movements. Distracted by the shuffle of black stockings near her desk, she wasn't sure later if she entered the account number incorrectly or if her pronunciations were too Indian, but while Bitty said, 'Sure, we can do that, sir. Just give me a few minutes while I retrieve your account,' the American client sprang from her seat and ripped off her listening headset, face blanched.

'I need to get back to the hotel,' she said. 'I feel unwell.'

Several calls later, the Team Leader hauled Bitty in for a private meeting. 'Bitty, what the hell, you messed up when the firang female side-jacked your calls. CEO's pissed, Area Manager's on fire. What did you say?'

'I didn't do anything,' said Bitty. 'I was reading from the script.'

'Maybe that's the problem. Americans don't like agents reeling out scripts. You should learn to speak naturally.'

There were more meetings after that including a one-on-one with the Area Manager.

'Who trained you?' he asked.

'Yvette.'

'Ah, that explains it. Shit man, don't know what it is, but Yvette's trainees are always weak on accents and lingo.'

Eventually they assigned her for reinforcement training. 'Akriti's a fundoo trainer, much stronger than Yvette,' the Area Manager said. 'If she can't change you, you'll have to find another job.'

Bitty was moved into the training cubicle to watch the trainer's 'live demos'. The agent listened in while Akriti responded to callers. To Bitty, who always faltered on scripted replies, Akriti's fearless rapport with American callers was fantastic. She was as relaxed as Bitty was with Indians.

'You have a date today? Wow, that's cool? You've been seeing this guy for some time? So where are you going? Reee-ally, he must really like you. That's wild. He sent you that? No way! Oh, me? You know, I mean I had this date, but we hadn't really fixed it, you know what I mean, and he hasn't called and you know, I'm not sure if I should message him or call.'

Bitty was amazed an Indian could spill secrets like that. And not only that, counsel callers. 'You know, that happened to me as well, you know what I'd do, I'd just tell him, okay, I know this is advertising and shit, but

76

you know, I *need* those roses. I don't desire them, I need them.' She spent an hour with this customer who had a boyfriend in Iraq. 'Yeah, I know what that's like but at least, can you call him? Oh jeez, that's tough. He hasn't called at all? Does he write? I hate it when that happens. But, hey, you know, at least your man's out there, doing something for the country, right? You should be proud of him' and so on and on and on.

With her unsteady 'Good morning, Mr Charles Dawson, can I call you Charles, which is your first name?' Bitty felt terribly inferior. Her eyes glittered when Akriti looked at her and said: 'Don't cry. You'll learn. Listen, you need a break. Want to go shopping?'

According to Bitty's father, the call centre with its unsettling shifts breached their well-regulated lifestyle with disease-inviting discordance: *Kala parinama*, the rupture of natural rhythms, recognized in Ayurvedic texts as a progenitor of ill health. Bitty, Dr Kutty said, had a *pitta* constitution. Classified as a warm body, she needed countering coolants mixed into her everyday food. To alleviate the spin-offs of night shifts, he added *Triphala Churna* and *Dashamoola Kashayam* to modulate her imbalance.

But her timings didn't distress Bitty, not as much as her father's close scrutiny of her 'unregulated' life. 'Yesterday you slept only five hours, you need six hours minimum.' 'You're not drinking water after meals.' 'Have you gargled with oil?' And worse, when she emerged from the bathroom adjoining her bedroom: 'What colour was your motion?' The toilet, recently made over with sky-blue tiles and a cobalt-blue western commode, was her sanctuary at home, a private zone that gleamed like her workplace. The rest of the house, coated in red-oxide flooring, carried the grime of previous owners. Unlike the neighbours, her parents rented two stories: downstairs, Dr Kutty's clinic and medicine storeroom, upstairs, their living quarters. The entryway above the paint-splattered stairway led to a sitting room that morphed into a dining area at meal-times and a bedroom at night, when her parents unfurled grass mats and cotton bedding. Bitty, who slept on a wooden cot, occupied what used to be the medicine kitchen.

It wasn't just the smell of medicine but her parent's questions that reeked of the past as well: 'Have you made friends in the centre?' 'What are their names?' 'Do you listen to your boss?' 'How are you ranked in the company?' It felt like they were trapped in another time, in her school-going years, when they badgered her with: 'Do you listen to your teacher?' and 'Have you done your homework?' She was too small then, but she saw it now, how simple they were. She wished they wouldn't stay up to see her off or eat dinner at odd times to keep her company. One night, after a shopping trip that didn't go well, she slammed the dinner plate when her father remarked between loud slurps: 'Bitty, your body needs minimum eight hours sleep. You must come home after your shift ends. Must stop needless outings.'

'Needless? Achan, how do you know my needs?' Leaving her dinner unfinished, she stomped to the bedroom that held her recent purchases and clanged the door shut.

After that night, her parents treated her with caution, mumbling when she was around, treading softly between the downstairs storeroom and home kitchen to mix new tonics for the 'rising heat'.

Bitty shut herself inside her bedroom to examine her recent purchases in the dressing mirror. No more brawls, no tedious fights. She slunk in and out like a paying guest, outwardly affable, sharing space and food for a hefty rent.

She was willing to put up with her dull home life, with abusive customers and Team Leader warnings because the weekly excursions made everything worth it. She did not need Akriti even, not for shopping trips. In fact, she preferred to shop alone.

Each time Bitty walked into a mall, caressed by air-conditioned eddies that cushioned her from the outside heat, she was caught in a swirl of excitement: fibreglass panels, swivelling racks, skeletal mannequins, lush fabrics, swank windows cloaked in styles unknown to Shivajinagar stores. Everything there – even a bottle of shampoo or a plastic hairclip – acquired an ethereal quality. She wasn't sure what it was, the spiffy packaging or exquisite backdrops, ravishing smells or haughty salesgirls; she carried out, each time, in carefully tagged bags, a wedge of ecstasy. Her crowning moment was when the card zinged and the machine blinked 'Approved'. It was a rush that stayed till she carried her bags home and tucked her new stuff into a steel chest in her room. Her parents weren't the prying sort but she stowed her eight sweaters and twelve scarves and jumble of semi-precious earrings out of sight. They wouldn't realize a job like this required a certain appearance.

'Americans are more materialistic than Indians,' her first trainer, Yvette, had said. 'When an American is upset about losing a few dollars or few cents for a billing mistake, don't treat the problem lightly. Money, for them, can be a matter of life and death.'

Bitty could relate to that when she handled calls. She had customers, with reasonable balances, spending too much time on small charges. The phone call, in some cases, cost more than the refund. Some calls echoed in her memory long after she laid her headset down. There was an eighty-year-old lady from New York, calling during odd US hours, upset about a $1.71 due from the internet company as interest charges for a wrongly billed amount. The agent was impressed not only by the caller's sharp reasoning, but by her knowledge of the Fed's interest rates. Bitty's own grandmother, Dr Kutty's mother in Kerala, was removed from such concerns. But it was another call that underscored how different Americans were.

The caller was a woman in her forties.

'Hi, this is Kate Anderson here. I am calling to check on this number – 435-234-3423. It doesn't seem to be working.'

'Just a minute, ma'am,' said Bitty, 'I am pulling up the account for you now... Yes, I have it in front of me. What error message are you getting?'

'Oh... well... It says the line's out-of-order or something, you know, that standard error message when the phone's not working.'

'I see, ma'am. And what is your relationship with the account holder?'

'Well... she's my mother. She's seventy-eight and you know, she's livin' by herself and I'm kinda worried that her phone's not working.'

'Yes, ma'am. Well, I can authorize for a technician to go over and check the line. Shall I login a request for you?' said Bitty.

'Sure, that would be just great.'

'There would be a $15.50 charge for the technician visit. Would you like to pay for that by credit card?'

'Oh, really? A $15.50 charge? Oh, I don' know if my Mom would be willing to pay that. I'd have to check with her first.'

'You can pay for her with your credit card.'

'Uh, no, no, I don't wanna do that and I'm not sure if my Mom would want this. You know somethin', jus' hold on to this, okay? I'll call you back later.'

Yes, there were several calls like that. Nothing dramatic, but astonishing to Callus agents that Americans were unwilling to make trivial decisions on behalf of mothers, fathers, brothers, sisters. Indians wouldn't hesitate to pay for technicians or sign up on behalf of a parent. But these days Bitty identified more with the Kate Andersons of America than with colleagues at her centre. She was, after all, saving up every hard-earned rupee to pay for those new Gucci – pronounced 'gooch-ee' – sunglasses, the ones with the exquisite golden frame.

❧

Bitty's rift with Callus colleagues was conspicuous during a group outing when her team decided, impulsively, to go out for dinner. It was a new-age restaurant with silk blinds, glass walls and a large silk mural framed with coloured lights. Bitty ordered a soup and a sandwich, no drink, thank you, and no starters. Each entrée a steep 350 rupees, no, she wouldn't waste her money on food. The rest, in an indulgent thank-God-it's-Friday binge, ordered fresh lime sodas, beer, paneer pakoras, sizzlers, steaks, biryanis and pastas, an intercontinental hodgepodge that presented itself in a whopping Rs 5,387 total. They divided the amount by seven: 'Guys, 769 each,' they said. Bitty added up her orders that night, a careful 230 rupees. 'I think we should each pay for what we've eaten, not divide the whole thing equally,' she said. 'Some of us skipped drinks and starters and dessert.' She heard a petulance creep into her voice but didn't care. The team gawked, dropping dessert forks with a clatter, as if Bitty were from a strange tribe. A teammate finally spoke up:

'Bitty, what's wrong with you? We've never done that before, why are you acting so American?'

'It's not fair,' said Bitty, 'I've only eaten for 230 rupees.' While the words rushed out, her eyes were lit with shaming tears. Why demand an explanation? 'Oh, shit, man, she's crying. Listen, just let her pay 230,' said another teammate. 'We'll divide the rest.' Bitty paid her share but was not invited out the next Friday. Not that she cared. She was, in any case, saving up for other stuff.

At the mall that week, a jewellery salesgirl introduced her to platinum. At first, Bitty thought the pendant was highly polished silver. 'Silver?' the woman laughed.

'Madam, you are holding one of the most expensive and precious metals known, many times the worth of gold. Look at the way it sets off the diamond – brilliant, isn't it?' The greyish-white looped pendant with a colourless diamond tugged at a thin chain. A poster near the counter had rainbows tumbling off the milky-white neck of a 'real platinum woman'. The salesgirl held it against Bitty's neck and directed her gaze into a hand-held mirror. The agent's chiselled features, thin lips and ruler-straight nose, blazed inside a white fire. She throbbed with an insane desire to possess it at once. But 38,000 rupees? Could she afford that? 'I'll take it,' she said, her voice leaping from her throat to squash her qualms. Her fingers shuddered when she handed over the credit card. They froze when the machine rolled out an 'Approved' slip. 'Sign, madam,' the cashier prompted. On the auto-ride home, Bitty peered into the packet several times, lifting the lid of the leather box to make sure it was really there. Her parents did not know it but her life had changed forever.

During a pre-Diwali visit, when Shopper's Paradise was dressed up in firecracker tinsel and flowery lights, Bitty spotted terms that sprung from a prickly past – tulasi, chywanprash, guduchi – surely, she was misreading the names? Ayurvedic labels on stylish displays?

Inside the shop, against splashy Diwali tinsel, Bitty spied a new counter – Le Ayurved – a display as uppity as Chanel, Gucci and DKNY. And all the ingredients, she realized in a feverish astonishment, were straight off her father's shelf: amalaki, haritaki, brahmi, chitraka, the same contents in stunning new forms. Foggy liquids and pastes altered into neat plastic bubbles, noxious brown thailams into translucent oils, greenish-brown powders and juices into colour-coded pills and the logo, a poetic fluttering of two leaves. Ayurvedic chic fit for Parisian counters. They even had a website, www.leayurved. com. Later at the office, between calls, Bitty browsed through their webpages. They offered gift-wrapped, home-delivered packages for the ailing and unlovely, with Achan's murky ingredients highlighted for their skin-cleansing properties. Moreover, their exclusive outlet on upmarket Commercial Street was right next to her house. During her lunch break Bitty resolved to surprise Dr Kutty with the new shop and buy him a gift package from her bonus earnings.

Achan agreed reluctantly. Dressed in his only pant-suit – Bitty pleaded for him to change out of his untucked shirt and obsolete baggies – his reading spectacles on, his wiry Malayali hair plastered with oil, he entered the sprawling outlet on Commercial Street. He paused for a minute to read the signboard – 'Lee Ayurved?' – then walked hesitantly up the granite steps. Though Bitty had visited all of Bangalore's multiplexes and malls, this store made her gasp. The high door framed in stainless steel led them into a three-storied grandeur beyond anything she'd seen. She couldn't say what it was, the tall steel shelves or metallic murals, the skylit courtyard or health café, everything in this store cloaked her father's life in a new elegance. Her father, his expression blank, moved to the medicine shelves and meticulously scrutinized each bottle and package like some government inspector. Bitty hung around the grass-skirted mannequins with an eye on the doctor, watching for his reaction to the spectacular restyling of his concoctions. He moved slowly, examined each formulation, replaced it carefully in its original slot. Wasn't he interested in buying anything? Perhaps he was so taken in, he wanted to remake his outdated storeroom. Then she could invite Akriti home.

He bumped into a section for pets, herbal painkillers and sleep inducers for dogs, cats, horses and cows. 'You can be an Ayurvedic vet, Achan,' laughed Bitty. Dr Kutty grunted. Achan was like that, always serious, rarely expressive. Except when he cackled at Malayalam movies, pirated versions relayed by the local cable man.

'Would you like to buy something?' Bitty asked. His silence, like her Team Leader's pause while ruffling appraisal papers, was disconcerting.

'No... no, nothing,' said Achan.

'But Achan, you must buy something. Don't worry about prices, I'm gifting it to you.'

'Nothing, nothing,' insisted Achan, walking towards the exit.

Bitty grabbed his sleeve. She rarely touched him these days. 'Please Achan, buy *something*, don't worry about prices. I'm paying for it with my personal money.'

'Bitty, I don't need anything. Don't waste your money in this shop,' Achan replied, stalling her pleas in contemptuous Malayalam.

At home, Amma asked Dr Kutty about the Ayurvedic shop. 'It's not Ayurvedic,' said Achan. 'There's nothing Ayurvedic about medicines there. It's inauthentic.'

'How can you say that?' said Bitty. 'They use the same ingredients you use.'

'Bitty, you have no knowledge of these things. Ayurveda does not consist of a few herbal ingredients, it's a way of life. Such things cannot be sold in a showroom.'

'You are jealous,' said Bitty, crossing the limits of past altercations. 'Because your medicines don't look or smell as good.'

'Jealous? Bitty, you don't know what you're saying. I feel sorry for those shopkeepers. They don't know what they've lost,' Dr Kutty responded with an annoying composure.

Bitty could feel a migraine coming on. 'Leave me alone, I have a headache,' she announced, and banged the bedroom door shut. Authentic! What did her father know about authentic? He couldn't distinguish an original Levi's from a 'Levvy's'. The pain in her head splintered into a thousand memories, all those childhood quarrels with her father. She was in the fifth standard when Achan challenged her General Science lesson. The topic was Food and Health and the section, 'A Balanced Diet'. Bitty was saying it aloud, word for textbook word, while Amma with her feeble grasp of English, barely kept pace. 'There are five basic food groups and a healthy diet must contain foods from all the groups. The five groups are: one, breads and rice, two, fruits and vegetables, three, milk and dairy foods, four, meat and poultry, five, fats and sugars.'

Achan, engrossed in a Malayalam translation of the *Charaka Samhita,* suddenly looked up.

'No, no, that is wrong. That is not a correct diet. You cannot mix all those different types of foods together. Milk cannot be taken with oranges and lemons,' he said. 'Melons cannot be eaten with grains. Melons digest quickly and grains slowly. Such a combination will upset your stomach. Also, milk and meat proteins cannot be mixed.'

'Achan, this book is correct. My Miss said we should eat a balanced diet.'

'Is your Miss a doctor? Has she studied Ayurvedic texts?' countered Achan.

'Don't confuse the child, let her be. She has to study what the school teaches,' said Amma.

'This is your fault,' said Achan, his rage deflected to Amma. 'You were the one who insisted on this English school. Kannada was not good enough. See what they're teaching them.'

'Kannada schools teach the same thing,' said Amma. 'Do you think they teach Ayurvedic principles? No, just English science translated into Kannada.'

Each year, Bitty's resentment had accumulated into week-long migraines, beating against her father's unflappable ways. But with the call centre job, the frequency had increased. Her father suggested *Chandanadi Thailam*, an oil to be massaged warm. Tonight, when Amma walked in with the scalding liquid, Bitty heaved the brass bowl against the wall, watched hot oil spurt into jagged Himalayan stains. 'Don't want his bloody thailam.' Bloody, the word, unthinkable in their house, rested in a terrified silence. Her vein throbbed unabated.

Six months later, Bitty's treasure chest had a mounting pile of unopened envelopes. Annoying orange envelopes with her name and address printed inside a transparent window. It was best, she found, not to dwell on their contents. Credit card companies were greedy wolves: besides interest charges, there were overdue fines, late payment fees, a host of baffling numbers scaling into shrieking 'OVERDUES'. They were hysterical too, these card people, capitalizing every line in bold fonts. But her card still worked, they approved her weekly purchases with consoling *cha-chings*. End of the day, nothing else mattered. It was the platinum pendant and the instant credit approval of a quick impulse that egged her beyond the usual aisles, the well-known racks. Hadn't they empowered her, set her thinking anything's possible – surely a real, platinum woman couldn't be hedged in by credit limits? Besides, why bother with murky numbers when she could sink her head in the rabbity crush of her 'Dry Clean Only' Angora vest?

At work that week, the Team Leader announced extraordinary incentives for agents willing to work double shifts. Apparently a hurricane had hit Galveston with extra calls being routed to the Bangalore centre.

'Our team has to handle the maximum calls, the MOST, understand? Each of you must do your best,' he'd said. 'The winners go to Florida; it has to be this team, I want us to plant the Indian flag in Florida, understand?'

Bitty couldn't understand why the man was so worked up that night. She was hardly inspired by his flag-planting mission but Akriti had told her about malls in America. Indian malls, she said, had a long way to go. Bitty was determined to endure the twenty-four-hour assault at any cost.

But the night was worse than other nights, almost as bad as her first month. The blitz of irate customers, screaming into clogged lines, spoiled her satisfaction scores. Enraged by long wait times, customers were unwilling to simmer down. There were moments when Bitty wanted to pour *Chandanadi Thailam* with its temper-cooling properties over the lines. She smiled when she pictured alarmed Americans wallowing in Ayurvedic oils. In the midst of all that abuse, Bitty wondered if she'd been too harsh with her parents. They had, in spite of her moping, buffered her night shifts, waiting always with medicines and warm water for the cab to depart. It was Amma who turned the heater on at 2:00 a.m. while Bitty snatched more sleep, Achan who laid out her 3-inch heels from the heap that crowded their doorstep. They didn't intrude into her life anymore, no questions about the new hairstyle or shoulder tattoo or hip-hugger jeans. Apart from Achan's long-forgotten comment on 'needless outings', they ignored her shopping trips. Once, Achan asked how much her pendant cost. 'Oh, this? Fake, just 300,' Bitty responded. What would Achan know about yellow-blue flares that scattered off the stone's edges?

A 46-year-old woman from South Carolina spoke into her headset. Bitty rubbed her eyes.

'Good morning, this is Betty here. How can I help you today?'

'Well, you know, Betty, you can organize express deliveries for Father's Day, right? I want to send my father a Bonustalk prepaid card? Can I order that here?'

'Sure, ma'am,' said Bitty. The Bonustalk card, which offered unlimited talk time for six months, cost $1,200 – a large amount even for Americans.

'Great, thanks. And will this make it before Father's Day?'

'Yes, ma'am,' said Bitty. 'I'm sure your father will be really happy.'

'I wish I'd done this earlier, many years ago. He has Alzheimer's now, doesn't know I send him anything. Anyway, can you confirm when this gets there?'

'Yes, ma'am,' responded Bitty, reading the sign-off while her mind wandered to that faraway father, indifferent to his daughter's late-life attempts to reach him. Could that ever happen to Achan, the unassailable doctor? Rarely visited by infections that sapped his patients, she hadn't imagined a future when diseases he combated in others would trounce his toughness. Would he, at some point, be immune to his tonics and special diets? Would his senses fray, his thinking decline, would he swallow willingly the 'destructive pills' of an allopath? Easier to imagine Amma aging with her varicose veins and progressive arthritis. But Dr Kutty's withering was impossible to contemplate.

Bitty discovered a new resolve. She'd buy her parents gifts, something branded, not cheap Shivajinagar stuff. She handled the rest of the calls with a missionary zeal and high-minded fervour that lowered call handle times below her everyday average. She could barely wait for the shift's end, and her trip to Bangalore Mall.

She spoke to Akriti, the first time in several weeks, who was taken in with the idea. 'Great idea, Bitty, your parents will be blown I'm sure. What will you get them?' The women spent four hours at the mall, wandering from the men's section to the women's section, from general household to specialty products. Her parents, with their simple desires and pedestrian needs, were difficult to shop for. After several to-and-fros Bitty decided on a silver ring for Amma, cuff links for Dr Kutty. 'You have to buy flowers as well,' added Akriti. 'I mean, come on, can't give them gifts without flowers.' So Bitty picked a basket of red chrysanthemums for a whopping 400 rupees.

The man behind the machine swiped the card several times. 'No luck,' said the cashier. 'Your card's not working. Can you pay cash?'

Bitty felt a redness rise in her cheeks. 'Not working? I've never had this problem earlier.'

'Happens sometimes. You can contact the card company.'

She fumbled inside her purse and found a single 500-rupee note. 'I'll take the flowers,' she said.

Once home, she walked in behind the generous flower basket, through the stairway and into the family kitchen where Amma heated dinner. 'Oh, what are these?' said Amma.

'Flowers,' said Bitty, 'for you and Achan.' Dr Kutty looked up, his pen tucked into a tear on his banian, the Sanskrit–Malayalam dictionary open on his lap.

'Flowers? For us?' repeated Achan. 'We don't have any need for flowers. How much did they cost?'

'A hundred and fifty rupees,' lied Bitty.

'One hundred and fifty? These will dry up in two or three days. Bitty, you might be earning a high salary but don't waste money like this.' He didn't even thank her.

Later, as she lay in the bedroom, her migraine unrelenting after Hurricane Ike, she heard Achan justify his stance to Amma. 'We have to do our duty. We must teach her to be thrifty, not throw money away on frivolous things. I don't care what she's earning, at this rate she won't save anything.' Bitty let Amma rub in some thailam in that night, willing for anything to break the unrelenting pain.

Next morning, Bitty stopped at the treasure chest. The latest credit card statement lay on top, ripped open. Who was prying into her mail? Achan?

'How dare you read my mail?' she said, bursting from the bedroom. 'You have no right to intrude into my life.'

'Don't talk to your father like that,' said Amma, emerging from the kitchen. 'It's disrespectful.'

'I don't care. He has no right to open my mail.'

Achan stayed silent, tucked into his Malayalam text.

'Besides, I'm the one paying for your household expenses. You're living off my earnings. At least stay out of my space.'

Bitty retreated into the bedroom and shut the door. The ceiling fan clattered at the highest speed. The credit card statement beat against her pillow like a trapped insect. Seizing the damn paper to shred it into a million pieces, she was taken aback by numbers in the last column. There was something wrong. Instead of the 76,000 or 85,000 or whatever ridiculous lie the company printed, there was a Rs 0.00 in the Total Overdue box.

She rushed out of the room again and knew instantly from her father's expression, from the way he looked up from his text and looked down again, he had paid the bill. The entire amount.

'How did you pay this? Where did you get the money?'

'From your 9,000 rupees,' said Amma, emerging

again with a ladle. 'We haven't spent a single rupee, we were saving everything in a Post Office bond. For your future.'

Bitty rushed back to the room. They expected her to be remorseful, grateful even. She was filled instead with a rage, a frenzy that made her jerk the satin-lined pendant box from inside her treasure chest and stomp back to the sitting room. She flung it at him, and it bounced across the sitting-room mat with emphatic thumps. 'I'm paying you back. Keep this – worth half my credit card bill. I don't need your charity.'

The leather box rolled near her father's feet and the clasp clicked open. Her father looked at it and curled his lips. It took several seconds for Bitty to realize the box was filled with a yawning blackness. She picked it up quickly, clawed inside the shiny lining while a terrible bird thrashed inside her stomach. 'You've stolen it,' screeched Bitty. 'You've stolen my platinum necklace.'

'Bitty, watch your tongue,' said Amma. 'We don't even know what you buy. We've never touched your things. How dare you call your father a thief?'

'In a few more months, I'm moving to my own place,' said Bitty. She shut herself into the bedroom with a loud bang that rattled her cupboard hinges. She sunk to the floor, her back sliding against the door. She knew he hadn't taken it, knew it before the words escaped her mouth; she must have lost it, dropped it in the van on a ride back from work. But she wanted to hurt him, pierce his unshakeable morality, his preening righteousness, abuse him the way she was abused on the lines: 'I don't bloody care what you say, you've bloody stolen it.' The statement flapped on the pillow, the Rs 0.00 glaring at her with a belligerent clarity. She crumpled the paper – the aggravating whiteness of her father's debt-free life – into a puckered ball, dropped it into the toilet, yanked the flush.

Mirror, Mirror, on the Wall

At 9:45 a.m., Sashwath was on the last slide. His voice, initially booming, was now tinny and tired. 'I'd like to emphasize again, the ability of a company to innovate and create intellectual property will determine its survival in the new environment.' He stepped off the podium while his carefully crafted PowerPoint collapsed into a blue box. The backdrop receded into the satin-red *OUTSOURCE TO INDIA 2007*.

There was thin applause muffled further by the plush carpet in the five-star conference room. The chairs were not filled yet. Even the outsourcing crowd hadn't made it on time. Sashwath, initially pleased with the first speaker slot, had been hoodwinked. The room had some junior staff and a piddling MC, none of the sector's bigwigs. The damn PR team, instead of averting this early-morning dishonour – an empty hall with waiters clattering trays with soon-to-be-served coffee and biscuits – had trumped up his admission into the speaker list like some fantastic coup: 'Good news, sir. We've wangled the first slot for you, we think it's a great start. You can present your ideas to customers and industry peers. We're not sure yet, but we heard the Finance Minister may be there.' Worded like that, it sounded like an impressive debut for the Callus CEO, the right forum to flaunt his singular experience and unrivalled insights. But the whole morning had fizzled into a no-show. He made a mental note to blast the PR goons.

After his laptop was switched off and the projector screen dissolved into a tea-break whiteness, the crowds started pouring in, just in time for the 10:00 a.m. coffee. He should have known the Indian predilection for food and five-star freebies. Even CEOs and VPs hovered around waiters, indifferent to skipped morning talks or the Industry's Outlook, the topic assigned to Sashwath by the absentee organizers.

The CEO stepped outside the conference room, into the hotel foyer, a Butter-Lite salt biscuit crumbling against his teeth. Under a severely blue sky devoid of clouds, chauffeured cars disgorged industry heavyweights onto marble steps. King-size Corollas and Mercs attested to the swift growth of a fledgling sector. TV journos, saddled with microphones and cameras, awaited newsworthy arrivals. While Sashwath wondered if he should introduce himself to an unsmiling man in a striped suit, a nondescript Fiat unloaded its driver and lined up for valet parking. Soon the cameras, all twenty or thirty, beamed blue-white flares at the Fiat driver: a stout man waddling up the marble steps. What? *Him? Basu?* His IIT college-mate? The man was still tubby like his college days, but imbued as well with a new gravitas by grey whiskers and salt-and-pepper hair. He brushed past eager reporters, his ears beet-red, but the journalists were a relentless lot.

'Sir, what is your view on projected growth rates?' 'Mr Basu, do you foresee any American backlash to outsourcing?' 'Sir, how will American elections affect the Indian economy?' Why were they hounding *him* like that? A mere upstart and they treated him already like Bill Gates? And besides, why weren't they badgering Sashwath, with his trim beard, boyish looks, and delegate badge flaunting his position – CEO, Callus Inc.? He knew more about projected growth rates and American backlashes than slow-moving Basu. Even now, as Sashwath followed the crowd of newshounds into the conference room, the bloke paused at the cookie plate and coffee table, headed straightaway for a snack. Why did they bother with his limited vision?

Sashwath feigned surprise when Basu swivelled in his direction with a plateful of samosas. But there was no glimmer of recognition there, the chap too full of himself to admit college-mates into shimmering camera lights. Did he know that Sashwath was *somebody* as well? A somebody who'd acquired ten million dollars, forty less than the targeted fifty, but when he bagged three customers, a second round of funding would boost his ratings? Who'd consider, given the reception he was currently getting, a hostile takeover of Basu's company in the near future?

The tea-break ended at 10:30 a.m. and there was a new MC on stage, more impressive than the scrawny mite who had introduced Sashwath. Idiot said 'Cahloose' for Callus. 'Ladies and gentlemen, I'm pleased to welcome you to the keynote address of this wonderful conference. We're glad to see this great crowd here. I can see you do not want to miss the rare opportunity of listening to Mr Basu Chatterjee of Bodmas Inc. Without further ado, Mr Basu, the podium is all yours.'

What? Basu? Keynote address? Why hadn't the PR fools apprised him of this? He wasn't even aware of a keynote address. There was a shuffle on the podium, the mic pinned on fatso's suit while Sashwath seethed at the organizers' lunacy. When he turned his head around the carpeted room, there were banners everywhere with Bodmas Inc. screen-printed on satin. All it took was a thirty-minute tea-break to plaster the room. On stage, Basu lurched like a ship, without crafted PowerPoints, cracking two-bit jokes snatched from the internet:

'And did you hear this one? The American caller says "I understand where you're coming from" and the Indian agent replies, "Bangalore, sir."'

Sashwath stepped out to the Men's room. He couldn't take this, the conference shrunk to a farce with men like him, men with keen judgment and real-world smarts suddenly obliterated into faceless listeners. When he returned, Basu was still on stage, talking about the need for a spiritual outlook when running a business. Not a word on shifts across the value chain or unique country propositions but some mystical balderdash, the guy arrogant and brash with his newfound wealth (how dare he forget Sashwath!) but as scattered and quixotic as his IIT days. Distracted by every stray idea, never focused on any one thing, how did he run a complex business?

Sashwath rubbed his stomach, moved his hand up his chest. A tart river rose inside, leaving an acrid streak on his tongue. In a few seconds, his thoughts dissolved inside a thunderous applause that echoed beyond the air-conditioned space rented for the conference. Did the local crowd have no discernment at all?

Basu's frostiness at the conference had done it. Sashwath was more determined than ever to steamroll Bodmas. As his chauffeured Honda Accord headed away from the deafening city honks towards IT Valley's soothing hush, he remembered the day Jagdish had called.

Sashwath was in Illinois then, headed out on Route 66 to a client site. He lost his grip on the steering when he heard the outrageous sum Basu had snagged from a Silicon Valley venture capitalist. A hundred million dollars, Jags had said. Even worse, contracts with two Wall Street banks. Fat Basu? Bugger, hardly prominent on the IIT grapevine, had suddenly overshot gold and silver medallists. Idiot hadn't made it to the US even, not struggled like others with MBA loans and green card waitlists. He was a take-it-easy sort while the rest slogged on college essays and GMAT verbals. 'Rather be my own boss, start my own business,' he used to say.

Sashwath had hardly paid attention then. A Bangalore business did not warrant the malice of McKinsey aspirants in those days. But twenty years later, this was a shocker: Basu, despite his contempt for American brands – 'Indian jeans are good enough for me' – had seized the world's attention and more significantly, its capital.

'Are you sure it's Basu? Hard to believe Butterball can raise that kind of money,' Sashwath had said when

Jags reported the news. A man like that, a fatso without ambition, how had he garnered the interest of money-grubbing VCs? 'And what the hell are *we* doing *here*, man?'

Even the 65 mile per hour freeway or the dependable garbage truck – the lush efficiencies of an American existence – were less alluring than a power-starved, potholed hundred million. For a while there had been a curious buzz about India – the country suddenly pitched from third-world squalor into a knowledge hothouse. TCS, Infosys, Wipro all jostling with Global Greats, snaring *Fortune* covers. And Sashwath's consulting bosses, suddenly fired up by his Indian origins, prodding him to partner with 'enterprising Bangalore businesses'.

For many months, Sashwath hadn't succumbed to the hype. He couldn't envision the India he knew – awash with undrained monsoons, tarpaulin tea-shops, rambling bureaucrats – leaping into the 21st century's techno-buzz. He was better off in a place where winds and ocean currents seemed to submit to the weathercaster's whims.

But the phone call had done it. Those vague notions of a rising India had been fleshed out into a distinct image: Basu, take-it-easy Basu, careening across recently-paved Indian highways in a silver-grey Merc, flush with Valley funds; back-bencher Basu attracting global attention, bloating in a manner his IIT mates hadn't foreseen; the kind of image that jangled Sashwath's green card complacence. A hundred million dollars was not a small sum. Man hit the jackpot, a lucky conjunction of time and place. If *he* could do it, anyone could. And Sashwath definitely could, Wharton MBA, McKinsey Partner, people-charmer, ace-salesman, ops-guru – a man imbued with a vision that Basu with his bumble-bee eyes could hardly conjure up. If they were slinging it in spadefuls, then Sashwath Tejpal, resident of Springfield, Illinois for twenty years, deserved to rake it in.

As his olive-green Porsche bounced along the two-lane Route 66, his future had billowed across the historic bumps of the Illinois road: a Bangalore call centre for internet and telecom companies, Sashwath Tejpal, founder-CEO. A steel-glass tower looming over the city's pancake rooftops, grateful locals lifted from sordid slums into snazzy cubicles. Despite his American green card and Texan twang, he was an Indian patriot, a new-age Gandhi returning to his homeland. It wasn't money, money was the least of it. It was his vision, his fortitude and Jack Welch daring.

What puzzled him then was how bumbling Basu, certainly without a rolodex of moneyed whites, had acquired clients. Sashwath recalled the way he had slobbered at college meals, the only one appreciative of hot canteen lunches: oily dals and thick, leathery rotis slapped out by disgruntled cooks. He was most likely as well to interject a discussion on Kurosawa, Fellini and Ray with: 'Have you seen *Sanam Teri Kasam* man, awesome songs, no?' In those days you were either a pragmatic go-getter or pretentious intellectual. Basu was neither. Not even the third kind, a nerdy brain who grappled with warps in space and parallel universes. Just a no-good drifter headed to the business world. How had he bamboozled Wall Street sharpies?

The CEO looked up when the car turned into the IT Valley gates, and the security guard snapped to brisk attention. The sight of those steel-glass towers looming over immaculate gardens filled him with a choking pride. Callus leased one floor in one structure: the 8th floor in the Cupertino Building. But one day, his company would outgrow this campus, would spill beyond those four towers, would create its own self-contained green city, a first stop for visitors and world leaders. He turned to his laptop deck: Callus at 2010, at 2015 and 2020. By 2015, earlier even, they'd overtake Bodmas. In 2007, they had 300 agents handling two small clients. By 2015, they'd have 100,000. And 300,000 by 2020, spread across 40 countries.

He directed the chauffer to crank up the volume on the CD player. For twenty years in the US, he had tuned into the National Public Radio or some local pop channel. In India, he played his wife's Hindi CD. Because bloody hell, yaar, *yeh swadesh hai mera.*

Sashwath thought the PR firm was doing a reasonable job. They made up for the washout conference with three or four interviews – one with a nervous man, another with a starry-eyed woman who reinforced the CEO's sense of the market. 'Unlike others, you have a roadmap,' she acknowledged in silky tones.

The coverage overall was moderate, not outlandish. A low hum to keep Sashwath ticking. Until he emerged one evening from an MG Road pub and spotted a chubby face on the magazine stand that leaned against a telephone pole. He rubbed his eyes and then he saw the same face, recast over and over again, on the front cover of some business mag. He'd only had a few beers, so it couldn't have been his fuzzy vision. He pummelled his way across the footpath crowd till he stooped over Basu – swollen like a cancer – on the *Dalal Street Buzz*. On the cover, on a leading business mag, Basu, Basu, Basu clogging up the city's newsstands.

'Not a three-inch write-up on some dinky back page,' he told the PR team, who fidgeted in his presence the next morning. Who seemed suddenly, despite their pointy shoes and spiffy suits, like overgrown adolescents. Idiots had no inkling of the sudden spike in Basu's publicity. 'What the hell are you guys doing?'

It only got worse. On Sunday, there was a barrage of Bodmas articles, on centrespreads, across front pages, colour inserts in business sections. All parroting the same theme: 'The Balanced CEO: A business that rewards its employees with time'. *The New Delhi Talk* screeched: 'Work-life Balance: An Indian business sets new trends'. The *Cityplus*, the *Indianow!* magazine, all taken in by the 'Multidimensional CEO: Integrating the Personal and Spiritual'. He heard as well from a connected snoop that Basu was slated for the next *India Current.*

Sashwath called up Jagdish that evening. The man shuttling between Paris, Cincinnati and Hong Kong didn't get it at first. 'Basu on *Dalal Street Buzz*,' said Sashwath, his voice whipping through white noise.

'Who? Boss who? Oh, Basu? On what?' When he finally got it, he laughed. 'Man, Sashwath, you have to give it to the bugger, he's come a long way. Do you remember the night at Saras, when we ragged him, made him dance to film songs?'

Sashwath had forgotten but it came back to him now. The night their group, flushed with dope, wrestled Basu into a ghaghra-choli and goaded him to imitate Sridevi's swaying hips. The CEO remembered the music blaring from a cheap audio system drowned out by lewd whistles. There was a reason that night for ruthless hoots: fatso had licked Reddy's impossible Fluid Mechanics paper, the only one among forty kids to be awarded an 'A'. The only one who cracked the killer question about tapered pipes positioned one on top of the other. 'Easy, yaar,' he'd said. 'Total energy per unit mass at the top minus total energy per unit mass at the bottom.' An 'A' when more than half the class had flunked. So swing and twirl and wriggle he did, with the same even temper that cracked Reddy's fundas. There were many snipes that night, coarse comments about Basu's total energy at the top minus his total energy at the bottom. 'Keep at it, man, till you're at 30 joules per kg. More action at the bottom.' Sashwath remembered something else; such memories, dredged up after so many years, should have been foggy, but they surfaced with astonishing clarity. It was the day after the ragging, when everyone felt vaguely guilty about the night's misdoings, and he bumped into Basu at the tea-shop outside campus. He expected recrimination of some sort, a cold shoulder or a deadpan look, but there was the usual cheer, his trademark bluster unaltered by the night's harassment. 'Want to see a flick tonight?' he said while Sashwath spilled his tea, the entire plastic cupful, on a hand shaking with remorse.

How did a guy, so unconcerned at one time about his standing in any circle, become this Machiavellian self-promoter?

On Monday, the CEO appointed a new PR agency. 'For heaven's sake, send me people with experience. I don't want a bunch of kids fiddling with my rep,' he said to the agency's chief on the telephone. 'I need a more aggressive approach, not two-bit snippets here and there. Something that can get us onto magazine covers.'

'I can't believe this,' he said to the new PR team seated in the conference room. It was a couple, a man and woman, older than the unworldly bunch that managed his account until last week. They filled the room with the scent of fruity deodorants. He hoped their grey hairs and sallow, pinched faces would deliver results. The CEO did not mince words: 'This other company monopolizes the nation's papers, and look at us, we have a far richer background and we're nowhere.'

At least the new team had a point of view, a rationale for the ludicrous aura that surrounded Basu. 'You see, Mr Tejpal, journalists today are looking for angles. Mere success is prosaic. Too many successful Indians these days, so success is not a story. You have to project a personality, some kind of difference. And Mr Chatterjee does that superbly. He combines high growth with spirituality and awards people with personal time. Reports say he grants sabbaticals instead of pay raises, offers free meditation classes, encourages hobbies – readers appreciate the difference.'

'Fine, give me an angle. How will you project me?'

'We can't do that, it has to come from you. We can weave a narrative based on something you believe in, a story centred on a core value.' The man spoke in a ponderous baritone and the woman droned like a background tanpura: 'Imhmm, Imhmm.'

'Core value? I believe in hard work. In growing investor value. Yes, shareholder value – why don't you use that?'

The woman looked at the man, the man looked at Sashwath. The chap's gaunt face looked like it was going to crack. 'That's already taken, Mr Tejpal. The biggest Indian business family has a huge headstart on shareholder value. Besides, that works if you have aam aadmi investors. You don't stir hearts by making bankers richer. Now take Mr Basu, he's integrated his spiritual beliefs to create a different kind of workplace. It's a fascinating story.'

Why cite Basu again and again when they'd been hired to dislodge his presence? 'In that case, you need to come up with something. What are your fees for? I hardly have the time with my packed calendar to fabricate quirks.'

Blokes had no idea what his life was like, the PR meeting one of several tasks he juggled in an overfull day. And no day like the other – internal meetings, operational huddles, banker calls, industry dinners, investor to-dos – did they know what it took? Take this instance: the PR team seated around his conference table, the screen filled with a coloured pie-graph that read, 'Competitor's Share of Shout' and his mobile throbbed. A banker asked him to summarize attrition costs. Sashwath buzzed his secretary to fix a one-on-one with the counsellor. Woman said she was fixing the attrition issue. The CEO had no time for details, for how things were done, he needed results. Clear outcomes. He turned to the PR team again:

'Don't really care how you do it, but I need, in six months' time, wider coverage than that idiot... I mean Basu.'

'There's something else that we've heard about Mr Basu. Apparently his success is largely due to Vaastu changes he made to his office layout.'

'Vaastu? What's that?'

'Haven't you heard, sir? Traditional architectural norms that align energies for optimal outcomes. Many Indian businesses have benefitted...'

Before the CEO could respond, his phone vibrated again. His Operations Manager this time. 'Boss, the disaster management clause with Beam America. We agreed to raise headcount by 30% during crises.'

'So?' His Senior Managers lacked judgment. They couldn't determine when they needed him and when they didn't. Why call him, directly on the mobile, about some clause in an agreement already signed?

'Storm's heading to Galveston. We need to increase headcount in two days.'

'So do it.'

'We can't. We don't have anyone on the bench.'

'Why not?'

'You refused, boss, in the last meeting, to hire anyone. You said we cannot have people idling around the place.'

'I'm in an important meeting. Think of a solution and come back to me.' Sashwath disliked this about his managers. Why were they paid such whopping salaries when they couldn't solve their own problems?

Chap wouldn't hang up. 'Boss, this is important. We might lose our biggest client.'

He turned to face the team. 'So, what were you saying about Vaastu? And how did it help Bodmas?'

Beam America was moving its 3,000-agent account to Bodmas. Sashwath's relationships didn't carry the same weight anymore. Not after the hurricane fiasco.

At first, the CEO thought Callus handled the crisis well. Exceedingly well, in fact. A 40% increase in call rates and they hadn't made customers wait. Not one bit longer. And they did this with the same headcount. With a 24-hour notice after the hurricane hit Galveston. Sashwath attributed it to focus and diligence, the results of a passionate leadership. His Team Leaders and agents worked on double shifts that night without tea-breaks or dinner-breaks. He promised the best team a trip to Florida, a generous reward for a night's exertion. They received a laudatory note from the Beam America VP: 'Congratulations to the Callus Team for their stupendous effort on the night of the hurricane. Without you coming through, we wouldn't have made it.'

It was after the celebratory party, funded by the company for all employees, that other reports started creeping in. Something about Callus agents disconnecting calls without resolving problems. Some calls disconnected as soon as they landed, so that customers, who were promptly received and greeted by a machine, were stalled from explaining problems by resounding clicks. 'Customers report they were disconnected again and again. Some had to re-enter the queue five times before reaching a human voice.' Call handle times – the time agents spent chatting with customers – were shortened because calls were not handled at all. 'Your guys hoodwinked the system,' the Beam America VP hollered on the phone. 'We don't understand how you allowed this to happen.'

Seated at another outsourcing conference, the VP's words rang inside Sashwath's ears. It was not easy, after all, when the largest client threatened to pull out. It was Basu again on stage, rambling about some Schumacher's economics, but Sashwath was devoid this time of his earlier revulsion. He watched slide after slide drop on the screen like chunks of his life. Perhaps that's how his future would flash by, condensed into bullet-point text. He was hardly taken aback, when a few minutes later, Basu thumped him on the back.

'Hey, Sashwath, didn't realize you were in town. When did you get here?'

'You're a big man now, why would you notice people like me?'

'I didn't know you were here, when did you move to India?'

'Been here for two years,' said Sashwath. Around them, waiters cleared conference tables, cleaners swept crumbs off shiny floors. 'I'm running Callus.'

'A call centre? Good for you. You're exactly the kind of person this industry needs. How are Rohini and Karan?'

'I hear you have 50,000 agents?'

'You know what these businesses are like. Before you know it, they balloon into something uncontrollable.'

'I have a question, how do you manage your PR? You're all over the papers?'

'Frankly, have no idea how that happened. This reporter bunch blows everything out of proportion. Just hype, nothing else. Hey, let's meet for dinner sometime with your wife and son. So glad you're in Bangalore. How about next month? Are you free? Next four weeks, I'm not here – I'm off to Omkareshwar for a 30-day retreat. Meditation camp for advanced students. Don't tell anyone about where I'm off to, last thing I want is journos hounding me.'

After Basu buzzed off, Sashwath watched cars recede from the foyer. His thoughts, usually teetering between this and that, paused on the recent conversation. Basu hadn't changed. The guy was still Buddha-like, immune to the rules of the community. Unconcerned by his own heavyweight position, by the distance between them, he'd been genuinely pleased to encounter Sashwath. His meditation retreats were anything but a PR ruse. Waving to his chauffeur, Sashwath felt, for the first time, envious not of the man's success but of Basu himself. He possessed something Sashwath would never have, an inner resistance, a dispassion that would always elude him.

Inside the car, he wondered what he should wear for Basu's dinner. Something informal, casual chic or handwoven ethnic? Where was that fair-trade, green boutique Akriti had mentioned?

Magic Mushrooms

He ruled the van, he was king. Other dudes, call centre agents, software morons, oily-haired suckers were tuned out. Grating voices inside the van, *your Team Leader, my manager, this report, that score, his salary, her promotion*, tedious talk, prosaic minds. He shut them out, rarely let them in. His ears were filled with Jimi's thick sounds, the strumming guitar screeching, roaring, billowing inside his earphones. Jimi had flair, flying fingers, guitar around his neck, throbbing like a pulse. Jimi, Jimi, Jimi, Jimutha, the sound of clouds, a child with a thunderclap voice, a boom as expressive as the Master, the one and only Jimi Hendrix.

The van stopped. Akriti climbed aboard. She was okay, the trainer chick, had fizz. Jimi himself was trained by an Anglo-chick, an Yvette something. Not that he needed training, all that drivel on Yank history, 12th and 14th presidents, doddery men fighting wars and freeing slaves, two goddamn weeks irrelevant to his work. Even worse, imbecilic accent classes for dudes who didn't speak English. Where did they grow up, Indian mutt-heads who stumbled on *How-are-yous* and *What-do-you-dos*. Akriti was okay, he'd spotted her at clubs. Drank beer, smoked, spoke decently. Couldn't have been a trainer otherwise. Now she smiled at him, lifted her skirt an inch, sank into her seat. Knock-kneed spindly legs. Not sexy but flirty. Her neck twisted to peek at him, turned rapidly back. A chick coaching other chicks yet invariably drawn to him. Who else on this van could give her that kind of kick? He scanned the rest – mother-tongued vernaculars – would any others join this moronic business? Dudes in his garage band – Guru, Ketan, Cariappa – had spunk; not deadheads like these numbskull operators. He wouldn't be here if his frenzied parents weren't screeching about his 'aimless drifting'. It was funny the way their remarks had deflated from 'You're worse than useless without a degree, you'll never get anywhere in this country' to a mellow 'A call centre job is *good*, Jimutha, at least the sector's growing. So what if you don't have a degree?' The change ushered by his short stay at the rehab centre and his therapist's remarks: 'Let the boy be. Too much pressure and there might be a relapse.'

A relapse? What did she know, the white-coated specialist, about psychedelic trips? Her hair tucked into a crocheted net, the woman rarely journeyed outside hospital walls. Did she know he wasn't addicted? That his trips were driven by a deliberate will, not by desperate cravings? Not just her but the centre's doctors, with chunky Tamil accents and weary morals, tiring him with raspy dictates: 'You need to start working, you need to have a purpose.' Strapped to a steel bed, his eyelids scarcely unglued, he heard primitive rumbles and laughed inside. *Purpose?* How would those dudes, humdrum medics from Bangalore colleges, apprehend purposes grander than doctor salaries? 'We can put you onto recruitment agencies to find a job,' they'd said. His fingers strumming his hospital gown, he counted necks: necks with thick folds, necks with bumps and grooves and ugly rashes slung with stethoscope-snakes, thinking all the while of Jimi's neck, the Master's muscles rippling in a V, his black marble skin made taut by his guitar. *Purr-piss*, the syllables strung out like two chords, stayed stranded like his parents' expressions when they found his new stash.

Purpose: a word he muffled with Jimi's 'noise' or Magic Mushrooms' new album, the psychedelic band he currently grooved to. The cool thing about his garage gang was they dug the same beats, shared the same vibes. If they disagreed, the boys deferred to his sound sense. They were not born like him with a visceral sense for rock, real rock.

The van stopped again. Jimutha removed his headset. They had shortened his name at the call centre. Now he was Jimi like the Master. The trainer suggested it: 'Call yourself Jimmy,' she said. He quickly agreed, not sighting her misspelling. A week later, when the Admin bloke handed out badges, he was aghast to find 'Jimutha – Jimmy'.

'It's not Jimmy, it's Jimi, J-I-M-I,' Jimutha said.

'No, no,' responded the Admin dork. 'Normal American spelling is Jimmy only, J-I-M-M-Y. Anyway, you won't spell your name to customers, why should it matter?'

'Because my name's Jimi. I can't wear this badge, it's moronic.'

The fellow's face puckered like a leaky balloon. 'You must learn how to talk to Senior Managers. Anyway, company cannot sponsor fancy spellings. Every badge costs 35 rupees.'

So Jimi fixed it himself with a roadside badge-maker, a blazing Jimi on purple, 'Purple Haze' for those who knew.

Akriti turned her head again. The woman was coming on to him. Her eyes shimmered but he was not swayed by her reedy legs. Maybe some other time, tonight he was figuring out tunes for the weekend bang-up. The boys were stale, even with the new sampler and MIDI controls, their tones were jaded. They needed to shift scales, try something else, stop parroting the same crap. He wanted sounds keeping with his moods and the pulsing traffic of a teeming city. Perhaps even call centre sounds, a trainer's rap or telephone jazz, a mixing of workplace clatter with drums and guitars.

Brakes screeched, the van lurched and Jimutha bounced in the back seat. Outside, flyover builders crouched around a smoky midnight haze punctured by headlights. An auto-driver, jostling in narrowing space outside metal pilings, squeezed his balloon-horn. Everything was here, the sounds he sought, in purring scooters and tooting autos. He shut his eyes and bulky pillars merged with shrapnel, metal pounded on tar, metal on concrete, metal with metal, rock with rock, music to crack through irksome lives and the tedious

114

night. He almost had it, a new melody to pump the boys and just then a spasm, a disruption: a blasted Telugu song in his tunnel. 'Swamiye Ayyappa, Saranam Ayyappa.' He opened his eyes. The driver, the infernal rogue filled the van's cavity with tinny film songs, godly music. What was wrong with the bugger, didn't he realize Jimi ruled the van? He'd tell the twerp at the next traffic light to shut off his infernal racket.

Like his father's loud knocks booming at his door: 'Jimutha, shut off that infernal noise.' His parents had been coddled all their lives in a clinical hush. Doctor parents, smug, moneymaking, public-spirited until he came along; a gynaec mother, a paediatric father, deft C-sections, six-pound babies, swift inoculations, regular hours, a stream of in-out patients. They had it figured out, all regulated till Jimi–Jimutha slid into their lives. Jimutha, a thunder-cloud with sinister curls, a dark puff that stirred them up. Much later, his mother told the therapist, she'd seen it in his wiry hair and clenched fists, 'a stubborn child'. But she hadn't seen the extent of his obstinacy, the 'unrelenting clinging to some blue-sky passion', his plunge from average marks at school into an all-consuming rock obsession. They were willing to put up with the rest, his admission into a small-time college, his indifference to their crazed outbursts: 'Do you realize how we've struggled to make it?' 'You... you have it too easy, that's the problem.' 'You don't realize how competitive India is.' His father retreating into a tart silence, certain it was the noise, the goddamn racket that spurred his son's cravings.

Fewer scenes after he signed up at Bodmas, the first call centre he'd worked at. At least, they rationalized, he had a job. Confined in a cubicle, curfewed by night shifts, he could hardly get into 'mischief' with his band-mates. Not the kind of job his gold-medallist parents once coveted but anything better than a void. They freaked again at his shift from Bodmas to the smaller centre. 'No one's heard of Callus, Jimi. At least, Bodmas has a great reputation. I hear American business schools favour Bodmas employees.' But Jimi had decided he didn't like that Bodmas place. Too much booming cheer, too gimmicky. Employees sucked in by the 'we are different' drivel. A goddamn cult, that's what it was. Jimi was happier in the beat-up Callus Matador.

He winked at Akriti who turned her head again. He slid into the seat next to her. 'Bloody awful hah, that driver's racket? Here listen, *this* will blow your mind.'

Some vodka, rum, lots of beer, a few strips of blotter with the real stuff – with police crack-downs, tough to hustle pure acid – drums, his electric guitar, guys he could groove with, and an empty garage. That to Jimi, was life, dissolution, escape. And the music, a harvest of happy tempers seized by a machine. No studio, no producers, no extras. For many months now, he had ditched all that. It was a democratic group, no bosses, no leaders but he guided them sometimes. They were caught up in 'sounding cool', giggling at night clubs, boozing at pubs, they'd forgotten the basics. The guts of psychedelic rock: numbing noise and a lick of Lysergic Acid Diethylamide. Like his doctor parents, he used a chemical name. That's all it was really, the ingestion of a complex compound by a living organism. Reduced the blah-blah to its scientific essence, nothing daffy like *Lucy in the Sky with Diamonds* or *Puff the Magic Dragon.*

This Friday, Akriti was there as well and Ketan brought a chick along, a family friend. A low-grade chick, maybe 5.5, if he was charitable, 6.0, lower than the 7.5 Akriti. The garage had oil stains – Guru's dad's cars were always leaking – cushions with silken covers from Jimutha's upstairs living room, a boom box, amps, the sampler, MIDI controls, his guitar, drums, and the new recorder with freaky feedbacks. His hair, below his shoulders, frizzed into a wiry puff. His denim vest hung loosely over his suede belt. Not for him the material sparseness of the American '60s or Gandhi's village living. He didn't really freak for things, but in the stuff he had, he liked quality – what else were his parents earning for?

Guru arrived with food. Not that Jimi ate on such nights but the rest couldn't conceive of skipping dinner. 'At least biryani and raita, boss, can't party without food.'

Magic Mushrooms played in the background. Their guitarist, a guy called George Fallows recreated Jimi's devilry. Of course, no one to beat the Master but still, this guy had that intuitive feel for slides and pull-offs. His solos ripped through Jimutha's cloud-head like bullets. He'd heard this song many times, 'It's coming on, it's coming on,' but for the first time, he picked up the rush of wheels – a car on a highway? an air instrument? – what was the source of the speedy whoosh, a drafty whistle smothered by the Mushrooms' drummer? And then Fallows with his guitar again, mind-blowing. Jimi removed his vest. The other boys waited for his command. They

117

were eager to chew the blotter but Jimi sucked up the sound, started the climb without chemicals. *Wait*, he flashed, his palms raised while Fallows seeped into his pores. For any journey, he told them, you had to be primed.

And then Ketan's chick, clearly a back-number, a vernacular recently risen in the ranks – he could tell by her unstylish jeans and flashy earrings – opened her foul mouth and started giggling. Loudly. A raucous laugh that crashed into Fallows's sorcery just when the notes were boring into Jimi's veins. Man, Ketan lacked taste. He couldn't bring anyone and everyone into the garage with no regard for anything. Why, this chick in the call centre would be a mother-tongue, a subnormal Telugu vernac, he could hear it in her voice, in her unchecked guffaws, the woman was a bloody local. More than anything else she was colliding with his mood, he was monkeying around in smashing blues, army-greens and now he saw blood red, angry STOP signs that halted his ride. He drew Ketan aside with a gesture and ushered him behind Guru's dad's car and told him to eject the creature.

'No way, yaar, that's not done. It's bloody rude,' Ketan responded.

Jerk didn't get it. If she stayed, he warned, no party, no music, no trip.

'Listen, what's wrong with her? She's not objecting to anything. Besides, I thought we don't have bosses here.'

Guru was high by then, his arm resting on Jimutha's shoulder. Guru kicked his dad's spare wheels, sent them crashing into the imported lawn mower resting against the garage door. Petrol vapours, rising from the garage floor, tickled Jimi's nose. He loved the smell. But Ketan was busting his mood. Of course Jimi wasn't the boss, but the woman didn't have *it*. As easy as that, no tall stories, the spare truth.

'What is *it*?' Ketan asked.

Blockhead. Did he need everything spelt out?

Guru helped him: 'Not our kind, Ketan, we don't dig her.' Guru had his contractor dad's calculating mind.

Yes, Jimutha added quickly: '*We* don't dig her.' Not just Jimi, the whole gang, a majority vote, a shared dislike.

'Bastards,' said Ketan. He walked into the garage and yanked the woman off her cushion, the chick already high, giggling uncontrollably without a smack of anything. He kicked the bass drum and the new 14" floor tom; cymbals crashed on oil stains. 'I quit, okay? Forever. Bloody find another drummer.'

Jimutha hurriedly chewed the blotter and passed the sheet around. Did Ketan think he was central to their band's success? Any guy on the street could pound those drums, but the guitar was complex and integral to the sound. But the bloody chick and Ketan's outburst spoiled his takeoff, he could tell it was going to be a bad trip. Not like the last one – an extraordinary hike across his poster ceiling into a Hendrix concert, guitar strings leaping from his fingers, Jimi outside his body, inside a throbbing mass, an orgasmic whole, the crowds, the swingers on the van, everyone had *it* – and now, shit, man, it wasn't coming on, despite Mushrooms, despite Fallows. His tongue grazed the blotter again, he'd never done this, a double dose of 100 ug LSD, it was that chick, man, she smashed his trip. He lost it, lost control. It was coming on, coming on. Oil-stains spread. Fattened. Rose. BLEW. Cushions gyrated. Floated. INFLATED. Bled. Oozed.

Pumped. Writhed. Breathed. Strummed. Hair, fur, roaches, worms wriggled crawled. Everything everyone squeezed out, compressed, suffocated, muffled. Goddamn awful goddamn awful, Ketan's chick-bitch bitch-chick her awfulness fused with Akriti's stick-legs.

The last call that day, a crabby customer. Jimi was sorting some agent's mess-up: a wrong billing address, an undelivered bill. 'These agents in India, they just don't get it. I spelt out my street name five times,' the white man said. He didn't know Jimi was Indian, so cramped was his vision of the archetypal Indian.

Not that Jimutha revered Americans, rule-followers of a different kind. In this job he rarely stumbled on anyone funky. Cribbing about a few cents here and a few cents there, they were snared by square bills in square worlds. He shrugged off his headset, the wires tangled in stiff curls. He was growing a moustache since the last trip. He needed to re-enter Jimi's world, bask in the ecstasy of pure sound. His hand slid into his pocket, a new Magic Mushrooms album, fabulous, he'd groove to that with Akriti. Since the garage bang-up he connected with the chick. In spite of a bad trip, they rode together, wave after wave, reading each other's goddamn thoughts, sucked into the same bogs, spooked by the same spectres. Perhaps a psychic link, he hadn't entered another person's mind till then. He logged out and looked across his cubicle, at vernacs all around.

The one next to him, a double-mother-tongue, a tenacious Malayali who stuttered on calls, stretched above his cubicle. Why did Callus hire such incompetents? The woman leaned into Jimi's space.

'Amerrricans are so rrrude,' she said.

Jimi lifted an eyebrow – *really?* How sad, poor girl. Tch, tch, tch. Hey, what was wrong with her? They shared a cubicle wall but they had *nothing* in common. *Nothing.* Yanks didn't give him shit, no way, not to Jimi and if they did, he didn't give a jot. He shrugged and moved away, aloof. Couldn't the female tell he was different, not one of *them?*

On the van again, he snuggled with Akriti. Man, she lucked out, finding him in this fossil factory. They were not dating or anything, just riding together in the van. He shared his headset with the chick, tuned her senses to the whole-bodied swells and thumps of Fallows's guitar, *real rock*, the kind that crept into your skin, pounded the universe, Siva's *tandava*. 'Hear that, baby,' he said, his hands groping at her skirt.

The van stopped at his place. 1:00 a.m. and several cars were parked outside the gate. Another party, his parents with their stuffy Rotary friends. It had been a long time since the last party, the doctors preoccupied by their unsettled son, rattled by his druggie trips, sheepish about his decline when other Rotary kids were headed to foreign MBAs.

His father leaned on the oakwood bar, custom-designed by an interior company that 'knows their stuff' and described his encounter with an Indian tourist group in Paris, a story Jimi'd heard many times over.

'You won't believe these people,' his father said, in his muddled Scotch voice. 'Here they are in France, surrounded by French restaurants, the best cuisine in the world, the lightest soufflés, rabbit pâté, salmon mousse – and what do you think they eat? Udipi idlis and dahi-vadas. They even take cooks with them. Beats me why they even leave the country.' Then he showed them the crystal bar shaker he had bought in Venice. 'Just look at the detail, that's what I love, their attention to detail. You see, Gopi, here, see this, the bottom's made of rubber so it doesn't scratch the oak wood.'

His father had strong opinions, things he admired, things he disliked. He admired cultivation, poise, objects imbued with taste. He disliked Hendrix, Fallows, Mushrooms, the posters, the sounds, the free-spiritedness, Jimutha's being, the *thing* his son had become.

Jimi slunk past that night, a soft shadow on the banister. After hundreds of calls and eight hours of strained politeness, 'You must smile on the phone, customers can hear you smile,' he couldn't act under his mother's fidgety eyes and his father's derisory breath: 'Yes, uncle, I work at a call centre', 'Yes, aunty, I love the job'. No, no, not in that mausoleum-like living-room with his father's mummified objects: a wooden turntable with Bach records, a rectangular coffee table with Egyptian prints, 'an elegance beyond Indian designers'.

He stopped near the stairs, unseen. His mother and a few ladies were hunched over the powder-coated CD rack: 'Hey, Pramila, what's this, a CD with Siva, Vishnu, Ganesha? Fusion music?'

'Honestly, I've no idea, those are Jimutha's. You know these kids, they listen to all kinds of things these days.'

'But, Pramila, have you seen this, a naked blonde woman among *our* gods? These Americans are shameless.'

His mother hurriedly wrested the CD from the woman's prying eyes. 'Is there? I don't know what this is. Only so much we can monitor with the internet and everything. Anyway the boy hardly has time these days. Such tiring work at the call centre.'

'So,' asked the woman, still fiddling with his CD covers, 'what does he plan to do next? An MBA?' Jimi knew it wasn't an innocuous question. Surely a call centre job wasn't a suitable life-station for *him*, the scion of two doctors with a booming practice?

'Maybe a Master's in the US,' said his mother, noisily shattering ice inside a bucket. A Master's? In the US? Jimutha had no such plans, his parents hadn't discussed this, they hadn't dared perhaps, so what was the doctor-lady talking about? His future, if he thought about it, was rock. For the moment though, he was beyond caring. Not for him, goddamn recordings, productions, concerts, CDs – the juice was in the making, in strumming the guitar and zoning out. *A Master's in the US?* A small lie, a mother's cover-up for 'her no-good son' but he was flustered, rattled, bloody damn pissed, whipped up to enter the room and spoil their goddamn party. *Nothing, aunty, I don't have plans, I live for the present.* He foraged inside his pocket, his knuckles white, trembling, there was the Mushrooms CD but where was the blotter, the blotter, surely it wasn't chewed up on Saturday, he could've sworn there was some in his pocket. The Callus ID, his car-keys, his cafeteria coupons, the chick's number, a few 500-rupee notes, ah, he found it, sprinted noisily up the stairs, didn't care about cloaking his presence, shot into the room, he was going, going, gone, blotted himself out.

Inside his room he seized the Vicks bottle, cough-soothing, chest-expanding vapours to jack up his high. It was here, release, deliverance, absolution. His walls covered in Fallows and Jimi posters, red and yellow spirals, a black-and-white Jimi with a suede-leather jacket, Fallows in Africa, astride a zebra with an eagle tattoo on his bare chest, Jimi as a Hindu god, many-faced goddesses slobbering at his feet, wouldn't the downstairs aunties freak out?

He plugged it in, Magic Mushrooms and his all-time favourite, 'It's Coming On' and glimpsed another face on the wall – Jimi inside his wrought-iron mirror? Jimutha, Jimi, the same moustache, the same thick lips, the smouldering eyes, the genius look, the narrow-necked Strat slung on his neck, the left-handed dexterity, the exploding sound that shot off the ceiling, sprung off the walls, slipped and slid across the floor, scampered down the stairs, trickled into the party, burst into their chatter, their kitty-cat talk and then the rush: winds whipped his face, fingers slid on strings. Crowds crooned. They-loved-him they-loved-him he jumped he bent he flexed played-it-forward played-it-back turned it upside-down downside-up that ways this ways anyways he was it, God, Jimi, Fallows. Cranked up the volume. Shot into space. All eyes on him, a million eyes with blue edges, fiery goddesses, knock-kneed chicks. He bent forward, crooned over the guitar, made love to the goddamn strings. They-loved-him, they-loved-him, they-loved-him, he hopped on one foot, then another, smashed the guitar, blasted the amps, struck a match, lit the wood, burnt the air, they were coming, they were coming, closing in, crowds, swingers, Mama, Papa, downstairs-aunties: 'Jimi, I didn't know you were home. *What* are you doing? Your hair's on fire.'

Six weeks and she was getting too close, too whiny, too demanding. The Akriti chick sliding into formulaic stuffiness, plodding womanly wants: 'You must meet my parents', 'Karan proposed to Ramya, isn't that cool, they're *actually* engaged?' 'We're going to be *alone* on Valentine's, right?' Worse, she was squirting her coaching shit: 'I think you should stop doing drugs, I mean Jimi, you have to grow up.' Did she think she was a goddamn parent? After tuning into his music, his CDs, his acid, didn't she get it? He was not on the same track, not like the rest – squashed inside squares – he was off the damn train. On the Callus van, she nodded at him, waved at the reserved seat, at the blank space waiting for him.

He ignored her, moved in next to the vernac chick, the one seated next to him at Callus. She was one of Akriti's trainees, the Malayali chick newly slicked at the Callus finishing school: mini-skirt, shiny top, plunging neckline. He flung his arm around her: 'Hey, have you heard this? Really cool sound, plug this in.' He watched Akriti, two rows ahead, her neck stiff, her head straight; he hoped she didn't erupt, he disliked raw emotion. Like his mother at the rehab centre, her doctor-poise shred into a million pieces, the tears, the ugly sounds, neurotic regrets: 'What did I do wrong? What did I do wrong?' and the flare-ups, the loss of control: 'Maybe, that music – we shouldn't have given in!' His parents feeling that the disease might have been warded off if they'd acted earlier. His father speaking with a specialist's swagger: 'It was definitely the guitar that infected his mind,' contradicted by his wife: 'Gopi said his son's keyboard lessons had a positive impact on his academics.' It was laughable to watch his doctor parents, efficient and decisive with patients, dithering at Jimi's resolve. Ironically, it was them, their white-coated sterility, their unshakeable faith in pills that inspired his trips. If chemicals could produce magical remissions then why not ecstasy, the simple next step?

Little did they know it was reality that was diseased. And their thinking, their clinical haze. On some trips he'd had such boundless clarity, such awesome visions – networks of light, the interconnection of beings, the goddamn web of life – stuff sadhus hankered for. He'd already made it, made it with his music, made it with this what's-her-name vernacular chick, made it in the only place and time that mattered, here and now.

Akriti hadn't turned yet. She was an emotional girl. She couldn't hold out for the entire ride. He talked to the mother-tongue chick, loud enough for Akriti to hear. 'So, what kind of music do you listen to?' She fumbled and stuttered, he could tell she was nervous. 'Listen, by the way, I'm Jimutha. I know we met at Callus, your name's...?'

'Bitty,' she replied. 'Bitty Menon.' His arm slung behind her on the rexine seat, inched forward, lightly brushed her shoulder. He wondered how far she'd go. One-eighth, quarter, half-way, maybe vernacs were far more willing these days? She was disconcerted by his nearness but fired up as well. Who wouldn't be, given the other clods around? She moved closer, her legs touching, pulpy thighs unlike Akriti's stork legs. That chick

hadn't reacted yet. Did the female think he'd plead for
forgiveness? She didn't know him, his shatterproof pride,
his iron-willed capacity to hold out; he hadn't asked the
idiot Ketan to come back, had he? Fool was back on his
own after a breakup with his woman. Jimi knew the man
wouldn't cope, no one did outside *his* shelter. Even the
Akriti chick, she was bound to break down, scamper back,
panting like a dog.

'So, Bitty, what do you say, want to hang out with us on
Friday – just me and a few friends in this garage?'

He was not serious of course. He hardly wanted her to
come. Ketan would have the last laugh if Jimi brought a
vernacular. On the other hand, Jimi loved to shake up
the blokes, break his own rules to unseat their thinking.
The woman had a decent face, neat features but he
didn't dig her, not enough to cart her around on a jaunt.
He was currently on a different trip: flog Akriti, shake
her trainer stuffiness, show her who's in charge. She
stayed with him on *his* terms or not at all, he flung her
out when he wanted to and she never, ever controlled
him. She could do what she goddamn wanted with her
whiny vernaculars. Her neck wobbled. In a few seconds
she'd turn her head. How could she ride out the journey
without looking at them?

'Where's the party?' the Bitty-chick asked him.

'I'll email the address, I definitely want you there,'
he responded, loud enough for his voice to reach the
driver's front-seat.

'What time?' asked the Bitty-chick.

Time? Man, the chick was regressive. They rarely met
at a scheduled time. There was a joint understanding that
people came when they *had* to.

'Time?' repeated Jimutha. 'Um, you know, I'll just pick you up. Send me your home address.'

'No, no,' she said. 'Don't pick me up. I'll come on my own. What time?' she persisted.

'Any time after 9ish.'

'Oh, nine at night? What time does it end?'

Nine at night? You had to give it to these vernaculars, they were an amusing lot. What time did it end? It didn't and that was the point.

'You know, don't worry about the time. I'll drop you back. Don't tell me you have a curfew?' he said, his eyes pinned on Akriti's stretched neck, stretched in the wrong direction, at an awkward angle. Was she asleep? Was the bitch unmoved?

He smiled absently at the Bitty-chick who jabbered on about start-times, end-times, this time, that time, time, time, time... time to rouse the other chick, shake her from her slumber. He shook his legs out, straightened all six feet of his hunky self to stop the driver's tinny music and play his CD while he grooved with this whatshername Menon. It gave him a reason to walk down the aisle and check on Akriti: was she knocked out, drunk, doped?

The man, the driver-man, the fool – Jimutha could not believe this – objected. He refused to play *his* CD. 'That I not put,' he said. Jimi was stupefied, almost forgot his original mission. Did the bloke realize he was not in charge here? Just because he controlled the steering, he didn't control their trip, definitely not Jimi's trip, no one did, not his parents, not Ketan, not the Akriti-chick. Not even the new Bitty-woman, obsessed with start times and end times as if she had a train to catch.

'Well, you have to, man, as employees we have rights.

128

What's wrong with this bugger, yaar?' he said, turning to see if Akriti heard. When the man resisted again, Jimi threatened to report his absurdness to the Admin dork.

When Jimi walked back across the van's aisle, the floor rumbling across a speed-bump, he glanced at the trainer-female who was scornfully awake. A disinterest initially puzzling, then annoying, now downright slighting.

He was enraged by her stiff neck, the obduracy of her ramrod spine. He'd teach her a lesson, the bitch. Did she think she was indispensable, central to his life? She was trashy, tasteless, 'middle-class kitsch' like his Dad said about gifts from patients. Jimi hardly missed her spindly legs. He had the Bitty-chick instead. She was not bad, might make a 7. Come to think of it, he really did dig her legs.

The driver he'd fix on the next trip. Till then, he'd groove with the new babe. 'Listen to this song, close your eyes and zone out,' he said, his spider hands trawling her skirt. 'Don't open your eyes, sit still.'

At 3:00 a.m., a redness blinked in Jimi's cubicle. Surrounded by a sea of vernacular voices, he battled ceaseless calls. What was wrong with the Yank buggers that night? Some goddamn storm in Galveston and a war with India? Shoot, shoot, shoot, the American way, a volley of words as harsh as their bullets, the job hardly a game like on other nights. No time to space out, to doze off or breathe, everyone keyed up, harried, vexed. He glanced at the neighbouring female – what was her name? – facing the brunt of their fury. After 45-minute

waits to reconnect phone lines, customers would hardly tolerate an accented squeak.

Jimi's phone light blinked. Shit, not even a second since he wrapped up the last one.

'Hi, this is Jimi here, can I have your account number please?'

'Uh,' the voice hesitated. 'Let me see... yeah, it's 2454332.'

'Thank you, sir. Your last name is Fallows?'

'Yes, that's right.'

Jimi scrolled through the screen. A customer from Dover. He needed to verify the first name before he proceeded.

'Can you confirm your first name as well, the one that appears on your billing records?'

'George,' said the voice.

'Thanks, Mr Fallows, can I call you George?' Jimi said and then stopped, froze. The computer screen lurched in waves, the cubicle crumbled, telephone wires, curly cords, goddamn confusion, my God, bloody hell, this wasn't happening, this man on the line, this American dude was George Fallows, *the* Fallows, Magic Mushrooms' Fallows. They were a Dover band, Dover, Massachusetts, how could he forget?

'Can you tell me my bill amount for the last month?'

Fallows, George Fallows, the incredible fingers, the magic guitar, *it's coming on, it's coming on*, Jimi couldn't stop it, the blinding vision, revelation, God, he was talking to God, and he could barely breathe... barely breathe...

'Hello? Are you still on the line? Can you tell me my bill amount?' he said, his voice rising like his incredible chords, his awesome feedbacks, his reverbs, his echoes, his pulsing voice strung out taut, man this was incredible, unbelievable. Jimi couldn't speak, his lips trembled, his voice sputtered.

'Ssss... sssiiirrrr,' said Jimi.

'Can you understand English? I need my bill amount.'

Jimi's voice buzzed like a trapped insect: 'Zzzzzsssss... irrrr.'

'Hey, listen, am I talking to an Indian? Can you understand English?' Fallows's voice sizzled and boiled, a steam engine, a steam train, *it's coming on, it's coming on*, he was getting there, almost gone, floating in space, a high without blotters.

'Ssssss...irrrhhh,' said Jimi, his response muffled by thick chords, his voice choked by goddamn wires.

George talked to someone else, offline. 'It's a goddamned Indian on the phone – doesn't understand a word I'm saying. Here, can you try?'

A woman on the line, Fallows's mother, wife, girlfriend, chick, my God, he was talking to Fallows's chick, he fixed his gaze on the Bitty woman in the next cubicle, on the numbers on his telephone pad, on any numbing detail so he could get words into his mouth, why was he speechless, incoherent the only time it mattered?

'Look here, we just need our bill amount. Is that a problem?' a voice straightaway aggressive, high-pitched and Jimi couldn't uncurl his frozen tongue. The words, shooting through his synapses at 1,000-miles-a-minute piled up in his throat – when there was so much to say, how could he fit it all into a two-minute response?

'Mmmmma'aam,' he mumbled.

'Hey, you, if yawl can't understand, can we please speak to yawr manager, someone who speaks English?'

'Are you getting through?' That was Fallows in the background, the bass, the boom, the underlying beat, the reason for Jimi's life. And then again: 'Honey, just hang up. Let's try later. Maybe we'll get someone who understands English. This guy's an idiot.'

A few seconds later, a soft click and the line was blank. No words. Only Jimi's thoughts snarled inside wires, a jumble, not the sweet obliteration of acid highs. He was left with the headset dangling and a sourness in his mouth.

An idiot? Jimi? It was strange, he didn't feel anything, not an immediate low, but there was a spreading numbness and then a spasm, a few seconds of nothing, a moment of relief and then a spiking pain like the waves that overtook his mother's patients. He needed a break. He clutched his abdomen and blankly watched the screen: Fallows, George, Account Number 2454332, 564 S. State Street, Dover, DE 19901 – DE? Massachusetts was MA, wasn't it? What the hell was DE? He googled the American states; DE: Delaware, shit this guy wasn't *his* Fallows, but a bloody George Fallows from goddamn Delaware.

He stood up, leaned over into the next cubicle, and rested his hand on the vernac's shoulder, the chick crumpled inside massive ear phones.

'Hey, how's it going?' said Jimi. 'Americans are jerks.'

'Yyyess,' said Bitty uncertainly. 'Many calls today.'

The wall between their cubicles buckled and warped like the stuff in his stomach. He looked into the chick's black mouth while she muttered in her vernac voice. He could smell her breath, a garlic-onion stench. She wore a shimmery lipstick that coated her lips with tiny frost particles. From the space between her teeth, from the top of her tongue, sounds drifted out with a Malayali lilt. He hadn't felt it before, the chick had chemistry. Vernacs had flavour, more distinct than grating trainers. He was turned on by her voice, her infernal mothered tongue.

'I'll see you in the van,' he said. 'Let's chill tonight at Guru's place.'

The pain stopped, he rummaged in his pockets, two CDs, Magic Mushrooms – damn them – and Hendrix – yes, Hendrix, he'd blast the van tonight, groove to Jimi with that Bitty chick. Ah, there it was. He needed only a few seconds in the Men's room.

Lakshya

Mani Muthanna turned up at work on time, every day. Even on this night shift job, he rarely slipped up on changing shifts. Peers and subordinates suffered scooter breakdowns, traffic hold-ups, sinister viruses; the latest was chikungunya, an infectious arthritis that immobilized many. But not Mani. Everyone conceded he showed up. Always reliable. Unlike vast armies of twenty-somethings who arrived these days with stupefying ambitions and appalling work ethics. He could not fathom why the new entrants were wired with an inbuilt disquiet. Inside a few days of arriving or landing a job, they planned on leaving, on moving elsewhere.

Mani hadn't moved to the call centre industry by design, such daring career shifts weren't his style. When the accounting company where he'd worked for thirty years closed shop, he was forced to consider other options. And the Callus company was suggested by an ex-boss. 'They're hiring in droves,' he was told. He was pleased by their offer: a Team Leader position with a starting monthly of 25,000 rupees. Enough to tide over his father's medical expenses – pills for Parkinson's patients were 500 rupees apiece. He wondered at such times how poorer folks survived. 'Don't get diagnosed,' the pharmacist assured him, stuffing receipts into a secured safe.

His father was at Stage Four, which a pamphlet from the specialist described thus: 'Severe. Walking may be possible, but limited by instability. Patients at this stage need help with all activities and cannot live on their own. Tremors may lessen or disappear.' What the brochure did not mention was the slow shuttering of responses to Mani's world, to anything he said or did and eventually to his being there at all. Each night, when Mani left the house, he handed the keys to a night-nurse, more expensive than day-nurses, so the extra income was already used up.

Despite what some would describe as a stodgy résumé or unexciting career, work was very important to Mani. It wasn't just the money, though he needed that for mounting medical bills. He simply liked work. He wasn't the kind who hankered for vacations or time off, or dreamt like his colleagues of eventual autonomy. He liked the buzz inside offices, the stir of moving targets, the sense of belonging to something larger than himself. A bachelor at 45, there were many pastimes Mani could cultivate – card-playing, billiards, chess – yes, anything was possible if his horsepower wasn't used up at work.

Ironically, Mani was the kind who was never promoted, the kind who was not noticed much. The only link between his past job and his current one was his anonymity. Despite his diligence, his constancy and other qualities that belonged to a quieter age, Mani remained unknown. Bosses who relied on his everyday availability, on his intense attention to all tasks, rarely heeded him. They took him for granted like the water in the cistern, which despite droughts in the state, came gushing out of the tank when it was flushed.

Peers counselled him on how to overcome his drawbacks: 'You're too shy and introverted. You have to be more assertive. For God's sake, learn to say *no*.' Others warned him that the environment had changed. In the old job, though Mani was less qualified than CA bosses, he was better at tallying ledgers, spotting slip-ups and exploiting kinks in tax rules or customs laws. But such knowledge and superior skills didn't take him far. 'You have to network,' wise entrants warned him. 'These days, no one cares about what you know. It's *whom* you know.'

And that, Mani knew, was a deep-seated flaw, not easy to correct. Even in the old office, his networking was clumsy. If he brought bosses home for lunch, they remained polite and uneasy, rarely opening up like they did at the homes of others. A colleague said it was the veggie meal and absence of liquor that put a lid on their spirits. Despite eloping with a carnivorous Coorgi, his Tamilian mother enforced the severe practices of a Brahmin kitchen: 'No meat in the house,' she said. 'Outside, you eat, drink anything.' Even liquor, tolerated when they lived in army colonies, was eventually banned. When Mani invited his bosses, the choice was 'Home-made lime-ginger or Roohafza?'

And it was awkward too in other ways, even with his mother alive. Seated before a glass cabinet that housed the family's 'military honours' – silver, nickel and copper medals glinting on green, saffron and blue ribbons, mounted in extravagant velvet boxes – his parents hovered like indulgent guardians, as if Mani and his colleagues were schoolboy miscreants, too young to be left alone. And those were his father's pre-Parkinson's days, when the major's brain fuelled a ceaseless banter about his Coorgi father and grandfather and their army skirmishes.

'It's funny Indians are proud of this call centre boom. Did you know more than a century ago my grandfather was writing letters for British soldiers posted here?' said Mani's father, his legs astride a worn sofa with new lace covers.

'But why?' asked Mani's boss. 'Didn't soldiers write their own letters?'

'You see, my boy, the British posted here were of an inferior stock. My grandfather was one of the first postgraduates from Madikere. He had, in those days – can you believe it – an MA in English? His English grammar was better than the British. Naturally, many were peeved.'

And then leaping over another quiet moment between Roohafza sips, he'd recount the Goa story – one that Mani and his mother had heard several times. 'My father fought the last war against Europeans. The last real war. Later wars against Asians – Pakistanis, Chinese – were nothing.'

It was India's last war against a Western nation, the major repeated to Mani's incurious colleagues.

Unmindful of their silence, he prattled on about the 1961 Goa liberation, keyed up by the non-alcoholic, ruby-red Roohafza. Like most army men, his father found jokes about air force and naval officers funniest. 'Air force officers are such fools. During that war, Toofani jet fighters flew over the Diu airfield. But that Toofani leader,' cackled his father, 'reported that the Portuguese were waving white flags of surrender. Foolish man dumped bombs in the sea; those were not white flags of surrender, they were ordinary dhobis hanging clothes.'

Mani hadn't turned out the way his father expected. 'Womanish,' was the major's dismissal of Mani's civilian career. And perhaps he was; his career and work-habits were so typical of his mother's side that most people assumed he was entirely Tamilian. 'Not a Coorgi gene in the boy,' his father decried, listing in descending rank military Coorgis Mani hadn't taken after. 'KM Cariappa, the first Indian Commander-in-Chief of the Indian Army, KS Thimayya, Chief of Army staff, your grandfather, a Quartermaster General, myself, an Army Major.'

Mani could put up with uncaring bosses, but uncaring subordinates were a new experience. And this was Mani's plight in the new office, where a group of five agents – all in their early twenties – winked and mumbled when he commanded them to do anything. In the old office, Mani wasn't a boss of any kind. The only person he ordered around was the office boy and even he rarely ceded to Mani's apologetic 'coffee *kodtheya*' requests. But in the Callus job, bossing around, commanding other folks was

Mani's only task, a job the Tamilian accountant faltered at. He wasn't scared of them. Why should he be when they were merely kids? But he couldn't fiercely impose his will like other hardnosed Team Leaders. His reportees pretty much thwarted his attempts, sometimes with open defiance, sometimes with masked manoeuvres, until his group trailed on all targets. His manager pulled him up at a review meeting: 'Mani, work on your scores or else... Thanks to your team, our ratings have sunk.'

Sometimes he wondered if it was age. Did the kids jeer because he was forty-plus, unlike the young jocks who led other teams? Or was it personality? In the old job, looks hardly mattered. But now, Mani was newly conscious of his undyed hair, of thick folds at his waist, of his short legs and boxy body. Working ten-hour days, paying household bills, administering to his father's nonstop disorders, fixing domestic hitches – one week the upstairs water dried up, then the borewell pump bailed out, then several fuses capitulated to the Electricity Board's voltage fluctuations – Mani hadn't signed up for gym lessons.

If not personality, was it character? Had he inherited his father's Coorgi temper, would that have made a difference? Surely Cariappa and Thimayya, with entire armies flexing at their commands, weren't weak-willed like him, hesitant to order men to the frontline?

Callus targets were simple: agent productivity and quality were all that mattered. Did they answer as many calls as possible? Did they resolve problems? Did they communicate clearly? Did they use the standard greeting and sign-off? Was the customer satisfied? This wasn't complex; in fact in his accounting job he had waded through greater tangles. The problem was in getting his team, naturally slack and lackadaisical, fired up.

They always had excuses, reasons for slip-ups. 'Sir, we can't bear it when the customer shouts at us in bad languages, we're not used to such shoutings. My login time was reduced because I was crying in the toilet.' That was Bitty Menon, a woman who always received negative ratings on customer satisfaction. Her customers cribbed about slow responses, her overall incapacity to solve their 'goddamn problems'. Mani felt sorry for the petite, fine-boned recruit. How could he scold her for crying in toilets when they were seated around a discussion table?

'Azeem, why don't you tell the team how you do it? You're the only one meeting targets. Maybe they can learn from you?'

'I just do my job,' said Azeem, in a matter-of-fact way that precluded discussion.

And then there was Jimutha, a fabulous communicator who didn't care about targets. When Mani addressed the team, he yawned or looked outside the window, his eyes glassed over in disdain. The Team Leader would have liked to suggest a haircut – his curls fled in all directions – but he feared an angry rebuff. 'Jimutha, why aren't you logged in for longer? What else do you do inside the office?'

'I'm *not*? Really? That's news to me. What else would I do in this place? Jam with office-boys? Maybe the report's wrong, *sir*?'

And that was the other thing. They all called him 'sir' though the practice had been dropped in other parts of Callus. Were they emphasizing that he belonged to an older time, to a time when subordinates weren't cocky and impudent, at least not to bosses?

But of the lot he found Bipin, the Bengali boy with hair flapping onto his face, the most impertinent. The others, despite their erratic ways on the phone, didn't look at Mani with such gleeful mirth as if the Team Leader were a comic presence rather than a manager.

'Bipin, what's the problem? Why have your Customer-Sat ratings fallen? And your average talk-time increased?'

'Oh, sir, Mani sir, I'm devastated. I don't know how that happened. Since I've seen my scores, I've been fully depressed. Can you please guide me, sir? I want to improve, I'm so eager to be the best Callus agent.'

An innocuous statement if it wasn't accompanied by the spark in his eyes, a glittering eagerness to make it inside the 'crappy, capitalist' company. Yes, Mani had heard about Bipin's Marxist views, the boy imbued with a natural intelligence and an unconcern more dangerous than Jimutha's.

'Bipin, this is not funny. You may not care about your job, but I care about mine.'

'Sir, how can you say that? I care about this job and this company more than blood in my veins. I have written to my village in West Bengal. They await my return with the best agent award. Please guide me, sir. I want to provide the best possible service to our American customers.' In Mani's absence, the Team Leader heard that Bipin called them 'white fascists'. But there was nothing he could do about back-talk and rumours when the agent's 'official' responses were faultless.

141

'Listen, guys, next week, you don't meet targets, you're *screwed.*' Even Mani was taken aback when the word popped out. The Team Leader was not even the *tough shit* kind and he expected the woman to trip into the toilet to weep at his 'bad languages'. But everyone was stunned, too stupefied to react. Fortunately, Bipin didn't say, 'Screwed, sir? What does that mean?' in careful, 'hegemonic English'.

The Callus business was growing every week with their largest customer, Beam America, sending more jobs to Bangalore. But operations were afflicted by a new problem: Callus agents, rapidly hired and trained, were quitting fast. The majority were headed to Bodmas, a centre that offered higher salaries, better buses, finer food. The latest buzz at Callus was about a budget sanctioned for 'fun'. The counsellor met with Team Leaders: 'You need to motivate them, create emotional bonds. We're funding picnics, movies, booze, what else can you ask for?' Team Leaders were ordered to spend fun budgets before the quarter-end.

Mani promptly announced the fun event: 'I'm planning a dinner at Murphy's and then a night-show, *No Country for Old Men* or *Atonement,*' he told the team at the next group huddle.

There were objections straightaway. 'Murphy's? Sir, I think they've closed that place down. Sometime in the 1920s.'

'Sir, you must be joking. Other teams are headed to pubs and you're lugging us to Murphy's? What will we drink there? Lime water?'

142

Hollywood movies were shot down for a hit from previous years, *Lakshya*, replaying at a multiplex. '*No Country for Old Men*, sir? That's rude, don't you think? In India, old men are respected, sir. Given jobs even. Besides, we'd rather watch desi rumps. By any standards, Preity Zinta's a goddess.'

The session was kicked off at the Star Wars pub. With its teak walls, tobacco stench, carpeted, liquor-stained floor, mini-skirted, stocking-clad waitresses, the place felt like another country. In a far corner, a large flat-screen TV relayed a cricket match between India and the West Indies. Every Indian boundary was cheered raucously by a group of expats who leaned against the tall bar counter. Mani, because his job hadn't required travel, had been to Illinois once, a rare trip sponsored by Callus. But the days were packed with training sessions and he'd hardly seen anything of Springfield. When he looked around the pub, he realized how little he'd even seen of his own city. He hadn't realized, in his home-to-work and work-to-home routine, how much the place had changed.

His team, lounging easily inside a wooden booth, was more familiar with such places. Even Azeem seemed snug and unfazed. Maybe his family was not strictly Islamic and permitted drinks at home? Bipin too, despite his Marxist leanings, smiled easily. Mani tried to keep the group engaged and the talk flowing but it was awkward. The men ordered whisky. Bitty ordered beer. Mani ordered a lime-soda then changed his mind: 'Make that a single malt,' he said, resting his arms on the curved wooden back of the booth.

'Get to know your people and tell them about yourselves. Be personal,' the counsellor decreed when releasing the Fun budget.

Mani fumbled for a beginning, for his father's slickness with words. Maybe it was the major's constant gush that curbed Mani's attempts; there hadn't been pauses for him to practise in. 'Did you know my great-grandfather used to write letters for British soldiers?'

Bipin perked up. 'Really, sir? What letters?'

'Any letters, personal letters, you know what it's like for soldiers, they'll do anything to communicate with families.'

'Such an honour for your family to have served the British like that. Did your family lose any benefits post-Independence?'

There was an edge in Bipin's voice and Mani quickly said: 'We never served the British. My grandfather and father fought for the Indian army.' Really speaking, that wasn't accurate. His father, despite his brandishing of Coorgi gallantry, never fought any wars; the major was expelled from the army after some brawl in Belgaum.

'Sir, that's something to be proud of. Were they also involved with local enemies, you know Naxalites, Maoists?'

Mani's tongue felt thick and heavy, unready for political wrangles. 'Bipin, tell me about yourself. Where are you from? Why did you join Callus?'

'Sir, there's nothing much to say. I am a simple peasant from a village in West Bengal. I've joined Callus because I believe in making American lives easier.'

Mani never knew how to counter Bipin at such times. That was the Callus vision: *To Make Customers' Lives Easier.* It was a vision Mani endorsed – that, after all, should be the final outcome of those calls. Except when the boy put it like that, it felt imbecilic. The Team Leader turned to Bitty. 'What does your father do, Bitty?'

'He's a doctor,' she said.

'Fantastic,' said Mani. He never imagined this shy woman had a doctor father. 'What kind – a specialist or GP?'

'GP,' she said, spilling beer on her white shirt. Her clothes had been getting tighter and more transparent. 'You know,' she added, smiling sweetly, 'there's something I like about Americans. They don't ask questions, don't intrude into your personal life.'

'Is that right?' said Mani blushing. Had he been too intrusive? It was normal practice, wasn't it, to ask what a parent did? Was he so tuned out with this Generation Y or whatever the advertisers called them? 'Let's move closer to the TV,' said Mani. 'I haven't watched a cricket match in years.'

An hour later, they shuffled towards their balcony seats inside the multiplex theatre. Fortunately for the Team Leader, the dense crowds precluded small talk. Flopping inside his bucket-seat, after late-comers stumbled across the torch-lit aisles, Mani expected to fall asleep. He hadn't been to a Hindi movie in decades. In the last one he watched, Shashi Kapoor was a svelte heartthrob. He was not familiar with the new actors or even with the wide-screen format and ear-splitting sound. However, despite his intentions, Mani was glued to the screen. Even credits in these new movies were arresting, slick. The 'sooo cute yaar' Hrithik Roshan, tied and untied a rubbery body, arched and buckled by a lack of purpose, asked himself, 'Main Aisa Kyun Hoon'. He was a drifter, a chap with no direction in life until he joined the army.

Mani was quite taken with the new actors. They possessed a chic Indianness that wasn't apparent in his younger cinema-going days. But Mani was truly enthralled when Amitabh Bachchan entered the screen; the actor, despite his age, had such a commanding presence. Mani clapped when Bachchan as an obdurate general who never lost a war imbued the flailing Hrithik with purpose: Win the Kargil war, keep the Indian flag flying. When the actors marched shoulder to shoulder on treacherous peaks and the music surged in patriotic fervour, the Team Leader sprang to his feet and snapped a salute. 'Sit down, sir,' hissed Bipin, yanking at his trousers. 'People behind you can't see.'

The next night, on the way to the office, the Callus van skidded across roads wet from a sudden, late shower. In a single-minded rush to reach the office, the driver splattered mud on scurrying walkers. 'Slow, slow,' Mani cautioned. 'Already late, sir,' he said, a short man with a short temper. He braked suddenly and a scooterist tumbled into an unseen pothole. The rain was not heavy enough to blind the driver and warrant such rash driving. A few trees had fallen, some power lines had snapped but the city hadn't plunged into its customary darkness.

Mani used to have a yellow raincoat which he hadn't found since his mother died. He'd worn instead his father's military blazer and beret, for which his father had no use anymore. When the van reached the IT Valley, the rain stopped. The sky was blank and devoid of stars. Mani's team alighted from different cabs and gathered near the building's foyer, where, for a short moment, reflections shimmered inside puddles. Mani quickly retreated into the building, to the lifts and to his busy work night.

Upstairs, while the Team Leader wiped his wet soles across rubber bristles that spelt out 'Welcome', the security guard directed him to a meeting room: 'Sir, big boss calling for all managers,' he said. There was a crisis meeting, a special gathering of Callus senior managers and Team Leaders. The CEO of the Bangalore centre, rarely visible to Team Leaders, stood at the head of the conference room table while everyone else loitered nervously. 'Guys, there's a special crisis tonight. Some of you might have heard in the news about Hurricane Ike, a very large storm that's hit the United States. Our client's call centre in Galveston has been closed and calls are being rerouted to Bangalore. Our call traffic has grown by more than 300% and is going to climb higher during US peak hours. We have to, absolutely *have to*, outperform ourselves tonight. Every agent and every Team Leader will work a double-shift. And I want you all to focus on one thing, handle the maximum number of calls in minimum time – short handle times, get me? And really drive productivity, we can't have any slacking off tonight. We're dedicating a special budget for this, remember this is a life-and-death situation. The most efficient team wins a reward,' and he smiled, 'a trip to Disneyworld, Florida. Now, go for it, guys, I know you can do it.'

Mani had no views on fate or divine designs, not even on afterlives despite his mother's passing away. He vaguely believed in some kind of God but couldn't defend his faith to a zealous atheist. And yet, after the CEO meeting,

Mani believed those Texan winds were blown in by a Greater Force – inside a grand scheme unapparent to human vision. Suddenly it fell into place, settling in on Mani like snow on Himalayan slopes. He had it now, a means to incite his kids, his call centre team: they needed a lakshya, a purpose loftier than weekly targets, and tonight the winds had handed it to him.

Drawing himself up on his block-heeled shoes, the Team Leader sucked his belly in. His adrenalin rose as he entered the call floor where numbers tripped rapidly on the electronic wallboard: *Calls in Queue: 79; Average Talk Time: 5.4 minutes.* Announcers sounded alarms across the loud-speaker system: 'Guys, calls are jumping, please get on the lines, right now, there are 78 customers in the queue. Hurry, login.'

He asked his team to log off and gathered the group inside the discussion room. Usually the teams met at the end of their shifts, but tonight they needed inspiration. In his deepest Bachchan baritone, Mani briefed them on the crisis: 'Guys, this is it, tonight is THE night. We have to handle this call surge and prove we are the best. I personally believe that each of you can do this. Remember this: I'm a Coorgi and Coorgis don't lose wars. Never. I've given my word to the Chief that we will do it. I am sure you can and you will. You will not let me down. Now, go. You get a five-minute break now and after that no loo stops, no cigs, no tea breaks. Our team has to handle the maximum calls, the MOST, understand? Each of you must do your best. The winners go to Florida. It has to be this team, I want us to plant the Indian flag in Florida, understand?'

148

'They allow that, sir? Planting the Indian flag in Florida?' asked Bipin.

'Don't be so BLOODY literal, Bipin. Now get to work, move.'

'And Mani sir, later if we need to, you know, do we piss in our pants?' said a lingering Bipin, reluctant to leave the discussion room.

'D'you think our soldiers in Kargil had loos on icy slopes? Piss inside your cubicles for all I care.'

Another Team Leader interrupted, 'Mani, why hasn't your team hit the floor? Calls are crazy, shit, yaar, scrap speeches tonight.'

'Okay, team, your five-minute break is off. Bipin, you've delayed us with questions, now HIT THE FLOOR.'

Mani's team, only four that night with Kannan on sick leave, walked slowly towards their labelled lockers, the only physical space assigned to agents inside the centre, to retrieve their headsets. Azeem walked back to Mani, headset in hand: 'Sir,' he said in a shrill squeak, 'I have a sore throat today. I need a break every ten minutes. I can barely speak.' Azeem down and Kannan absent. A battle more impossible than the Kargil war.

'Azeem, you decide. Remember, this is for the service of your company, your country. If necessary, I will organize for the office-boy to bring you warm water every thirty minutes. Are you on antibiotics as well?'

'No, sir, but I have some Unani tonics,' he said.

'*Unani* tonics? Those are placebos. I'll get you something stronger, you'll do fine,' he said. 'I'll be watching you from the control tower, I mean the command centre. Team, you will login near the electronic wallboard.' Mani pointed to a cluster of orange-purple cubicles near the large screen that scrolled numbers like a stock exchange ticker. Usually agents picked their own seats inside a cubicle cluster but tonight the Team Leader would assign them.

'Bitty next to Bipin, Jimutha next, now Azeem, no, not there, Bipin, over here, next to Bitty, yes, this cubicle and now Jimutha near Bitty and does anyone have Kannan's mobile number? I need that guy to come in NOW even if he has to drag his dead body over.'

'How that will help, sir?' asked Bipin, defiantly flicking his headset off.

'Bipin, turn that instrument on and LOGIN. All of you, no more small talk, LOGIN.'

Mani, who normally retired to the centralized command centre along with other Team Leaders, hovered anxiously around the group tonight. Bipin rushed through his scripted greeting like a bullet train: 'Goodmorningthis isBeamAmericamynameisBenjyhowcanIhelpyouthis morning?I'mverysorrytohearthatIwilltrytosolveyourprob lemtoday.' Good, thought Mani. At least he was going to handle more calls. But Azeem, he noticed, inflated his talk-time, repeating himself over and over again, his hoarse voice not carrying across the wires. He needed to fix that.

He buzzed the emergency doctor, on standby in the company medical room. 'Can you suggest something for a sore throat... err... what? NO, you can't see the patient, he cannot logout tonight. Lozenges? No, that's too mild, I need something STRONGER, how about antibiotics? Can you send me a strip? I know they take time, no, you CANNOT see him, just send me bloody antibiotics, I'm sending the office boy. What is the dosage? Okay,

okay, that's fine.' Lozenges on a battlefield when the boy needed a quick fix? Had the man never treated soldiers?

Bitty, in the meanwhile, was marooned with a fuming caller. She hollered to break into the customer's monologue: 'Sir, IF YOU CAN PLEASE LISTEN TO ME, I know you have been waiting on line for fifty minutes and we apologize for the inconvenience... Sir, I completely understand, but IF YOU WOULD LISTEN FOR A MINUTE...' The woman could not break in like that. Mani grabbed a free instrument from an empty cubicle, punched in his Team Leader password and barged into Bitty's conversation. An American man shouted: 'I've been waiting on this fuckin' line for fuckin' fifty minutes and if you don't fuckin' call your manager, I'll make sure that I fuckin' sue you.' 'Sir, I'm the manager and can you fuckin' SHUDDUP?' yelled Mani. The voice suddenly dropped. Bitty stared at her boss, aghast. 'What are you waiting for? Go ahead and solve his problem,' said the Team Leader while he placed the receiver in its slot and slid out.

Kannan's mobile number was SMSed to Mani by the HR department. Kannan's mother picked up the phone. 'Sir, I am very sorry but he is very ill, he cannot come tonight, he has hiiiigh fever,' she said. 'He cannot lift phone also,' she added, 'he cannot walk even... No, sir, please don't send company cab today, he will not be able to work... Sir, I know, today may be special for company, but Kannan CANNOT come.' If mothers had their way, armies would be soldierless, all battles lost. He'd send the van in any case; would she dodge his summons then?

The watchboard flashed '180 Calls Waiting'. A Senior Team Leader shouted out the latest metrics on the central speaker system. 'Guys and ladies, this is a dire situation. Our Service Levels are dipping. Please watch the numbers on the Board. And keep taking those calls and keep talking. Watch your Average Talk Times. We need to remain the Number One Centre in terms of Service Levels. Remember, the best team tonight goes to Florida.' For most agents inside shouting calls, surrounded by lapping noises of the FM 91 radio station, the announcement escaped their attention. But the excitement was palpable. This wasn't just another night. Another Team Leader scribbled updated team results on a white board. He drew a table with several squares, titled 'Are You Going to Disneyworld?' – apparently the CEO's idea. Teams that worked for the Beam America process were named after American basketball teams and the board listed results for the night, so far: Kansas City Knights – 108 calls, Los Angeles Stars – 94 calls, Mississippi Stingers – 88 Calls, New Jersey Jaguars – 78 Calls, Las Vegas Rattlers – 76 Calls and Mani's team, lagging behind the rest, the Ontario Warriors with only 68 calls.

The antibiotics arrived after two more calls to the unobliging doctor. Mani stood over Azeem like a fretful nurse while the boy swallowed the pills during a two-second break between calls. But the Team Leader's attention was quickly diverted: Bitty had logged out, her face frozen into a mulish silence. Her eyes, under thick lashes, glistened. 'Some customer insulted her,' explained Bipin. 'Used the b-word.' Near the coffee machine, with Bitty's red, bulbous nose cloaked with several paper napkins, the Team Leader assured her it wasn't personal. 'It's just a job, for God's sake. Maybe the man has a problem, maybe he always speaks like that to Americans as well.'

Bitty was restored after a vexing fifteen minutes. The crew returned to the reassuring hum of polite responses: 'I know you have been overcharged, we will refund the money.' 'I'm sorry, could you repeat that, please?' 'Yes, the technician charge has to be borne by customers, I'm very sorry, sir, but that's company policy.' Faster, faster. Mani circled their cubicles and drew their attention to the scoreboard with an agitated finger – they needed to keep the finish-line in sight. They raced through the scripted parts, especially the legal disclosures, the parts that customers rarely heeded in any case. 'Mr Jackson, before you hang up, I would like to repeat that you have agreed to change your tariff plan to the Master of the Net Plan and the charges will be automatically...'

The white board hadn't been updated for the last half-hour. Mani logged into the central Call Distribution system to check individual scores. Bipin surged ahead of the rest with 24 calls, Mani noted, as the list filled out in grainy detail. Bitty lost time because of the b-lady but was doing okay at 17 calls. But the rest languished at a pathetic 12 or 15 calls each. As he pencilled in the numbers, Jimutha interrupted him. 'Sir, desperately need a loo break.' 'Jimutha – you're at 12 calls. You can take a loo break after 24,' responded Mani. 'Sir, it's bloody urgent.' 'After 24, Jimutha, and tell Azeem the same thing.' It was 12:00 a.m. already. Another Team Leader shouted across the floor – 'Mani, any loo requests? We're trying to schedule them across the floor.' 'NONE,' replied

153

Mani. 'Water,' squeaked Azeem. Mani personally carried over a warm water jug, and handed out filled paper cups to the team. 'Bloody handing out water when we need to go to the loo,' said Jimutha.

'All of you get a loo break when the team reaches 150 calls,' announced the Major.

'Loo break like Florida trip,' muttered Bipin between calls.

'Want a cig, Mani?' said another Team Leader who passed by the Ontario Warriors territory. 'Not now,' said Mani, his hand resting on Bipin's swivel chair, 'not today.' He couldn't desert the front while his team lagged behind.

At 2:00 a.m., Bipin was still leading, at a staggering 47 calls and Bitty was at 38. Jimutha however hadn't progressed beyond 18. What was wrong with the guy? Mani walked over to his cubicle and found his head swinging, his headset askew, wires stranded in mid-sentence – was he dead? – and then heard rhythmic wheezes. In all this noise, the man was asleep? 'Ice, get me some ice,' barked Mani, at the office boy who roved between cubicles with several paper cups of pre-sweetened, machine-mixed coffee. Jimutha's unplugged mouth shivered into shocked wakefulness. 'Holy shit!' he spluttered, his eyes popping open.

'Okay, everyone, time for a five-minute break. One by one, of course. I will be timing you on my digital stopwatch, no one can stay out longer than five minutes, not a second more. Hear me? Jimutha, you're first. Please wash your face, wake up for heaven's sake.'

Jimutha was out for a mutinous seven minutes. Mani paced restlessly near the loo exit. What was he doing in

154

there? Before the door opened, the entire floor was filled with a ear-splitting jangle: a bomb, a terrorist attack? No, an alarm. 'Shit, man, fire alarm,' shouted another Team Leader. Others continued to speak into their wires, immune to the shrieking siren. A process trainer, an American expatriate also on the floor, rushed towards the exit.

'Why aren't you guys moving?' he asked, his face blanched.

'Just a fire alarm, chief, nothing to worry about. In India, we move when we see smoke.'

'Man, it's from the loo, somebody lit a fag in there.'

Jimutha walked out, awake, a chemical stench on his breath.

Other teams trooped in from lunch, in twos and threes. 'Yum, man, today veg biryani is damn good and gulab jamun with ice-cream,' they muttered, taunting the relentless Ontario Warriors who hadn't stepped out for tea, or cigs or lunch. But the Warriors were inching ahead, moving from the last position to a respectable third. 'I'll take you guys out for dinner tomorrow, Chinese food,' said Mani, 'wonton soup and gobi Manchurian, much better than biryani and jamuns.'

'Not needed, sir, we can eat in Florida,' said Bipin, 'Big Macs.' Mani smiled. The boy after all was ahead of the pack. 'Bipin, no more jokes,' he said, patting the boy's back. Not a bad sort, really. One could count on him in a crisis.

By now the Warriors, with one loo break, were ahead of the Los Angeles Stars but slightly behind the Kansas City Knights. There were only two hours of American daytime left, after which calls would sink into low night levels, when only a few drunks and insomniacs would call to squabble about charges. He walked past the City Knights cubicles to see how they were doing. Like the Warriors, they spoke nonstop. But they also had an extra agent. Mani logged into the Central system to check who was leading the City Knights team. A few minutes later, their leading agent received a scrawled, hand-written note, unsigned: 'Call home urgent, emergency'. Strangely, her mobile was missing, the landline at the reception didn't work. She returned, baffled and breathless after sixteen wasted minutes.

Azeem in the meanwhile had completely lost his voice. He gestured wildly and logged out. Mani asked him to refill crushed paper cups with coffee. The company had run out of cups that night. Surely they couldn't lose on the last lap. 'Guys, faster, speak faster and DON'T drop your accents, we'll lose points on quality.' 'Sir, don't care if I lose my job, can't speak another word tonight,' said Jimutha flinging his headset aside. 'Jimutha, an hour more, that's it and guess what, I'll login myself to give you guys a lead,' he said. The Team Leader was uncomfortable on the phone but he knew of wars where generals themselves faced assault.

At home that night, Mani snatched the house-keys from the night-nurse. She looked at him strangely, like she'd never seen him earlier. The glass cabinet reflected the pink flush on his cheeks, the boyish gleam in his eyes. 'I've fed him half the soup, you need to finish the bowl.' Yes, he nodded, and scampered up the stairs, to the large bedroom where the Major sat up on his bed with the short table adapted for bedside feeding. 'Major,' he said, spooning the sweet-corn into the large plastic soup-spoon. Mani always called him Major, not Papa or Daddy or Dad. 'I fought my first war today.' The soup dribbled out, a little more than usual. 'We won, the Warriors won.' Mani thought he could see a light in the left eye, but the soup was hot; maybe it was just that.

Other Moons

What Allah took away He gave back manifold. He took Azeem's legs but bestowed wings that carried the polio-stricken boy into places inaccessible to his able-bodied brothers. 'Look at him now,' Abba said. 'Earning ten times more.'

At Callus, his call centre workplace, Azeem had a different name. Aaron, an American name, cool, rounded like the curled American 'aaahrh', a sound foreign to his cramped home off Tannery Road. Like his name, there were many things about Aaron distinct from Azeem. He wasn't like Azeem, a submissive son, a doting brother. Or even Faithful. And more than anything else – and this still appalled Azeem after many months – Aaron was a voyeur, obsessed with women, American women. With listening ears he prized from them private thoughts, gossipy secrets rarely shared with strangers on phones. 'Yeah, my boyfriend's kinda weird, I've never spoken about this before, but you know, how you know somethin' and you don't really think about it, you know what I mean?' 'Yeah, I've been thinkin' about seeing a counsellor but I don't know if that would help; it's deeper than that.' 'I used to have this crush once, on this guy from high school, but now, I'm meeting him after fifteen years and it's really funny, I mean...'

Such access had taken months of practice, cues tested till he had mastered the words, the right mix of tone and interest: not too curious, just listening, the careful dampening of overt absorption. In the Callus world, Aaron wasn't breaking rules. He was, in fact, one of the centre's best performers. He received gushing emails or thank-you calls from customers with bills revoked and charges cleared. Most of them, at least the gullible ones, rarely guessed who he was. Aaron smiled when he thought of Azeem's family: Ammi in her burkha, Abba with his Tazcat cap. 'Are you Arab? Do you live in Iraq?' his customers would have asked, if they'd seen a family photograph.

Such access wasn't risk-free. The first few weeks, he was shunned by callers, rebuffed by angry Americans for 'intrusive' questions. During his artless early days, he was too hungry, too quick.

'You're living with another man?'

'Excuse me? Why do you need to know that?'

'You're married?'

'I'm sorry? Hey, that's really none of your business.'

Even the words were wrong, Aaron knew that now. These days, Aaron spoke about himself first, let them in on a hurtful secret. 'I was seeing this woman, and it was incredible and I don't know what happened but...'

'Oh, yeah, that's terrible, I know how you feel.' He picked his targets carefully. Not like earlier when he was fumbling and indiscriminate. He liked longer calls, relished the sway of their voices, soft and almost touchable on the phone. They treated him like a man, hulking and virile like his brothers.

The job, in a strange way, fulfilled a childhood dream to roam with camera eyes into the homes of relatives, to visit aunts and uncles who greeted him with tiresome compassion: 'Are you still going to your school, Azeem beta? Can you manage on the buses with crutches and all?' He wanted always to unravel their secrets, to pry into private frailties with a high-powered lens, the camera hoisted above *The Universe*. He loved that sixth standard book with pictures of distant moons and extinct stars, of limitless voyages into velvety space.

Now Aaron was doing exactly that: coaxing out confessions from foreign people. Of course, Aaron never came home. Wily Aaron, who played tricks on the phone to gain their trust, 'a listening kind of man', was out of place in his family. An Aaron Abba and Ammi hadn't met, of whom they were unabashedly proud. So proud, they'd alienated neighbours in the colony. 'Never let him join that industry, those kids have low morals,' mosque-goers hissed. 'He's lame, they'll take advantage.' They were shocked too by his work schedule and cab rides. Mostly they were dismayed by his incredible income; their kids wouldn't bring such monies in their lifetime. Such low thoughts hardly bothered his parents. They'd shrunk, like Americans, into a self-contained existence, severed from a seething community. An existence which Aaron preferred.

Asma lived in a world with few sounds. The street dog's growls, the Fajr call to prayer. Not the milkman's cries, not the sound of her own voice. In her world, she saw what others didn't. Pipal tree shadows scampered in the courtyard, indigo frills peeped from under Ammi's burkha, mountains capered, rivers pranced on Azeem's lungi. Sometimes she was so taken in, so possessed by romping lights, skittering shadows she hardly stopped talking. Talking with her hands, with unstoppable fingers, special signs she shared with Ammi.

Ammi said she had been babbling like this for as long as she could remember. It took her longer to fathom what her last-born was saying but Asma was even then gesturing wildly, expressing with stubby baby fingers flashes of sight: the flick of cows' tails, the rushing flight of pigeons, the flutters of patterned hankies as men kissed the earth jointly in praise of Allah. Asma was lucky, Ammi said. Allah granted her a chamber, a den that none could enter, not her three brothers or two sisters. Certainly not Abba.

Deaf, her father called her. Unlike Ammi, he couldn't see she was born with a sign-language engraved in her brain. She hadn't thought herself disabled till Ammi explained what her brothers and Abba said. Ammi was her interpreter, the intermediary between her special place and the cacophony of hearing people. On many occasions, vexed with Abba, riled by her brothers, she preferred to shut them out.

She'd been most provoked when she was eleven and her uncle visited, an uncle from a distant town. He hadn't seen anyone like her, he said. With strange finger talking and ugly mouth sounds. There must be a cure, he told Abba. Unani medicines, special oils, bitter tonics, some means to expel her silence. The doctor gave her ear drops, *Roghan Sammat Kusha*, and her brothers and Abba set her down each night, while her fingers protested at Ammi who watched from a distance. The drops didn't hurt but her body and her world, the tiny cocoon she'd spun for herself was trampled upon by these unfeeling men. They tried garlic boiled with hot oil, odious flavours poured into her ears. 'Do you hear anything?' Ammi signed. 'Hands clapping, feet stomping?' How would she know? Her ears hissed and buzzed – skies pounded, earths split – but she'd never in her life heard their sounds.

But Allah have mercy, Asma had yearnings, frightening, unthinkable for a deaf girl. Not the yearnings Ammi imagined her daughter had when she settled her dupatta against a swelling chest or yanked her sticky hair into childish loops. Yearnings spurred by a school-going Azeem, the polio-ridden boy singled out among her brothers to attend a Special Ed English school. Every night, when the moon seeped through their tin roof, she crawled from her gunny sack bed and hauled the jute bag he lugged around on school days. While her brothers twitched and wriggled inside restless dreams, she tugged it into a dark courtyard where bandicoots fled behind unwashed aluminium vessels. She scraped a match, shone the kerosene lamp with a trembling flame. Squatting on the granite washing stone, the hairs on her arm lifted by breezes, she pored over sphinx-like shapes and mystic letters, over irregular patches diffused in blue. 'Our universe,' Azeem had told her one day. The physical earth a tiny orb in a space more immense, more perplexing than her street's bounds or the Colony's market.

Azeem did not tell her much. 'Not for you,' he said about the enthralling worlds he'd encountered at school. Thin, small-boned, clean-shaven, he slammed the book shut, pictures of inky skies with barbs of light, stars, moons, planets swirling in orbits. She held it when he was asleep, traced captions below rippling blacks, vaporous mauves; she longed to prize his deftness with books, rapid eye movements that dredged meanings from scribbles.

Once, when Azeem was in the sixth standard, she'd climbed unseen into his school bus. And wandered unnoticed into the vast school grounds, among square buildings and chanting classrooms that imbued Azeem with fantastic powers. She saw kids prattling, some like Azeem, lame, some with jerky movements, others with heads unfixed on sloppy necks, but tumbling and gambolling in slides and swings and grassy patches, their differences forged in enviable belonging. She was beaten that day by her parents. Ammi berserk with worry, Abba humbled by the police. A deaf girl missing, her body mutilated, defiled? The fault, they said, was theirs, not hers. They never imagined for a moment even that her body was hers to carry wherever she wished.

After that stray absence, Ammi watched her carefully. And since then, she'd been truly disabled, desires boxed inside the tiny house on the alley behind the main road mosque. Her brothers and Abba left each day for their welding work and Azeem for his call centre shift. It was only Ammi and her, trapped in domestic routines,

163

stoking flames, boiling water, frying fish while she plotted her getaway into *The Universe*.

The pink, raw insides of the Callus trainer's mouth – 'Don't vibrate your tongue as in rrrrrr, softly curl it upwards, say aaahrh, that's right, that's the American aaahrh' – reminded Azeem of Ammi's nagging sessions with Asma, the last baby in the house, grotesquely denied normal speech. Asma was not mute, only deaf. For several months, Ammi tried to modulate her sounds, so harsh, so jarring to the family. Silence her till marriage, Abba said, and after that, another family could look out. But Asma was obstinate: the more they tried, the more she shrieked, the noises ugly and untamed. They willed her muteness until she wore it like a veil. They tried to silence her fingers too, hand signs unseemly for a woman, but her fingers were resistant even to Abba's coercion.

It was during training, his first few weeks on the job, that Azeem had been inflamed by his new income, many times greater than his father's salary or his brothers' welding commissions. He hurried home on pay day like a frenzied fairy, his arms filled with gifts for the family: a shirt for Abba, a sari for Ammi, lungis for his brothers and for Asma, a hearing aid, a new-fangled digital device more expensive than Ammi's sari. His brothers never wore those lungis, they resented his sudden ascent and fortune. Ammi and Abba were silent, but Asma was most offensive: she ripped the sponge off the phones and refused to allow them in her ears. The cardboard box, the bubble-wrap, foam and instruction manual lay mangled behind their stove.

At work, Aaron rarely thought about Asma. There was no time in his jostling world for the likes of her. At home, he treated her like a vagrant cat. Anyway she lived in a woman's world, sequestered with Ammi in a curtained space. Aaron had calls to answer, problems to solve.

Asma convinced Ammi to take her to the Deaf School, a school so distant from their house the journey was like a trip to another city. A local relative told Ammi about the school. Asma's pleading signs wore away at Ammi's objections. Without leaking their intent to Abba or her brothers, they emerged from their street, their feet skirting the dips on uneven pavements. On the main street, near the bus stop, crowds surged, heedless of electric sparks from welding shops. Men, mostly bearded, in long kurtas, heads covered in embroidered caps, fused white-hot metals into popular arcs, the latest in window grill designs.

The bus was late. They waited, Ammi jittery, Asma resolute. They rushed in when the bus arrived, dodging the censuring eyes of the welders. They rumbled across roads and sights Asma had never encountered in her life. From the upper deck of the double-decker bus, she scanned neon signboards and sky-touching towers, streams of metallic car-roofs stopping and surging at the policeman's signs, hand movements more juvenile than her flittering talk. Over years, Asma's hands had sprouted

165

wings; her fingers rippled in flight, movements Abba noticed but wilfully ignored.

The school's cheerless entry barricaded by a tall iron gate and barbed wire fence frightened Ammi. She turned back, ready to depart on the next bus. But Allah willed their journey on and Asma clambered over the piercing barrier, sprinting towards the classroom windows.

It was a single-storey building with peeling whitewash, stained black by the grime from leaking pipes. Asma did not waste the short wait before the next bus. Hoisting herself on a brick ledge that wove through the parthenium field, she peered into a classroom. A classroom, like those in Azeem's school, boys and girls with small desks and chairs, a teacher and a blackboard. But there was something else, something unimaginable, the unfolding of a magic that exploded inside her ears. Everyone in class was chattering, mumbling, shouting, laughing with fingers. Like Asma, in her finger talk. Not just the students, the teacher too. She drew on the board a hibiscus flower and signed with finger movements, names for each part: the rounded bottom, pollen-carrying stems. Asma was so excited, she lifted Ammi's burkha and Ammi barely protested. She too was taken in by this new world of classroom signers. A language scorned by the men in their house, sanctioned by a real school.

As they stood there, nearly bare feet on sun-baked bricks, Asma saw the signs were different, distinct from her invented signs. She understood their fingers less than her family's lips. A language as remote as Azeem's English was to their parents. And yet she was hypnotized, captivated by the easy exchanges, by flushed, fluid expressions of a people she imagined as wholly silenced.

Not just their fingers, but her discovery of them, a world, a family of people who shared her being in ways her brothers or Ammi never would. They were hounded out quickly by a uniformed watchman, a lip-moving watchman who flung curses at Ammi's feet, her one visible body part brazenly treading forbidden grounds. Asma stayed rooted on tiptoe with devouring eyes. Why heed a lip-mover?

She wasn't admitted to that school. Such twists of fortune, in their house, were reserved for men. But Ammi and she heaved themselves on the same bus every day for a week, dodging the watchman, dodging school dogs, peering into the finger-talking classrooms to seize forever a place she'd visit in dreams. Ammi shared her rapture. Inside her burkha, she entered the thrall of her daughter's silence.

They never told Abba or her brothers about the world they'd visited. They'd confine her again, Ammi warned. Banish her to a faraway village or her uncle's town. Asma squashed with shuddering fingers the thought of such appalling futures.

Like Asma's, Ammi's fingers had grown swifter over time, her hands more expressive than her mouth. They had signs for everything: Asma's sign for Ammi was a burkha, her hands gliding like a wave over her face. Her sign for Abba was a beard, her fingers closing under her chin; her sign for Wasim the cap, the pink cap he rarely left without; her sign for Afsar an arc, she carried lunch every day to his welder shop where he twisted hot electric bands. No signs for her sisters, they left home soon after she was born and they'd remained strangers to her. Her sign for her uncle was a twisted ear, her face contorted in pain when she signed his name. Her sign for herself was a finger pointing at her heart.

Asma had signs also for the mosque, and a sign for the Big House where she was once a servant. She was fifteen then, Ammi's helper but otherwise excluded from their Colony world. A man offered to hire her to wash vessels, sweep and mop the floor for a generous weekly sum. Asma was terrified; she understood sounds and sights around her home, on her street and in their market but the Big House was unfamiliar. In her home, she did not hear vendor jingles but felt the stirrings of Ammi's burkha. She spotted water droplets trickling through walls before Ammi heard the new rains. She sensed the slow crawl of millipedes before they were stomped upon by her unseeing brothers.

But in the new house, cavernous with many rooms, she hadn't learned the sounds. Or their meanings to lip-moving people. She was scared but more frightened of Abba and the ear-wrencher uncle.

She worked only for a week. The man hadn't touched her but he watched at all times with touching eyes. Eyes that polluted bit by bit in a puncturing gaze. When she came home each day, her fingers were still. Ammi worried, she wasn't used to her daughter's lifeless hands. She thought something worse had happened and shunned the money Abba thrust into the cashbox. Asma stopped working after that and returned to her nightly browsing of Azeem's books.

Azeem, her sign for him was a crutch, metal supports Abba bought by pawning his watch and Ammi's jewels.

Azeem was gentle, not like Wasim, Afsar or Abba, he rarely intruded into her world, rarely hushed her hands or bristled at her sounds. She held him in high regard, his special knowledge, his foreign words, English lip movements exalted by her parents, revered by large companies.

But after the new night job, Azeem was different. Not just physical changes though there were those too: lotions dabbed on cheeks, gels slathered onto curls, spicy fragrances sprayed into armpits. They knew, Ammi and herself, they needed a new sign. At home, he wore the same lungis, rested on the same jute cot, his crutches propped against the wall and yet he was different. She saw a faraway look in his eyes: he looked elsewhere as if beyond the sky into some distant world with the same sinful glint as the Big House man. Azeem had never been like that. He'd become too suddenly like the others. Even his smell, he had about him now the odious male stench of her brothers.

At work that day, Azeem could hardly breathe. The stream of calls overflowed like the sewage drains after the monsoons. Aaron's voyeuristic instincts were quelled, customers were angry and abusive. He was held late at work that night and there wasn't any way to call Abba. Their Team Leader had told them to work double shifts. There was a hurricane in Galveston and an overload of calls at the Bangalore centre. To top it all, Azeem had a sore throat. The Team Leader personally administered hot water and blue pills. 'Swallow,' he commanded, dressed in a military outfit. What happened to the fellow that night? He was usually unimposing. The electronic wallboard flashed dire numbers: 102 *Customers in Queue*, 43 minutes *Average Wait Time*. The command centre screeched special messages on the central announcement system: 'Come on, guys, handle those calls. Reduce your handle times, increase productivity. We've got to do it tonight, faster and faster.'

In all that noise and unceasing excitement, he could hardly focus. His customers' problems were poorly resolved. As the hours wore on, Azeem strained to stay awake, to understand what the Americans were saying. After fourteen hours with ill-tempered voices, he was suddenly aroused by a sugary 'Hi.'

'Good morning, Aaron here, how can I help you this morning?'

'Hi. This is a relay call. Will you be willing to handle a relay call?'

'A relay call? Can I put you on hold for a minute?'

'Sure.'

He shook his colleague at a neighbouring cubicle. 'Hey, yaar, quick, what's a relay call? Don't know? Shit, man.'

'Hi. Yes, I can handle this call. Who am I speaking with?'

'Laurel Swift.'

'Okay, can I have your account number, please, Ms Swift?' said Azeem.

'Yes-it-is-898809802'

'Thank you Ms Swift. How can I help you today?'

'I-think-I-have-been-overcharged-on-my-previous-bill. Can-you-please-explain-the-charges-to-me?' Maybe it was the time of the night in Bangalore but the voice had a lilt to it, a young, teasing voice that felt like a target.

'I need to verify your billing address first. Can you tell me your current address?'

'Department-of-Physics, 0354, University-of-California, San-Diego, 9500-Gilman-Drive-La Jolla, CA 92093-0354.'

'Thank you, ma'am. Your charges last month include a $50 monthly fee for voice service, $15 for text messaging, $32 for international calls...'

'Really? I-have-a-problem-with-that. I-never-make-international-calls.'

'Oh, we'll have to explore that then. Do you have anyone else living with you?' There, Aaron, inquisitive as always. He could see this woman, bikini-clad, muscular, sprinting barefoot down a beach. Like *Baywatch*. Though the call had a strange staccato feel.

'No-I-live-alone. I'm-the-only-one-who-uses-this-phone.' The voice, bewitching again, he'd have done anything to prolong this call. Damn the *Customers in Queue*.

'Anyone else who has access to your phone?'

'No-I-already-answered-that-question.' And suddenly the upper right hand corner of the computer screen flashed. The customer's age, damn it, her age was 73? How could she possess that young, syrupy voice?

Aaron was flushed when the call ended. Of course, he remembered now, a relay call, his trainer had mentioned it. 'Deaf people in America relay electronic messages to voice operators,' Yvette said. 'Please be slow and clear on such calls.' The teasing woman-voice belonged to an operator.

Four hours later, Azeem negotiated the van's steel steps with his clumsy crutches. Climbing into the van was an everyday challenge. Twice, he'd almost fallen back on the road. Someone had mentioned that Bodmas, the other company, offered disabled agents vans with extendable ramps. Azeem didn't think it was possible, such extravagance in India. Surely, the job itself was largesse enough?

While the van inched through packed evening streets, he watched dusty fogs gather beneath a building half-demolished. There was something about that relay call, something incredible but also disturbing. That 73-year-old physicist woman, that Professor Swift, was deaf? She'd been so articulate, so much in control. A deaf person in such a high position was unthinkable in India. In their house, Asma had always been treated as an unfinished person. Could it have been otherwise?

'He's home, he's home,' she signed to Ammi, her hands twirling in rushing circles. Azeem was home, safe and untouched. They'd been so worried. Abba travelled to Azeem's office to enquire about his missing son. Ammi buried him in her burkha, she was so relieved.

Later that night, Azeem removed *The Universe* from his old schoolbag, moth-eaten now; Asma hardly opened the book these days. Despite the faded colours the pictures were enchanting. But Asma was distracted. By Azeem's hands. For the first time in her life, her brother explained with excited, soaring fingers about vast skies and unnamed worlds. She didn't know what happened to him in those tense sixteen hours, but he spoke that day without lips. He spread his arms and pointed upwards, the limitless black space above their home, the sky. And then five fingers, inward, clenched and spread outward, flat, stars, a sign almost like Abba's beard. Then his hands cupped like the mosque's dome: the moon? No, no, not the moon, he signed, other moons, other worlds. In her language.

Deodorized

No bus to catch, yet Rani was late. It was getting dressed that took her longer and longer every day. Scrunching her face in the oval mirror that rested against the steel trunk, she twirled brushes, dabbed powders, squeezed scents. At first she had one lipstick, one face powder, one scent. Now laid out on the uneven surface of the trunk, she had four lipsticks, two powders, five scents. Like the madams at her workplace, she combined colours: today, brinjal purple on her eyes, a pomegranate flush on her cheeks and a scent like ripe grapes.

Nestled inside the Whitefield slum, her home was fenced off from the IT Valley's tidy gardens and mirrorwork towers by concrete walls and barbed wire. The walls were too tall, the barbed wire too spiky. If not she'd have hurled her body – lithe and muscular under the drab Callus uniform – away from the non-stop cries of untended waifs, from snapping dogs and growling drunks into the muffled English of her nightly workplace.

When she was almost done, a scramble for her office badge. Only one room, one steel trunk, yet nothing could be found. *Aiyyo*, there it hung on the metal hook that held her father's shirt; she slung it on her neck, a plastic card with her unsmiling photo attached to a yellow ribbon: *Rani Kampanna, Contract Worker # 343, Housecleaning, Callus Inc.* In the stamp-sized photograph, of which she had five copies, her ears, weighted down by hefty earrings, were large loops of flesh; she was only seventeen, but her ears were those of an old woman. Her eyes, because this was her first studio photo, were creased by blinding studio lights. In the photograph, she wore an orange-pink China silk but to work she wore her Callus uniform, a blue-grey sari with a grey overcoat hanging below her knees. Rani liked large prints and radiant colours, turmeric yellows, chilli greens. The uniform, stark like cement, had a Callus logo embroidered on the front pocket of the overcoat shirt. No flower motifs to dress up the border or sari pallu.

But the photo-badge she wore like a garland; inside her neighbourhood, it granted her a special standing. Strapping boys, recently outfitted in jeans pants and slick hairstyles, tracked her movements. They followed her each night, when she walked to work, with hoots and whistles that halted at the Valley's gates. She was the only one among several hundred slum-dwellers permitted entry into a world so tantalizingly close, yet soundly secured from hovering outsiders.

At first, some slum men seemed overly rattled. There were discussions in beaten pathways, between beedi puffs and the night's last swig: how did she wrangle access, when several of them at various times approached gate security guards for any kind of work and were beaten back by a gruff 'No work for you here'? How did Rani, a girl at that, receive official sanction for her nightly entry?

'Don't give anyone,' her mother hissed, 'the contractor's contacts. You cannot trust anyone here.' Rani, who heard of the recruitment agent from a school friend, had given a false address for the ID card. Her friend said the next-door slum was avoided by IT Valley contractors. 'They're being told not to recruit nearby troublemakers,' the friend said. 'Better give a different address.' The troublemakers included Rani's parents, construction workers who once roamed freely inside the Valley's boundaries; who reared their infants among its sand pits, metal pilings and granite heaps; who bore on bumpy turbans, flat pans of liquid cement to fuse puzzles of brick and glass; who stubbornly refused to shift their tin and tarpaulin homes for vague promises of alternate housing; who belonged to the IT Valley Construction Workers' Union, an unregistered body even after fifteen years of fighting for unpaid wages, disputed lands.

Still, despite her lying and cheating and false address, despite her accidental crossing into the gated campus, Rani felt finer than her neighbours. Even if singled out only by fate, she was singled out nonetheless and the difference between her and *them* showed in small ways: the way she brushed her teeth in the morning – her brush moving up, down, all over her mouth with lips clamped to keep the foam from dribbling – the way she wore her sari a few inches below her waistline, the way she combed her hair without a parting, the way she walked on high heels without tripping or falling, differences apparent only to the keenly observant but more obvious with each passing day to a changing Rani. When she turned into the IT Valley grounds, flashing her contract badge to the gate security, her gait altered. Swaying from side to side on brick walkways, she goaded the slum-boy stalkers into soaring frustration. Inside the lush gardens, even the night was different; from under the street lamps, the sky had a purplish gleam. Near her feet, silver jets sprayed a mist on bluegrass blades. She didn't turn back till she reached the Callus building, the distance between her and the gawking boys growing with each step.

She'd been warned by the contractor not to use the elevator, to 'use the fire-stairs', metal steps that thumped like drums till she reached her floor and entered the office through the swivelling door. There was a brief sign-in at the reception where Rani carefully signed her name. She lingered, for a brief minute or two, smiling coquettishly at the door security guard before turning left and left again into the Ladies, the Callus territory assigned to Rani.

For the first half-hour, inside the long corridor of flushing stalls, the contractor's instructions beat inside her head. She was a schoolgirl performing a drill: first dry sweeping with coconut bristles of the main area outside stalls, then wet wiping with a handle-cloth, then sponging with Phenyle and new disinfectant, then the inside stalls: wet mopping, dry rubbing, toilet seat disinfecting, then Harpic blue swirled inside bowls, then brushing, flushing, rim spraying, lid cleaning, many, many jobs at the start of each shift. Other duties too, swapping toilet rolls and paper towels, cleaning sinks, wiping long mirrors, refilling soaps, a beehive stirring before the crowds stomped in.

When the doors swung open, in that impatient, feisty manner of the night's first shift, Rani squatted and waited. Trampling on still-wet floors, they trooped into her cleaned stalls and dangled from toilet-seat perches. Rani could see many feet from under the stall door frames: some curled inside jewelled shoes or splayed out on flat sandals, some pinkish white, some coffee-coloured, some glossed and polished, some reddened with henna spirals, all clean and scrubbed and dirt-free. None with the deep cracks that split Rani's heels into wide cliffs of rubbery skin. Feet that scurried out from swinging stalls to prettify faces and preen bodies – handbags tipped out onto sink counters, hairbrushes held in fists, sticks shimmered on lips, brown and white powders brushed on necks and noses, eyes and chins. She watched keenly, rocking slightly on her squatting heels, slick, glorious toilet-goers while they fiddled with bra-straps or tucked shirts into squashed waistlines.

She took it all in: curled lashes, pencilled eyebrows, outlined lips, pointers to refine her own walk, her facial expressions, even the turn of her wrists. She stripped one glove to examine the single gold bangle her mother retrieved from the pawnbroker. It was clunky, so unlike the sleek bands that glinted by the washbasins. The gloves, foisted on her hands by the slobbering contractor, were awkward at first; she giggled when she first wore them, so strange the reptile skin that coated her fingers. In her second week, flustered by the slithery feel, she spilled a whole bottle of Harpic bleach on the toilet floor. 'Wasting means salary cut,' the contractor warned. But when she wore the gloves now, her nails were filed into careful half-moons under the translucent plastic.

Midway into her shift, Rani propped up the contractor's yellow sign outside the door: *Cleaning in process, please wait.* This despite two or three toilet-goers shut inside the stalls, legs swinging, pants heaped at ankles. A few months ago she would have waited for the place to be wholly empty before hoisting her cleaning sign and fastening the door; now the traffic was nonstop and quiet moments were rare. Besides, the contractor's brazen urgings had steeled her responses: 'Time to clean means cleaning time. Put the sign out to keep them out. At all times, toilet has to be fully clean.'

Early in the job, she was shy and fearful, yielding to knocking women even if her wet-wiping had to be done again and again. She was daunted by urgent knocks. And forceful shouts: 'Ayah, urgent, let me use first.' Moved by desperate pleas: 'Ayah, please let me, please only few seconds.' Now she was unflinching till the cycle was complete and her hands had been scrubbed. Rani, who studied only till the eighth standard at the Corporation School, could read English. She didn't need the contractor to explain: 'Please wait means please wait, no need to open.'

Tonight the voices were insistent, almost plaintive but she delighted at their disquiet, basked in the fleeting emptiness; with one hand, she wiped with scented Lizol, with the other she examined her new find. A bangle, a thin silver loop that encircled a green stone. When she held it up to the white mirror light, the sphere changed colours, revealed yellows and oranges, dipping suns, rising moons – colours so fantastic, her glove flapped like a netted fish. The women continued to knock: 'Ayah, fast open.' 'Ayah, quickly, have to get back to my desk.'

Rani tucked it into her waist and continued cleaning. Before they burst into the room, she squatted on the floor, her stomach heaving softly. How careless of the woman to carry her bangle in her handbag pouch. Didn't she know anything could happen, the bangle could drop, wash into the drain? If Rani hadn't rescued the silvered treasure, who knows which swampy waters would have tugged it in? She wondered if there were matching earrings on the woman's lobes, in her handbag, her jeans pocket or somewhere in the toilet, already abandoned. It was likely with such an expensive bangle to have matching earrings or a necklace. But the woman, a short creature with blue hair tints, didn't visit again. The bangle stayed single and unattached.

At home, Rani wordlessly tucked it into her mother's steel trunk, under cotton bodices, a faded curtain, a torn mosquito net, giveaways from houses where her mother worked as a maid. She rested it carefully among other finds from the Valley toilet: three bracelets, two pairs of earrings, one anklet. She was bolstered by her mother's belief that at one time their family was privileged, this life a brief slump in a cycle of ups and downs. Her mother had relics of a bygone prosperity, an ivory lice comb and a brocade sari blouse. The blouse, because it was too large for Rani, was consigned to the trunk. But the ivory comb her mother used; when she ran its pointy teeth against her daughter's oiled scalp, examining each swipe for scampering bugs or bloated eggs, she spoke of earlier times, when their family didn't worry about next day's water or the evening's dinner. The cycle, she said, had turned with Rani, the girl so clever, she had a job in the Valley. With each toilet treasure, they repossessed the past.

With so many handbags carelessly flung on washbasins, it was easy for Rani, who was bolder and quicker with each passing night, to unzip pockets, search pouches, snatch shimmery lipsticks, earrings, eye-liner pencils, leather-strap watches, nail files, silver hairclips, an assortment of trinkets that dazzled slum-dwellers. Because the objects were small and her coat over-sized, the security disregarded small bulges in her sari. Most weeks, she acquired a thing or two, sometimes more when crowds were thin and mirrors empty. She knew the stall time of each woman. The plump jeans-pant rarely emerged before three flushes, the pony-tailed horse-face, two minutes then a double flush. With newcomers, she first studied their toilet habits: were handbags left at washbasins or slung on stall doors, one, two or four flushes, how long were their mirror routines, how often mobiles rang, how long each call, small details that Rani filed before picking targets.

Inside her neighbourhood, Rani had acquired a filmstar glow. Even her hair was redone, with eye-covering bangs fashioned at a beauty parlour in the market. Her saris were lighter, more chiffony, her blouses newly cut. On her off-days, the difference between Rani and a Callus toilet-goer was difficult to tell: the same jewellery, the same makeup, the same gold-dial watches accentuated by jasmine bunches, perfumed hair-oils and silver anklets.

Every off-day, she watched a movie, often the same film three or four times. In dark halls, she filled the screen, lovely, radiant, the fancy of many men.

She was bolder with the lecherous contractor, no longer cowed by his decrees: 'Use Harpic twice, mix Lizol with water.' The man never visited the Ladies, never stepped into her stalls. Why should Rani heed his commands? She skipped one or two cleaning duties, displayed the cleaning sign five times like always, lingered before mirrors, doing up her face or brushing her hair, flicking wavy tresses behind her shoulders like those women.

One night, there was a cockroach perched on a toilet seat. A chocolate gleam with translucent wings, rubbing its forelegs, shaking its antennae at stall door entrants. The toilet-goer, a wide-girthed hysterical creature, screamed. As if her throat was being slit, as if she'd seen the Byappanahalli ghost, as if the stall door shuddering in her hands was chewing her flesh. The cockroach, unruffled till then, was frightened into flight. There was a flurry after that, the whole Ladies a chaotic stir, while the insect flying from face to face and light to light, landed on a mirror. A harmless, brown whir but one would have thought it was a blinding fire or raging storm, the way they stomped out, their handbags strewn, their lipsticks half-done, their hair-clips abandoned. Rani trapped the creature in her broom and slid it into her money pouch. Near her home, kids had cockroach races; plump, flying ones were specially prized. The creature wasn't the night's only bounty because she also stumbled on something extraordinary – a special find. A silver chain with a diamond pendant – what a chain, what a pendant! Prized from a dark blue box, this wasn't like anything she'd acquired. Cast off in the scramble of handbags, the silver glowed more brilliantly than the noon sky.

Hoisting the *Please Wait* sign, she emptied the toilet and adorned her neck with the thin loops. Rubbing a coloured stick on her cheeks, she mimicked their frantic cockroach expressions before the long mirrors. 'Eeeee, aaaaah, yuck.' This was a story her neighbours would relish. Jumping so high, screaming so loud at an insect. Not even a biting one. How would they react to the rats and leeches that inhabited her streets? She ignored their knocks for longer than usual, 'Ayah, open, please fast open.' When she eventually let them in, she was startled by the contractor's shirtless chest. He always spoke to her in Kannada: 'Rani, can you come to the reception?' he said, thrusting his hairless body through the crowd. To the reception? Now? In the middle of a shift? What could the man want? Was it a festival bonus or a good job bonus? She heard the Men's cleaner received extra monies for 'good cleaning job'. Retouching her lipsticked cheeks, yanking her petticoat a wee-bit lower, Rani marched on high heels, her stomach churning.

The man's gold watches and many finger rings flashed near the telephone desk. Nanjundappa slobbered at Rani, his eyes fixed on the flesh above her navel: 'Varghese sir is complaining about the Ladies. Today there will be a toilet inspection. Ten more minutes, keep it fully ready.'

Uncaring about hoisting her petticoat or tripping on her new heels, Rani dashed across the hallway, barged into the Ladies, stomach churning, heart pounding. For a few seconds, she leaned against the door, breathing fast. A toilet inspection? Why? Why tonight? Was it the cockroach, the creature's harmless presence on the white toilet seat? She was doing everything she could to clean the toilet: dry sweeping, wet wiping, sponging, disinfecting, mopping, rubbing, brushing, flushing. She could replay the routine if the contractor desired. Her eyes ran through the toilet paper holders, the paper towel rack, the soap trays. Everything was filled. Could she help it if the insect found its way through an open drain, perched itself on a toilet seat? If the girls hadn't run around, hysterical and screeching, the creature would have tucked itself into some dark corner.

What if the inspection had nothing to do with the cockroach? Had they complained about the waiting time, how long she took for cleaning? Surely the contractor couldn't fault her for that? He gave her the sign, asked her to use it.

In a few minutes, the man knocked on the door and walked in before she could heave it open. He said Varghese sir would visit next week if the complaints persisted. He shuffled as if sent inside against his wishes. He entered the first stall, slapped the stall door, lifted the toilet seat, yanked the flush. Did the same thing in the second stall. The third stall and fourth stall he inspected from outside. The fifth stall was a shower stall. He thrust his head in and out, then walked towards the washbasins and examined his two nostrils in the long mirror. While the contractor was prying his hairy voids with fat fingers

184

she glimpsed a row of lights. The necklace, the silver necklace, she'd forgotten to pull it off. She was wearing it still, with its shiny diamond and curly loops and intricate metallic twists. Her hand rose to clutch the heat rising in her neck and her arm swivelled across one breast. The contractor coughed up his paan and spattered his red drool on the sparkly white basin. He tilted the liquid soap and squeezed rose-coloured fluid on the rim.

Then he turned around and puckered his nose. 'There are complaints about the smell in Ladies. So bad they're saying an animal has died. Have you checked fully for dead animals? Lizards or rats in pipes?'

Rani shook her head. There was no dead animal here – what was he talking about?

'Are you cleaning properly? First wet wiping, then dry wiping, Harpic, Lizol?'

'*Howdhu*, sir.'

'Five times all nights?'

'*Howdhu*, sir.'

His eyes shifted from the washbasin rims to her navel. 'Clean two more times and I will send an air-freshening scent. Spray the full toilet.'

Rani shut the door quickly, then rushed to the mirror to undo the clasp. The man entered again without knocking. 'No jewellery for work, only uniform.'

The spray did not work. The toilet-goers whispered outside stalls, their murmurs misting her mirrors. The contractor called again. From his mobile to the reception phone. Complaints, he said, hadn't stopped. It was the smell, a stink apparent to everyone but the toilet-cleaner herself. Didn't she know it was there?

When Rani entered the IT Valley, it was like piercing the skin of a magical other-world. The whole place, starting with the pathway outside, was redolent with scents: wet grass, fallen leaves, blooming flowers, everything touched by a godly incense. Even cigarette fumes around the fountain were steeped with special flavours. Inside the office, the reception smelled of rose petals, the polished marble of tangy lime. On glass tables, there were indoor flowers of every conceivable colour and shape. But the headiest odours were toilet vapours, Lizols and Harpics, deodorizers and air-fresheners that made her head light, so light she soared like a bird. The women, when they came in, left sharp trails of body sprays and perfumes, the room at all times soused in spicy, flowery smells so spine-tingling, she couldn't fathom what stink the ladies were talking about.

'You only,' the man continued on the phone. 'The madams are saying the smell is you. How often do you have a bath?'

'Weekly twice,' said Rani, unprepared for this new assault.

'*Weekly twice*,' the man screeched. 'You must have daily baths, otherwise your smell will be too much.' If complaints did not stop in a week, he threatened to replace her.

Weekly twice was a lie. Rani had a bath once a week in a pond that was used for morning jobs, washing clothes and drinking water. It was a trudge from her thatched-roof home, behind the wholesale market, plastic pot and soap scrap in hand, with three other women into a field covered with thorny bushes and stinging leaves. It was where they went each morning, for big and small jobs, the women taking turns to watch for hissing twigs and ogling boys. There were signs outside, 'Private Property – No Trespassing', signs gummed over with film posters. Earlier, the plot had granite slabs and grape vines strung along wires, while now white-flowered weeds concealed squatters. These days the plot swarmed with pigs as women scrambled for clean patches not already sullied by yesterday's job.

Before they found this plot with its concealed pond they had to walk a greater distance, beyond the bridge, into sunken railway tracks. Water mugs in hand, a few sprinkles for each squatter, they washed under fluttering saris before cargo trains sped across freshly laid slop. They bathed inside public parks and private gardens when security guards were shirking from 24-hour duties. They washed inside graveyards, crouched behind marble slabs with pots hoisted from salty borewells. Many times they paid for the water, three rupees a pot from tank-loads ferried by private trucks.

Baths, because they took longer and required a sari strung across wires, were taken once in seven days because the women couldn't afford, with the wholesale market opening at 7:00 a.m., to linger beyond the arrival of the morning's first trucks. The others who sold jasmine flowers, garlic pods and pearl onions on the pavement couldn't make allowances for the night-shift queen. They sneered if her washing took longer, 'the mighty wall-crosser', the only woman in their vendor community who made her living outside the market. She ignored their jibes, their jealous put-downs and she couldn't, even if she hoisted their unsold wares or cleared their pavement space, wrangle extra bath days.

So when the contractor ordered Rani to have an everyday bath, for many days she wrestled on her own with a fluttering sari and footpath sounds – were those a man's footsteps, tromping into her grapevine hideout? Did the bush part with a sibilant menace? Did the main road watch with glowering eyes?

A few weeks later, Rani found a new place for her bath. It was on a night when there was an inexplicable slowdown of toilet traffic. When she entered the toilet, there were new stickers on the toilet mirrors, and inside stall doors: *When you can be in Florida, why spend time here?* Below the printed English text were pictures of blue waters, a white beach and several palm trees. That night, stall-sitters came in bunches, quickly in, quickly out, no lipsticks redone, no powders patted, no hairs brushed. What was it that checked their loitering? She examined the picture stickers in greater detail. Rani had never, in all her seventeen years, been to an ocean. But her mother, who grew up in Mangalore, spoke of it often. What struck her most about the Florida pictures was the vast emptiness, long white stretches of sand without people. Could it really be that empty anywhere on the planet? Were agents sucked into that blue-white emptiness from white-white toilet seats? Rani could not imagine going to a place without people. No one to talk to, no boys to dress up for. She wondered how they dressed in this Florida *ooru*. She pirouetted before the mirrors, tied her sari in three different ways, each style more daring and revealing. Like this or that or this?

Two hours later she was unnerved. Was there an

inspection tonight? Would the contractor knock again to sniff at her navel? After three disconcerting hours, she tripped across to the reception.

She asked the reception lady, a four-flush woman who made many calls from inside stalls. 'Why aren't ladies coming to the toilet?' she asked.

'Tonight?' said the receptionist. 'I really don't know, there's so much chaos. Something about a storm.'

Rani asked her about the toilet stickers. 'Oh, that,' laughed the receptionist. 'That's an award. For the best team tonight there's a reward. The company will pay for a trip to Florida.'

Where is Florida, she asked.

'It's a faraway place, in America. Very far away, two days by plane. Would love to go there.' The reception lady looked wistful. 'After marriage, I plan to go there for my honeymoon.'

Rani re-entered the toilet and ran her hand across the stickers. Perhaps that place was beautiful, more appealing than it seemed. Two days on a plane, Rani couldn't imagine what that would be like. She'd seen planes rumble through Bangalore skies. It was difficult to imagine such tiny streaks of light carried people inside. It must be stomach-churning to be so high in the sky. Flo-ree-dah, she repeated the word to herself, rolled the syllables inside her mouth. She pressed her nose closer to the sticker. Surely those ocean winds and palm-tree breezes were scented, fruity and flowery like her toilet.

It struck Rani then, when she looked around the empty stalls, she could use the shower-stall for her bath. Ladies used it after gym workouts. Rani locked the main door and stood under the hot-cold gush. She was lavish with liquid soap, with the new bottle from supplies. When she emerged, wet and lily-scented, she thought of her walk back home. She wondered whether lurking slum boys would sense the difference. She'd stop to buy jasmine strands to accentuate her smell.

The next night, Rani didn't make it to work. It started with a small flicker outside a house with a thatched roof, a smouldering beedi or a dry twig lit for cooking. She knew how quickly it spread, how rapidly heat destroyed their propped-up shelters, dry coconut-leaves the first to gather sparks and carry flames to cow-dung cakes spinning like night-sky chakras. The last time they had built their dwellings closer to a railway track and all the homes were reduced in a few hours, into a heap of ashes – grey, powdery dust that settled on nearby rooftops.

This place they built after the IT Valley construction, after their temporary tin-roof shelters inside the Valley's grounds were outlawed by the project's completion. Eight years they'd lived and woven their lives into the wholesale market and garlic trade and cement carriers. Were they to be transposed again by a spreading heat? There was no time to think – only act. The fire hadn't reached Rani's home, not yet while she stood with a neighbour's baby on her hip, kids crouched at her feet. Was there anything else to gather, anything to possess?

The steel trunk was too large to carry. But she quickly stuffed her trinkets, necklaces, earrings, bangles, lipsticks, perfumes, powders into a cloth bag, a large one that held onions and potatoes inside their curtained kitchen.

She heard crackles – and then a shuffle, a blur of bodies – large men, with clubs and sticks, urging them into one of five lorries, parked near the edge of the slum. They prodded them in – gently at first, viciously when they resisted – 'You have to move, danger, fire, go, go, go, get in.' A jumble of shapes, young and old, sick and hungry, deformed and half-bodied piled quickly into the safe harbour of a lorry's four wheels. They didn't ask why the men were there or how they arrived in time to deliver them from a swelling heat.

When everyone was gathered, crushed like wholesale sacks – some sitting, some standing, some fallen down – the lorry sped away from the hissing sparks at full speed. They rumbled and crashed inside the market's narrow streets, knocking off a few abandoned garlic carts. Of what use were they anyway, when the owners were fleeing to some distant unknown place? Rani then remembered her trinket bag. She'd stuffed it all in, left it standing on the trunk. Also her Callus badge, her passport into the IT Valley grounds, she had it secured under the aluminium pot where she stowed her monthly wages.

Wherever the lorries were taking them, down the main road, under the bridge, by another railway track, it was already too far from Rani's Valley toilet. Children sniffled, shivered in the night breeze. They whizzed past telephone pillars, tall spires, domes of strange temples, large parks, government houses, tyre shops, plywood heaps, open grounds like her morning vineyard, then into a lorry mart where a thousand other lorries, roaring with cement bags halted for a few minutes. Rani fell asleep, her back propped against wooden planks.

191

When she woke up, the city was gone, the crowded buildings erased forever. They were speeding across fields, rice fields greener than IT Valley lawns, towards a large body of water reddened by morning skies. She looked at her leather-strap watch, 8:00 a.m. The fires must have reached her treasure chest, melted its dented surface. Her mother, hanging on to the side of the lorry, was hunched over. People in the lorry were stooped in despair. Where had they brought them? Here? Into this barren field? There was nothing here. What about jobs? Buses? How would they make a living?

Rani's high heels clapped the ground. She undid the black buckle strap and walked barefoot to the edge of the lake. Nothing else in the field but a few palm trees. Straggly palms with a few coconuts. Her face rose in the water, her smudged lips, her smeared cheeks. She squatted on her heels, the way she used to in the toilet, splashed water on her arms and neck and face. Colours trickled down her cheeks and ran into the whitish soil that surrounded the lake.

Others stumbled from the lorry with glazed eyes, fearful of the new surroundings. Rani waded into the water, lifted her sari to wet her legs as far as her knees. It struck her then, waters, palm trees, white sands: the toilet stickers. Rani had moved, before Callus toilet-goers, to that distant *ooru*, to that faraway beach on earth-rumbling lorries. She turned her head to the sky – a bright, acrylic blue like the stickers – and laughed out loud. '*Idhay namma* Flo-ree-dah,' she said when her mother reached the edge of the lake. This is our Florida.

Very, Very Varghese

When folks said, 'That's so very, very, Varghese,'
the Admin Manager basked in the compliment.
Yes, he was singular and indispensable, as he had always
been at all the companies where he had worked. Nearly
fifty-five, but versatile. Up with the times. He paced the
30,000-square-feet office with the brash, foreign-returned
CEO who hopped lightly over plywood stacks and carpet
rolls. Drawing himself up to his entire five feet two inches
inside his striped Allen Solly shirt, the manager slapped
on his yes-boss face, his expression heightened like those
of Kathakali dancers in his native Thiruvananthapuram.
Their talk was punctuated by the uncaring thwacks of
Rajasthani carpenters who beat nails into teak window
frames. Using his contractor contacts, Varghese had
sourced these chaps and organized for their transport all
the way from the dusty hinterlands of the North to the IT
capital. Unlike the overfed locals, the sinewy Rajasthanis

worked hard. 'Runs in their blood,' Varghese explained to the NRI CEO, who hadn't appreciated the manager's genius in curbing costs *while* upping quality. 'Entire villages in Rajasthan are devoted to carpentry.'

The pounding stopped when a chap came in with a rattling tray of tea glasses. A few ceased work to slurp tea under an unfinished door. Varghese wanted to review progress with the supervisor, a fierce moustached man driving an electric drill through an aluminium sheet. But he couldn't stop now because the sprightly CEO was at the other end of the room, leaping across cardboard boxes stuffed with floor tiles. Varghese, careful not to spoil his black Hush Puppies, gently stepped over a clutter of buckets. Despite his caution, a bucket tipped over and the smell of turpentine oozed into the room. He moved a hand to block his nostrils. The CEO, unruffled by the strong blast of solvent, held the office blueprints against a paint-splattered window. The window frame was stuck over with brown paper and masking tape and a muted light filtered through the draft layout, spotlighting white dashes.

'Very good idea, boss, everyone in same-size cubicles. I'm fully in favour of equality. But not sure if local people are cultured *yet*. If we expose ourselves like that, they'll be coming to us for each and every thing,' said Varghese.

The CEO, after twenty years in the US, had strange notions about employee seating. He wanted the whole place democratic, everyone equal. He wore collared T-shirts and rumpled cotton trousers while Varghese maintained workplace decorum with a black-orange paisley tie. The first few days, the Admin Manager wore YK Ramu suits, carefully tailored in high-quality Raymond

194

wools to camouflage his paunch, but was forced to renounce his jackets after Sashwath's chaffing: 'Varghese, we're not so formal inside Callus, I'd like to promote a dotcom sprightliness.' At home, the manager moved six new coats, all custom-made with shoulder pads and faddish elbow patches, to the attic. 'Will require later for foreign travel,' he told his disbelieving wife.

But some decrees could not be broken, so Varghese was privately resolute on Senior Manager seats. Having settled himself inside a teak-wood cabin, the CEO insisted Senior Managers – Varghese included – mingle with Callus riffraff inside regular cubicles, brushing aside the unfitness of American norms in the Indian market.

'That's the whole point. I want you guys accessible. Not shut off inside closed rooms,' said Sashwath, marking out with a pencil the grassy undulations of a nine-hole golf course that encircled his corner office. The CEO's hair, Varghese noted, had been carefully plastered over a looming baldness, a bluff the manager could barely pull off with his two or three remaining tufts. 'Two basketballs,' said his wife, 'your belly, your head.'

If Sashwath had his way, Varghese would be caged inside an 80-square-feet cubicle, the same size as call centre agents. 'Personally I don't need 80 square feet, can manage with a desk and chair, don't need a cubicle. But subordinates here are troublesome, they snoop into conversations. At times we'll need privacy, room for strategic discussions,' he said, while the unfeeling NRI pencilled in French windows to fringe his golf course sweep.

'And that's why we have discussion rooms. Anytime you need private space, you can move into a discussion room.'

That wasn't the point. How do you convince a numbskull foreign returnee that Senior Managers in the Indian culture couldn't demean themselves in small cubicles because it wasn't *done*? As it is, engineers and agents were a pesky lot. If there was nothing marking out seniority, there'd be scant respect for bosses. In a city where everything was hemmed in – concrete buildings jammed inside illegal sites, pedestrians squashed out by cars, cemeteries dug up for new constructions – space was *power* in a manner that people from the vast, open plains of America would never understand. Erasing a person's standing would result in the sort of chaos that Sashwath with his McKinsey vision could hardly foresee.

The supervisor arrested their talk. Money for Fevicol, he said, in guttural Hindi. He addressed Sashwath when he knew it was Varghese, the Admin Manager, who was in charge of their activities.

'Don't disturb, will talk to you later,' said Varghese, glaring at the man's gashed vest. That was the point: not just employees but rogues like these – carpenters, dealers, printers, transporters – who'd disregard managers squeezed into commoner slots.

But those weren't gripes Varghese could deploy to wangle larger cubicles. No, such arguments wouldn't wash with a freshly-arrived half-American. Lost inside his globetrotter bubble, the man would discount centuries of thinking and Indian attitudes: 'Minor issues, Varghese, about time the country changes,' he'd say in that dense American accent.

The Admin Manager sneezed in the sawdust. 'I completely agree, boss, we don't need separate Senior Manager cabins. Let everyone sit inside cubicles. Of

196

course, there will be blokes who may not join for that reason. I hear companies like Bodmas are spoiling managers with closed-door cabins. Ridiculous.'

His statement for some reason riled the boss more than anything else: 'Really? Is that what they do at Bodmas? Where did you hear this?'

'Have my sources,' said Varghese. 'But no need to get influenced by that.'

'Do you think I can have a small terrace outside my office? The view would be terrific.'

'Why not? Absolutely. This is not confirmed but I hear in Bodmas some Senior Managers have private terraces. Of course, there's no way we can afford that.'

'Afford what? Sometimes, I wonder if the terrace will obstruct the view from my desk. Of course, if we can create a nice lawn, a small garden, it can work. Do tulips grow here?'

'Yes, yes, why not? This is the garden city, we have all the flowers in the world – jasmines, roses, marigolds, orchids – name it, we have it.' If NRIs could uproot themselves from green-card habitats and plant their pestilence in a new India, why not tulips?

While the CEO turned his back to re-examine his marks on the paper, Varghese coughed: 'So we have concluded with our limited funding we can't attract the best Senior Managers?'

'Funding? Who says our funding's limited? I can raise a 100 million if I need to, I'm waiting for the right time. And of course, we need the best talent. You know, I suggest we go ahead with larger Senior Manager cubicles. But not closed door offices like those Bodmas morons.'

'Yes, yes,' nodded Varghese, hiding his glee as best as he could. 'Let's not imitate Bodmas. Maybe larger-sized cubicles with visitor space, high walls and sober colours will do the trick. A few signs to denote seniority, that's all.'

Eight months after those artful preliminaries, Varghese was seated inside a 200-square-feet cubicle, on the phone with a transport contractor: 'Yes, fifteen Matador vans to begin with, working on four night shifts. In six months, we'll increase to fifty vans.'

The 200 square feet were sufficient for a visitor's chair and a small corner table besides the built-in desk and filing cabinet. What was bothersome, after all this effort, was the person seated across his cubicle inside a Senior Manager space: a numbskull woman with a gangly body and vexing hair colour appointed as a 'Trainer cum Counsellor'.

When he saw her several months ago at the Callus lobby when the office was still being set up – foam boards piled up at the entrance, marble unpolished – he thought, sweet, apt for a candy-voiced receptionist or dumb secretary. Short skirt, cleavage-showing top, coloured cheeks, streaked hair, chunky clogs, the kind that prettified lower rungs. The carpenters, bloody Rajasthani rogues, had halted their work, stretching sweat-streaked necks to ogle, unabashed.

'Are you here to meet me?' asked Varghese. He was polite then, kind even.

'No, I don't think so,' she smiled, her voice doe-like,

masking the wickedness that emerged a day later. 'I'm here to meet the CEO,' she added, as if the meeting were an everyday banality, not a crafty encounter arranged by a cunning creature. A straightaway meeting with the boss for an unknown entrant was preposterous but what else would one expect with a bearded NRI willing to humour anyone and everyone?

And then a bigger blow when the boss asked Varghese to order her '*Trainer's*' visiting card. It took him several cups of dark, unsweetened coffee – there wasn't anything more numbing inside the office – to recover his thoughts. Varghese was not a smoker but he almost considered that day a trial pack to break his vexation. The nitwit woman a *Trainer* – what was the man thinking? Varghese was not sexist or patriarchal or whatever the blasted word was, but surely the workplace needed to put a lid on feminine wiles? His wife, for example, had greater license than his mother, who had never assailed her husband on trumped-up defects: 'You eat too much,' 'Why YK Ramu, why not an ordinary tailor?' 'Warned you not to stitch six coats, told you they were a waste.' But he allowed her that, did not clamp her mouth shut. But infernal upstarts like this – young and *female* – could shatter office decorum.

'Found this great trainer,' the CEO said when ordering her visiting cards, all misty-eyed. 'She also has counselling experience. She can function as a trainer and counsellor.' The manager's feet wobbled. How could one explain to a headstrong NRI: this is India, not America, folks don't need counsellors for slight irritations. 'Can't get along with my mother,' 'Wife's a nag,' etc., etc. In India you just managed, took whatever life doled out to you. Besides, these agent kids were overpaid. What problems could brats who earned ten times his 1973 starting salary possibly have? And what kind of oversight would this female provide when she needed direction herself on dressing for work? What qualifications did she have for this Trainer/Counsellor position? Did Sashwath ask to see her certificates? References? Counsellor *indeed.* The woman looked like a school dropout. It was a problem with CEOs, they saw a pretty face, they lost objectivity.

The visiting card wasn't the worst, there was more to come. The first few weeks, tucked into a training classroom, the female was out of sight. Later, he thought there was a mistake when he found her walking into the next-door cubicle with an armload of family pictures and four or five smelly plants: 'Akriti, what are you doing here? These grey cubicles are reserved for *Senior* Managers. Feel free to occupy any of the purple or orange ones,' he said, waving his generous arms at empty agent spots.

'Boss asked me to sit here,' she said, hanging a creeper on the cubicle edge, a money plant with large leaves.

'No, no, I think there's some mistake. These cubicles are reserved exclusively for Senior Managers. I'll check with the boss. In the meantime, don't hang anything up. You'll spoil the walls for the next person.'

When he returned from the CEO's office, he couldn't decide which was worse: her cool disregard of his fiat, her obscene belongings – photographs, artworks, plants, feminine bric-a-brac that detract from a workplace's gravitas – plastered on those walls, or the CEO's thoughtless dismissal: 'Varghese, she's grown beyond her training role. And she needs a larger space to counsel agents. She's helping me on attrition. I hope you're not objecting because she's a woman, this is an equal opportunity company.'

In just twenty years in the US, these NRIs acquired an outrageous liberalness. Why not stay there then, these 'equal opportunity' people, in lands that brushed off age and experience and *real* seniority?

She'd been on board for six months and Varghese was cramped by no-good Admin reports. Why should he, a man thirty years older, report to that lipsticked woman on the state of toilets or cafeteria choices? What did a counsellor have to do with Admin details? And if the company needed a counsellor, why this creature? Why not Yvette, the other lady trainer who seemed more level-headed? When he'd suggested this once, the boss had rapidly dismissed the idea: 'No, not Yvette. Woman's too dowdy. This is a global business, counsellors need spunk, strong personalities.' Spunk? Akriti couldn't even count.

Instead of attending to weightier matters like van routes and driver shifts, Varghese sorted through dinner combos for the Callus cafeteria. The few tufts that stood up on his head now had several grey strands. 'The woman,' he told his wife, 'can turn a wig white.' Food choices, like graded agent voices, were no longer a simple matter best left to cooks. No, said the boss, it required complex plotting on Excel worksheets in light of the 'rating system' introduced by Akriti. There were, every three or four months, surveys dished out to clamouring agents to uncover employee dislikes. In the last survey, pre-cooked dosas wrapped in silver-foil were key contributors to agent distress.

'Increases our attrition,' expounded the bird-brain. This around an oakwood conference table inside the loftiest conference room, in front of a PowerPoint snapshot of the indicted wrap. Instead of rubbishing agent grouses for what they were – the product of drifting idle minds – the CEO dwelt on cafeteria complaints as if they overrode balance-sheet glitches or operational slip-ups.

'What else do they object to?' he asked.

'Some say samosas are cold and oily, some feel noodles are sticky.'

'*Really?*' said the man, as if the Callus stock were driven by such things. 'Varghese, you have to work on this, I want those ratings to rise by 50% by next quarter. Confer with Akriti for agent suggestions.'

The gripes didn't stop with food. A new grouse from the squawking bunch involved Toilets. The Men's toilet was apparently 'adequate' but the Ladies at all times had a bad stench. 'No problem in toilet. Ladies spend too much time in loos,' said the Admin Manager.

'Varghese, let's not get distracted. If there's a complaint about the Ladies you need to talk to the housecleaners,' snapped Sashwath.

Varghese knew the name Akriti called him behind his back: CTO – Chief Toilet Overseer. He heard her wisecracks when he left the office on time: 'Varghese hasn't gone yet, hasn't the school bell rung?' or 'Don't rag him, yaar, he's cute, he's our mascot.'

He ignored a reminder email that popped into his inbox, a new demand from the overgrown creature: 'To protect agent privacy, I need a private counselling room with soundproof doors and a comfortable couch. I would also like sufficient wall space for cheery posters.' It was galling enough that she occupied a Senior Manager's cubicle; there was no way the Admin Manager would assent to a closed-door cabin. The only other person who had a cabin was the CEO. Would he have her implanted inside an equal space?

Just then his mobile buzzed. Was the CEO, that weak-willed idiot, buckling already to her recent appeal?

'Varghese, I need to see you immediately. Can you come here?'

Folks thought Admin was a cakewalk, but the job was more complex than piloting a spaceship. Besides bus routes and office cleanups, the boss entrusted him with sundry matters, tasks that fell into crevices between departments. Some policeman's request to 'kindly consider a job for his daughter' or some ministerial lackey demanding bribes because records showed 'fire permits are not in order'.

'Just do it, Varghese, don't distract the others,' said Sashwath, as if the Admin Manager's head were not buzzing already with night-shift drivers and absentee cooks. 'In any case, these jobs are so very, very Varghese.'

When he popped into the boss's office this time, the CEO had stepped outside the French window to stare at the powdery golfing greens rimmed by eucalyptus trees. 'I want to visit the kitchen area,' he said. Was this a sudden hygiene check? Had there been a notice from government food inspectors? Varghese rarely wandered into the kitchen and shuddered at the thought of such spontaneous forays. Cooks were an uncouth crowd – there'd be unwashed dishes, yesterday's leftovers, piled-up trash, rats, roaches – who could tell what else? 'Kitchen, boss? I mean you're welcome anytime but is there any specific reason? We might disturb the cooks, we should give them notice first.'

'Rubbish,' said Sashwath, in that peremptory American manner. 'I want to see the place now, I'm moving my office there.'

'Your office? To the kitchen?'

In a few minutes, when they stepped inside the heavy steel doors, all Varghese could think of was the heat. It was the only room inside the office without A/C ducts. Steam whirled around his head and ears while pungent vapours from newly-cut onions clouded his vision. Two cooks in white uniforms with white aprons splattered with chicken grease and sunflower oil mixed dosa batter with ungloved hands while another stood near a flaming vat and dropped samosas into sizzling oil. Every two seconds he wiped a leaky nose with his fingers. Varghese blinked, teary-eyed, at the boss.

But Sashwath was distracted. He darted around the room, then stood on a cardboard box to peek outside the tiny exhaust window, unflustered by heat and fumes and oil stains that doused a wretched Varghese. What new scheme was he hatching?

He'd been asked to move his corner office to the North East by a Vaastu expert, he said. Into the space occupied by the current kitchen. He scurried among large steel tubs filled with fermented flour, chopped chillies, charred brinjals: 'Maybe I can have my desk here, get a French window installed at that spot. I'm trying to get a handle of the view here. Is there some ladder we can use to climb that ledge?'

For a man accustomed to five-star comforts, Sashwath was remarkably agile. He climbed nimbly out of the exhaust, using a shaky aluminium ladder some cook drew out from a dark corner. Varghese clumsily followed, breathing heavily when he landed on the sunlit strip. The place was sweltering and airless and he could hardly see in the blinding light, the arch covered by Sashwath's hands. 'Hell,' said the CEO. 'Bad view.'

Bad was hardly the term Varghese would use to describe the slum that had overtaken the barren land behind the IT Valley, reserved at one time by the BDA but under litigation for the past fifteen years. While courts plodded through many hearings, the acre of congress grass fenced by barbed wire had been captured for makeshift homes – corrugated tin roofs, thatched walls, sodden bricks, yards and yards of bright-blue tarpaulin stretched like a fallen-down sky – what did these people care about untried cases or BDA injunctions? Even under a strident afternoon sun, the place was filled with shadows. Three kids with bulgy, unfed bellies wandered outside the tarpaulin shelter and turned unblinking eyes at the two men. They smiled and waved.

'Foreign visitors can't see this,' said Sashwath, waving absently at the kids. It wasn't just the sight, rotten as it was, it was the smell – sooty kerosene fires, dried-up faeces, rancid trash piles, hundreds and thousands of unwashed lives – much more noxious than the fumes in the muggy kitchen. 'Can we do anything about that?' asked Sashwath, stroking his beard. 'Clean up the view in some manner?'

'We can, but it will cost us a packet,' said Varghese. He didn't ask at that point why the office was being moved in the first place. Or why the rational, business-school cracker had given in to ancient architectural norms, why, all of a sudden, good energies and bad energies mattered more than business plans or the logical workings of a modern mind.

'Who is this Vaastu expert?' he asked instead.

'Chap who designed the Bodmas office. He claims responsibility for their success.'

'Vaastu is a very good idea,' said Varghese. 'I've heard many offices have benefitted by reorienting structures. But some people say Feng Shui is more practical, should we try that first? Don't have to demolish anything for Feng Shui. A candle here, a wind chime there, much easier.'

'No,' said Sashwath, 'I'm impressed by Vaastu, it's Indian, Varghese, not made in China. In any case, let me know the costs to clean up the place. Of course, we don't want fallouts with NGOs or politicians. I'm sure you'll take care of that.'

The business, Varghese sensed, must be worse than he thought. Maybe funds were drying up or revenues tottering, calling for dire remedies, the auspices of greater forces. Varghese himself went to church once a week, but he was careful not to mix religion with work. Till now, he didn't think Sashwath was a follower of anything but stock values and his own share in the company. It had to be a deep crisis to hurl him over the edge like this. Varghese must chat up the accountant folks to gather what was going on. In any case, there was no talk about Akriti's cabin and back in his cubicle, the manager exhaled, popping a button on his collared shirt. He flung the woman's invading vine across the matte-grey wall but it sprung back with its insect-luring leaves. Arched on her wooden clogs, she peered into his space: 'Hey, Varghese, acting on my memo?'

He didn't look up from the laptop screen where food choices blinked in different fonts. He clicked the file shut and launched a new worksheet: 'Vaastu plan for CEO's office.'

'Varghese, did you get my mail?' The woman rarely slung her serpent neck over the cubicle wall unless she needed something.

'I'm busy, Akriti, please don't disturb me.'

'Also have you completed the test?'

The woman of late had been buzzing about some personality test she was handing out to all and sundry. Varghese did not subscribe to her bunkum, so why do it?

'No time, Akriti, I'm doing something serious.'

'Sashwath asked me to email a list of Senior Managers who hadn't completed the test.'

'Really? Last time I was scared of not completing tests was in the fourth standard. What does Boss plan to do – rap us on our knuckles? In any case, you'll have it by morning. I'm busy now.'

'Are you organizing janitor shifts? Sorry I disturbed you.'

'You have to move them quickly,' said the consultant, 'before they hear of your plans.' The consultant belonged to a firm that specialized in land clearance among other things. Varghese nosed out his contacts from an

Admin friend. In Admin circles, the manager was well networked.

'Why?' asked Varghese, standing up on his filing cabinet to peer into Akriti's office. He was glad she was away, couldn't have her listening into his mobile conversation. 'We'll sponsor more sanitized housing, the move will be a leg-up for them.'

'Jobs,' said the consultant. 'No jobs in the outskirts. You are uprooting them from their livelihoods.'

'Livelihoods? What livelihoods can they have in this place? Something will come up in the outskirts, the way the economy's pumping. And why can't they commute like the rest of us? Besides, I don't think these people are fit for any work. Or they wouldn't live there in the first place.'

'In any case, we have to act fast,' the man said. 'Otherwise, they will build a footpath temple or a shrine inside a tree and then it's a different game altogether. Religious conflict, riots, police, politicians, courts, even the State cannot budge them after that.'

'How quickly?' asked Varghese.

'Overnight. I know, I've done this many times.'

'We don't want violence,' said Varghese.

'Of course not. Our agency services multinationals, big-time real estate companies. Everything will be quiet, skilfully managed. You won't hear a whimper.'

'Can this be done during the day? You see, we work nights.'

'No, not possible, only at night,' he said. 'We can't act when there are crowds milling around.'

'How much?' asked Varghese.

'Such details,' he said, 'are best settled face-to-face.

But let me warn you, has to be all cash. I will give you an address in Jayanagar for delivery.'

'Boss,' said Varghese, calling the CEO on his internal line, 'I've spoken to the agency, fixed up all the terms.'

'For what?' he asked.

'To sanitize your kitchen view,' said Varghese.

'Sanitize? Only you can use a word like that. Anyway, good progress. By the way, there's a hurricane in the US, call overload at Bangalore. Need extra vans tomorrow.'

'All right, boss.'

'Varghese, wait,' said the CEO. 'Need your help on something else. Can you hang on a second?'

'Sure,' said the manager. This was a quality Varghese happily brandished: he thrived on crises. They brought a new vitality to his sagging torso. When confronted by big troubles his belly rumbled inside his tucked-in shirt and his chest swelled. At such times, he mourned the jacket's absence because his buttons inevitably snapped open. 'Tell me, boss, what do you need?' he said.

'It's about Akriti's request for a separate cabin, make sure you handle that.'

When Varghese clapped the phone down, he considered re-briefing the consultant on the neighbourhood cleanup. Let them go ahead with the shrine, he'd say. They had a right to that land, they had lived there for years.

He called the bloke. 'Not tomorrow,' he said. 'Maybe day after. Tomorrow we have a crisis.'

'I'd really like to give them a good time,' said the CEO. 'Kids worked really hard. Just for tonight, don't hold back on anything, make it grand.'

It was the night after the hurricane. Callus was having a Big Party. A mighty celebration of soaring investor values after such 'fabulous service delivery and crisis management on the hurricane night'. There was an email from the American client, printed in bold fonts and pasted around the office: '*Congratulations to the Callus Team for their stupendous effort on the night of the hurricane. Without you coming through, we wouldn't have made it.*' It took great effort for Varghese to mask his swelling irritation when everyone was gleeful and buoyant. There were trips to Florida – an outrageous reward for the night's best performers – and an all-Callus party to be organized by the Admin Manager.

The CEO was fussy when it came to parties. He liked them planned to the last detail. Varghese already had a checklist, gleaned from issues at the last party: Sashwath's complaints about appetizers served 'too cold', the barman fumbling with a Manhattan, metallic balloons flopping from chandeliered holds, green grime clinging to swimming pool walls. The CEO usually called personal friends: other CEOs, venture capitalists, PR advisors, theatre folk, poets and artists, moneyed people who didn't need jobs. Sashwath huddled with their murmuring fashionable wives while the Callus riffraff scampered inside with sponsored abandon. At the end of such nights there were bodies floating in pools, not dead but liquored up. 'Don't you think, boss, this is degrading for the company? What impression will we leave if employees behave like this?' asked Varghese after the last party.

'Relax, Varghese. It's a generation gap. Kids these days are different, they work hard and play hard.'

For tonight's party, most employees had the night off. The next-door golf course had a wooded harbour with a natural pool sunk into a rock face, the perfect setting for an outdoor party. The manager went to the venue six hours before the party started to get the place in order.

'No, not there, don't keep the orchids bunched up like that. Spray them around the place, on the walls, hanging from the trees, yes, a few on the fan, some on the light switch.' Varghese was getting the hang of it. Last time, there were streamers. 'That's childish, Varghese, this is not a kid's birthday,' said Sashwath. 'Next time, get something classy, flowers, orchids, be imaginative.'

Earlier, the DJ was a Callus agent. But for tonight, a professional was brought in from a local radio station, someone plugged into the latest beats. The man, a popular voice on the local channel, was a mini-celebrity and rarely acceded to *any* party. 'I'm into fusion,' he said. 'Not interested in film songs. If the crowd likes fusion, I'm in, otherwise count me out.' The man, fuzzy like the counsellor creature, expected Varghese to keep tab of musical leanings as if food choices were not knotty enough. How would the manager know if the agents were into fusion or anything knowable? They were to him a clamorous lot personified by the fuzzball woman. So he asked her instead, the eyes and ears of the feckless bunch: 'Are these kids into fusion music?'

'You know, that's a great question, I'm not sure. Why don't you run a survey on that?'

'Yes,' said Varghese on the phone, to the imbecilic DJ. 'Go ahead with fusion. Anything's fine, as long as it's loud.' You couldn't tell anyway, at that volume, if sounds combined into something coherent or merely heralded an apocalypse. The musical arrangements didn't end there. The DJ, showing up at the club a few hours before the party, carped about outdoor acoustics: 'Shit, man, this place is a disaster. There'll be feedback from this tree, an echo from that bush.'

'Do clouds bother you too?' asked Varghese. While the man with his long hair, one earring and torn denims grudgingly drew wires across trees, behind rocks, around flowerbeds and inside rosebushes, Varghese attended to the food, to what the boss termed a 'disaster' at the last affair. This time, appetizers served on three-layered trays were baked inside an on-site oven. There were whole mushrooms stuffed with cottage cheese, paneer kababs, chilli chicken, cocktail meatballs with mint leaves and artichoke roses to garnish the sides. The food, inspired by the DJ's ideas, had a theme: fusion. Tortillas with chicken tikkas, spicy pastas, paneer pizzas. The tables, sparkling with Diwali lights, were dressed in pleated whites with purple orchids pinned like brooches. Yes, thought Varghese, even the boss would be pleased.

A few hours later, everyone agreed the party was fabulous. Great job, said the boss. A big hit, said the agents. Even the Akriti woman was unusually fawning: 'Everyone had a blast, Varghese. Terrific party.'

But more delicious to Varghese's ears was a short conversation with the CEO, in the midst of the gaiety, 'Varghese, I need a word with you.'

He thought the CEO was going to point out, like always, some galling shortfall: 'Orchids are too pale' or 'Artichoke rose was dry at the centre' but it wasn't about the party at all. 'You know that request for Akriti's cabin, hold it. Let her continue to use the discussion rooms.'

Varghese was noted that night for his unbridled dancing, the manager supple on the makeshift dance floor. 'Go, man, go,' shouted agents, who surrounded him in skipping rings. When the music faded he flopped into a white wicker chair in cheery exhaustion.

That's when the consultant called: 'Sir, we're done. Can we start the demolitions?' It took a few minutes, near the swimming pool's chatter, to nail down the voice. Oh yes, that – the blasted kitchen view. 'Yes, yes, go ahead. The whole job, you don't need my permission at every stage.' Guys were good. There weren't any noises in the golf club, a stone's throw from the shacks.

On the way home, he paused outside the deserted thatched homes. There used to be, on other mornings, a welter of noises from the inside. Barking dogs, crying children, wailing women, sordid sounds refracted by streaming traffic. It was 5:00 a.m. and there was an eerie silence, a blankness settling on the shivering tarpaulin. A large crane and dumpster halted near the outside, ready to devour the one-time dwellings. He parked his car near the footpath and walked around the place: a few chickens, one or two mangy dogs, a goat, and piles and piles of rubbish, the remains of years of inhabitation.

He hadn't been inside a slum before. He wondered, as he crouched down to look inside, how they squeezed into these choking holes. Where did they shit, bathe, eat, sleep? And how did they do *it* with children watching? Difficult to believe there were minds inside those jammed spaces. He lifted up a tarpaulin sheet to look under it: a few unwashed aluminium vessels, a few grimy clothes. Hadn't they gathered all their belongings then? As he turned around, he realized the rubbish piles were not rubbish. There were tattered clothes, plastic boxes, kerosene stoves, torches, metal strips, tyres, tubes and something more astounding as well – five or six carved wooden cabinets, not sandalwood but plywood with rose and teak veneers, finely etched with flowers, leaves and grape bunches. Did they make those cabinets, scoop out the designs? Where did they sell them? Were the contractors wrong about local craftsmen? The finish on the cabinets rivalled the 'Delhi furniture' sold at discount outlets. A few sides were splintered. Was there violence then, despite the agency's assertions? What was his mother's dictum: 'What you don't know can never harm you'?

And suddenly, there was something on the ground, something among the wooden cabinets that caught his eye. A badge. A Callus ID inside this place? He stooped down to dust it off. Had it fallen from the kitchen, riding on breezes from the looming tower? There couldn't have been, among these people, a Callus employee, could there? When the consultant said jobs, the last jobs on Varghese's mind were Callus jobs. The badge read *Rani Kampanna, Contract Worker # 343, Housecleaning, Callus Inc.* Housecleaning was an Admin function. Indirectly,

214

the woman worked for him. The left-hand corner bore the stamp-sized photograph of a dark woman. He did not remember anyone like that. The expression was grim and he couldn't tell if that was a mole on her chin or a stain on the plastic. The steel clip was bent, the edge scratched, she must have worked for a few months at least. She looked young. What did she do at Callus? Assist cooks? Was she surprised when the agency came in? Would she commute from wherever she was? He tossed the badge back, kicked the shiny plastic under the rubble. Why should he worry about one person? With so many cooks, drivers, office boys in his charge, a Senior Manager could hardly dwell on a small-fry cook.

He remembered the naked kids, the three that looked up at the manager and the CEO. Were they engaged in cabinet production? Should he have stopped earlier, given those kids some money? Too late now, he'd never know where the agency moved them. Risky as well for the company to be overtly involved, there'd be zealous journalists or political protestors indicting them for illegal movement.

At home, his wife dusted off the mothball bits from his YK Ramu suits. 'Shall I exchange these for stainless steel?' she asked. 'Whatever you want,' said Varghese, who was filled that afternoon with an inexplicable gloom. There was no logical reason for his mood, the party smashing, the counsellor fended off. Like his wife said about the kitchen view, he was just doing his job. For that, you could hardly be damned.

FIRE 'n' ICE

Akriti could live anywhere in the world. She was at ease with all cultures, all people. No one could tell by looking at her that she was an Indian who had grown up in Bangalore. It wasn't just her poise, the way she carried herself, it was her international schooling that made her so cosmopolitan. For five years, she studied in this fabulous place: a 50-acre campus with horse-riding, golfing, swimming, billiards, classrooms ringing with many accents – Chinese, Korean, Irish, American – she was the only one at Callus whose contacts crisscrossed the globe. Oddly enough, Indians were a minority in her school, so much so that Akriti could hardly relate to locals. Her estate-owner parents saw value in an avant-garde education. She'd inherited their mindset, free-thinking and progressive. And that's what Indian companies sought, the recruiter said: 'People with a broad outlook, diverse experiences. People who can bridge gaps between cultures.' That was Akriti. Transiting from a school like that to a city college was not easy, not for most people. Yet even there, she was crowned Miss St Helen's; brown skin, yellow skin, how did it matter as long as you had *it*.

Inside the Callus conference room, huddled with Senior Managers, she sparkled in a sleek skirt and sheer blouse. She wore ethnic clothes but not to work. Since she was rising swiftly – a trainer/counsellor to an almost-manager, she was cultivating a global persona. A clutter of laptops and BlackBerry phones flashed on the polished oak table. It was a gathering of eight heads, some grey, some balding. She was the only woman, her layered bangs flashing with Revlon highlights. Heads turned to a slide projected by the Operations Manager: 'Too many agents quitting and joining Bodmas. The attrition rate is shooting up. Because of this operations are crumbling, we can't man phones with rookies.' The chap paused while Akriti scrolled through her BlackBerry to-dos.

'So what do we do about this?' That was Sashwath, snappy, impatient, welcoming any fix as long as it was instant. His lips stretched into a taut line. So boyish at times, he reminded her of Jimi, the musician agent she had recently dated. Jimutha had taken her by surprise; she hadn't expected to meet anyone so cool, so downright radical in that van. With his frayed jeans, spare denim vest, dragon tattoo and puffed-up Afro, he ballooned into an ache she never planned to have. Her feelings hadn't lasted of course. Long term, she couldn't stay hitched to an agent's earnings. As much as Akriti liked men, she also liked money. She planned to shrug him off, dump him gently. Why linger with van-riders when the CEO eyed her?

'Any thoughts?' asked Sashwath again. Other managers shuffled their laptop presentations. Someone sipped coffee with an uncouth slurp. The office boy slithered in with cream biscuits.

'I have a plan,' said Akriti, though attrition wasn't her responsibility, 'to shrink attrition rates in six months. Of course, I'll need the cooperation of all the managers in this room. We can do it if we stay positive.' Her voice knifed through the air-freshened chamber.

'And what's your plan?' That was Varghese, the churlish Admin man. He rapped the table with his mobile. Always had about him a nervous energy. Poor chap, trapped in the old ways. The world was changing, he had to accept that. She'd love to counsel him but he'd never admit to wanting help. Many of the fellows around this table – IITs, IIMs, foreign MBAs and what-not – needed help. Infantile EQs. In a workplace it was emotional maturity that counted, not exam-busting intelligence. Akriti could handle their moods and petty peeves because it was her strength, her ability to engage with all types.

Even at the Springfield training she was at ease with Americans, unlike her loud, back-slapping fellow trainers who became strangely bashful with Natalie and Michael. It was her charm, her counsellor's disposition, her attitude to life that gave her a leg-up while others remained agents or trainers. Mousy Yvette for one, mired in irrelevant concerns, would never get anywhere.

She turned to Varghese without a trace of displeasure. 'We need to keep agents happy to stem the tide. I have a list of chief complaints based on private sessions and surveys I've conducted across the call floor.'

'Excellent, Akriti, that's proactive,' said Sashwath. 'Can we see that?'

The men looked sullen. They wished they'd thought of this. Engineers all, they computed heights and weights, meaningless factorials but when it came to Life, they just didn't get it. Not a clue on the makings of Happiness. To curb attrition, satisfy employees; as easy as that, even her cat could tell them.

'The main issue is lousy cafeteria food. Especially pre-cooked dosas. I don't see why we can't give them fresh dosas.'

'You have to work on this,' said the CEO, turning his head to the Admin Manager. Across the boardroom table, the air was electric. Sashwath, with his salt-and-pepper hair and fizzy, adolescent energy was charming in a manner most CEOs weren't. She'd do anything to solve his problems. 'I want those ratings to rise by 50% by next quarter. Confer with Akriti for agent suggestions.'

'Easy,' said Varghese, 'to conduct surveys. Not so easy to fix their grouses.' He deliberately avoided the counsellor, turned his bald head and bulbous eyes to the CEO. Thick veins throbbed in his neck.

'Why not? Surely nothing's impossible if you have the right attitude?' When she looked at Sashwath, the NRI nodded. He shared her can-do spirit.

'You don't know this country, you don't know how things work,' said Varghese. His eyes crept over her face like he was studying an insect.

'What do you mean by that? I've grown up in this city.'

'You had it easy in that rich-kid school.'

Rich-kid school? How dare he dismiss her experience like that? Those were the best years of her life – poetry workshops, artist retreats, theatre camps – an incredible grounding that had given her the creative vision to fix any problem.

When she left the meeting room a half-hour later to pick up wine for her mother's party, the man's comment simmered in her ears. A few weeks ago, in a chat with the Admin Manager, she had described how exceptional her school had been, how state-of-the-art surroundings had shaped her differently, how she already had an American accent before the Springfield training. She'd even shown him the website, pictures of the sprawling campus, the humming Science Centre with enormous skylights, the multimedia auditorium, the Olympic-size swimming pool. 'That's where we played golf,' she said. How dare he sneer at her now?

More than anything else, what slowly trickled into her was the surprise, the solid certainty of the man's dislike. Akriti was a person who was used to being liked. Most people liked her straightaway, some liked her over a longer period. The CEO, for one, was taken in at once. It wasn't just her looks – though there had been comments on her pert nose, her big, fragile eyes, her slender neck, her 'too tall, too slim' body, even her slight resemblance to Audrey Hepburn – it was the way she engaged with people. It was the reason she was voted Head Girl at the Tulip Dale International School and Miss St Helen's at college. She thought Varghese was a rough sort, but she'd wear him down with attentive, doe-like eyes, with free advice on what to wear and how to converse. She thought he was enchanted by descriptions of her school, by the mere fact that a person like her was sharing so much with a person like him. But he was unshakeable, resistant to all charm, a rock in her path like nothing she'd encountered before.

Food choices were enhanced, dosas freshly fried, but agents continued to quit. In her counselling sessions, Akriti unearthed another issue, an issue so foul, it was disgraceful for a global company. It was the stench inside the ladies' loo. If only the Admin Manager did his job instead of poking around in nearby cubicles.

When she relayed the latest issue to Varghese, he shook his head: 'I think you give them too much leeway. Half our agents don't even have Western toilets at home. Why so fussy at work?'

She dealt with Varghese the way she dealt with the smell of urine and turds on Bangalore pavements – by blocking him out. She had this remarkable ability to expel the unpleasant from her life.

The CEO, on the other hand, was worth every minute of her unwavering attention. And that's why Akriti glided into his path when he ushered his PR team and some journalist woman around the centre. Sashwath guided visitors around his polished interiors with the zeal of a museum curator. 'These tiles, these Arabic patterns, these are world-class' and 'Note the contours on our cubicles, it's all modulated design.' The counsellor knew toilet odours, any blemish on his 30,000 square feet artwork, would rankle. 'Our Senior Managers occupy these cubicles,' he said waving at Akriti. 'It's an open office, everyone's accessible.'

'Sashwath, I need to talk to you privately.'

'Yes, what is it?'

'Privately, Sashwath.'

The visitors drifted out of hearing, across the hallway, towards the lobby. When Akriti described odours inside the Ladies she scrunched up her elfish face. 'A global company should foster a five-star work environment. Or people will opt to work in other call centres, especially Bodmas. Their facilities are awesome.'

Sashwath peered into the Admin Manager's cubicle for a response: 'Varghese, are you aware of the stink in the Ladies?'

The idiot, unmindful of menstrual cycles and the special sanitary needs of women, did not respond for several seconds. He did not stand up even. From his low-level sitting position, he dismissed the issue: 'No problem in toilet. Ladies spend too much time in loos.'

The CEO fortunately didn't heed his response. He asked Varghese to purge the foulness at once.

Akriti's family had always been to counsellors: marital counsellors, family counsellors, school counsellors. Akriti had many memories of counsellor waiting rooms and reception areas, of being plied with chewy toffees or the Disney channel, while her parents slipped behind solid wooden doors with brass nameplates. In the preceding weeks, they might have been shrieking at each other and shattering glasses, but after a 2,000-rupee session, they sank into a tolerable aloofness. Even the divorce was amicably handled – the arbitration sensibly settled out-of-court – because her mother had switched to a family counsellor who specialized in post-marital mediation. After the divorce, Akriti and her mother continued to seek external advice on various things: Should the child stay one week with the mother, and one week with the father? Or should she move on weekends only? What school would be best for a gifted child? Should foreign schools be considered, given that Indian teachers did not recognize her potential? The Tulip Dale International School, which also had a residential program, was suggested by a family counsellor.

The school, it turned out, was a great fit. In the more liberal milieu, having a parent who was divorced was no big deal. To classmates who had two mothers and three fathers, Akriti no longer needed to explain herself. At her earlier school, Akriti felt stifled by presumptions. By teachers who assumed all kids had two parents. By friends who sneered at her moves between her mom's place and her dad's. By friends' parents who were visibly separated but resisted the finality of a 'divorce'.

It was at Tulip Dale – where anyone could be anything – that Akriti discovered her passion. She didn't need a counsellor to tell her she was a natural at counselling. Her opinions were always sought out by friends: 'Does this colour suit me?' 'He hasn't called back, should I call?' 'Should I straighten my hair, it's so, you know?' She always knew what to say. And that's why she was fabulous at her job.

She found however, in private sessions with Callus agents, that their work was not fun. This, despite the facility – after several skirmishes with Varghese – being spanking clean, the food more edible. What they disliked now was the work itself, the droning monotony, day after day, week after week, crabby customer after crabby customer.

Callus managers and Team Leaders lacked imagination. You could make *any* job interesting if you were creative and inspired. But many, like starchy Mani, could hardly relate to their teams. Fortunately for this company, she had an intuition for what people wanted. She devised a new strategy: a 'fun' campaign. She directed managers and Team Leaders to deliberately inject fun into the job. 'Be innovative, be different,' she advised them. 'Look at it from the agent viewpoint.'

She convinced the CEO to create a fun budget. Wangling money from the CEO was more difficult than she thought.

'I trust you know what you're doing. We'll have to account for this under some other head. Bankers will freak if we have fun at their expense.'

The 'fun' budget had an impact, but it wasn't enough. The CEO was not satisfied with the 1% reduction in attrition levels. 'Not significant,' he said, his fingers twitching.

Akriti remembered something a marital counsellor had suggested to her parents. After several sessions, when the aloofness had waned and the glass-shattering resumed, the counsellor handed out personality tests. Her parents were asked to fill out – instinctively, without

224

thinking – a five-page questionnaire with multiple-choice answers. They were told therapy was futile if personalities were diametric opposites. Akriti was only twelve then, but she could see how revealing the tests were: there was no synergy between her father's timorous approach to life and her mother's fierce ambitions.

It came to her then, the reason for high attrition rates – personality clashes between bosses and subordinates. And perhaps, a few like Varghese were ill-suited to any job. The counsellor browsed online resources and discovered this fabulous workplace test. There were 120 questions in all, she did it herself several times, and she was astounded by the results. It reflected in four pithy letters, exactly what she *was* at all times. Akriti was a blazing FIRE – Farsighted, Inspiring, Responsive and Empathetic. Even her parents, who'd known her for twenty-seven years, could not describe her with such precision.

If she wasn't *farsighted*, which the site described as a *wise, forward-thinking* individual, would she badger Varghese for a response to her email? The stiff-neck had done nothing about her request for a private cabin. She copied Sashwath on five emails and yet the manager was unshakeable. Each time she talked to him, he had a glazed look as if she were speaking in a foreign tongue. Once, when she refused to stir, when she continued to stay in his cubicle till he looked up from his enslaving laptop, he said: 'Use the discussion room. That's what we do for closed-door meetings.'

'The discussion room is always booked.'

'If you plan your work, you too can book meetings in advance.' His neck patches traced the shapes of continents: Europe, Asia, South America. Did he oil his bald head or was that just some greasy lotion?

'I can't plan everything, employees come to me in crises. They need immediate support.' She wanted to add her meetings were more important, more sensitive than his tête-à-têtes with toilet cleaners and drivers. She bit her bottom lip, tapped her shoe. He had a visitor's chair, yet never asked her to sit down.

'Oh, I see. That's something I hadn't thought about. I have an idea. Why don't you ask the boss to provide an outdoor space, an umbrella in his terrace garden?'

The Great Wall could shatter but Varghese would not budge. It was surprising that Sashwath, an impatient go-getter, tolerated him. Such types were a drag on the bottomline. Varghese, she was sure, was an ICE: Inflexible, Closed and Emotional. The testing website said ICY no-gooders stonewalled high performers: 'They can douse FIREs,' the website proclaimed. There must be others like him – Team Leaders, managers – who contributed to agent attrition. No one in their right senses could deal with an ICE, let alone report to one. If she weeded out the ICE blocks, the attrition rates should shrink.

All the managers thought the test was a good idea, and all the Team Leaders cooperated. She hadn't realized she'd create such a buzz. 'Better than daily horoscopes,' said a Team Leader. 'Can't wait to see my type.' Agents, too, heard about the test. In the cafeteria, personality types outdid cricket stats. While she waited in line for her pan-fried dosa, she overheard their chatter:

'My Team Leader's a SUN, what about yours?'

'STAR, is that good?'

'What about that Tamilian fellow, what type is he?'

'Heard he's an ACE. Something negative.'

Everyone appreciated the truth in those letters, the new light thrown on characters. Everyone but the biggest, solid, block of ICE she'd ever encountered, her cubicle neighbour, the Admin Manager. Varghese had a hundred objections to taking the test. 'Akriti, I've done stuff like this before, it's bullshit. Doesn't tell you anything. Besides, how can you be sure people won't fake it – just provide answers the company wants?'

'Impossible, Varghese, I've tried it so often, even if you think you're faking it, you can't fake it. It's a great test, I wish we'd done this before hiring people.'

'Anyway, no need to waste Senior Managers' time on this. Do it with the lower levels.'

'Varghese, it's mandatory. The CEO insists that all managers do it.'

'Is it? All right, I'll do it but not now, not when I'm busy.'

Varghese stayed busy for several days past the deadline. She overheard the other managers say that Varghese planned to pick answers at random, by throwing darts or chanting 'eeny, meeny, miney, moe'. He eventually turned his test in when she was rounding up the company's scores. She seized his sheet with great excitement. She quickly added up his coloured circles and arrived at a result she could barely withhold from Sashwath. 'I need to see him immediately,' she told his secretary. 'It's urgent, we have to act at once.'

Inside his cabin, the CEO was speaking to his PR agency. Akriti, who could hardly contain herself, leaned into the visitor's swivel chair. 'Bloody front page on all business mags,' he yelled. When he snapped his earphones off, Akriti whipped out the manager's answer sheet.

'Varghese is an ICE, exactly as predicted.' She pointed out the result for the CEO to confirm. There was no way he could doubt the science behind the test, not anymore.

'Fair enough, Akriti, but what does it mean?' asked Sashwath.

'Don't you see, when you need people who are fluid and easy to work with, he's a roadblock? He's inflexible, which the testing site defines as *unwilling to change, obstinate*. And closed, not receptive to feedback or external triggers, *the kind of person who won't budge when the cheese is moved*. And emotional, which is irrational, impulsive, hysterical.'

'I get the drift. What are the next steps?'

'ICEs are immutable so it's best to ease them out.'

'We ought to warn him first, don't you think? Give him a chance to turn around?'

'Sashwath, the *I* in Varghese is prominent. Just look at that report, he's at the high end of the obstinacy scale. I don't think we should waste time with him. The site says ICEs that stay too long in the company become ICEbergs, impossible to dislodge. Seem harmless on the surface, but they can, with their sheer presence, wreck companies.'

'Still, he's an old hat. Let's call him in, give him feedback.' The CEO called his secretary. 'Can you send for Varghese?' He turned to Akriti again. 'So where are we on attrition?'

'It's the same thing, Sashwath, I've used the test to pinpoint Callus misfits. About 10% of Team Leaders have ICE characteristics. We need to warn them. I expect attrition to peak at 6% next month, then dip to 3% in six months.'

'Can I commit that to the bankers?'

'Definitely, Sashwath, the test is infallible. Look at the result in Varghese's case. We know it reflects his key traits.'

'Hmm,' said the CEO, heaving himself from the chair and walking towards his French windows. 'Come here, I have something to show you.' The terrace garden with its purple bougainvillea, red leafy poinsettias, yellow cannas and white lilies was a space Sashwath personally oversaw. A gardener, hired exclusively for the two-dozen potted plants, spent more one-on-one time with the CEO than any Senior Manager. 'This prickly pear is from Mexico and look at the way it's thriving.'

'Your garden is always beautiful,' said Akriti, who had started noting stuff she rarely attended to earlier: white spots on leaves, the shy blossoming of new buds, earthworm furrows on topsoil. The CEO looked at her with smoky eyes. They walked together, near enough for his cologne to mingle with her leafy, autumnal perfume. The sun settled behind thick pink-red clouds, golf course grasses gleamed orange. She wondered if she should invite him home for dinner. She rested her palm on the small of his back. Just then the Admin Manager stepped in.

'Boss, did you call me?'

'Ah, Varghese, just the man we were looking for.' Sashwath quickly turned back, returned to his revolving chair.

'I've found someone who can organize the movement,' Varghese said, ignoring Akriti's presence.

'What movement? Oh, that? Good, good.' He turned back to his laptop.

'Is that all, can I leave?' asked Varghese. 'I have lots of work.'

'She has something for you. Something about the personality test. Akriti?' said the CEO, peering into the far reaches of his email box.

'We have your results, Varghese. The test says you're an ICE, which means...'

'Boss, I can't waste time on this. I have important work to attend to. I don't believe in this personality crap. The person who created this test must be a NUT, N-U-T – Needless, Useless, Time-waster.' As usual he addressed only the CEO.

'This is a scientific assessment of your fitness in high-performance teams. This test has been used by Fortune 500 companies,' said Akriti. When Varghese was around, her voice lost its polish and became shrieky. What irked her as well was Sashwath, busy at his laptop like he was out of hearing, disconnected from whatever she was saying. She was doing this for him, relaying the bad news.

'I don't care who's doing it, the test is imbecilic.'

The CEO looked up from his computer. 'Varghese, give her a hearing. Maybe you can redo the test if you disagree.'

230

The Admin Manager laughed. 'Sashwath, have you seen this test even? Or better still, have you done it?'

'No, I haven't. Perhaps I should.'

'You should, you absolutely should. Then you'll know what hocus-pocus this is: *Are you an introvert or extrovert?* I'm an introvert when certain people are around. *Do you prefer working in teams or working alone?* That depends on who else is on my team. For questions like this, there are no straight answers. Boss, why don't you do the test?'

'Okay, Akriti, give me the test. I'd like to know what my key traits are.'

Akriti breathed more easily. She had the CEO's buy-in. She'd love to give him the test, the man was a raging FIRE. Charismatic leaders belonged to that breed.

A few minutes later, when the test unfurled from the shared laser printer, she thought of an expanded role for herself. Perhaps a new title as well. The CEO respected her, supported her opinions. Sashwath and she were of the same type. He might be lower on the Empathy scale but that was offset by his overall likeableness. When she handed him the test, Varghese was still with him. 'I'll do this right away,' the CEO said. Akriti looked at Varghese. Sashwath was willing to prioritize this, but the Admin Manager, distracted by toilets and cooks was 'too busy'.

Back at her cubicle while the CEO coloured his dots, Akriti listened to the Admin Manager's bothersome tapping. The man had lost it, he knew his days were numbered. The website had a diagram to chart the company's overall score. Most Callus managers clustered around WARM traits. There were, like her, a few FIREs. What surprised her was Yvette: woman was a FIRE, greater on far-sightedness than Akriti even. The counsellor couldn't believe the dowdy trainer had any leadership traits. She wondered for a minute if Varghese was right, if the test could be rigged? She quickly banished the thought when Sashwath's secretary called: 'The CEO would like to see you.'

Akriti rushed to his office with an excitement she hasn't experienced in months.

'Hey, was looking for you,' he said. 'There's a fresh crisis at Callus. Ike's moving from Cuba to Texas, client's shutting the American centre.'

'Who's Ike?' asked Akriti.

'What? Oh, Ike? It's a storm, a hurricane. The winds might hit Galveston.'

'So?' said Akriti, who tried to cover up the disappointment rising from her stomach and tying knots in her chest. The test lay untouched on his desk. Not a dot coloured, not a line filled in. This piece of paper was a compass to his personal life and the company's future and he was distracted by weather in some remote part of the world? 'How does that affect us?'

'Beam America has a call centre in Galveston, they're shutting it down, routing extra calls to Bangalore. We need to increase our headcount by 30%.'

'We can do that,' said Akriti, fighting the hardness seeping into her face. FIRE, FIRE, she repeated mentally, her self-awareness mantra. Farsighted, Inspiring, Responsive, Empathetic. 'Anything is possible.'

'No, no, I don't think you have the picture. We need to increase our headcount by *tomorrow*,' said Sashwath.

'Tomorrow? Have we already agreed to this?' Difficult, not impossible. Nothing could stop a FIRE. *All problems can be reduced to ashes*, the website said.

'Yes, in the original contract. We committed to ramp up staff with a 24-hour notice.'

'How many more calls will we get tomorrow?'

'40% more than usual.'

'Can't we have everyone work double shifts?' asked Akriti.

'Already planned that. We still need a 20% increase to handle additional calls.'

'What about trainees? Let's move them to live calls.'

'Also planned.' The CEO sounded tired.

'Agents will do anything if you motivate them. Give the team that handles the most calls a prize... A trip to America... to Disneyworld in Florida.'

'That's an idea,' he said, his eyes glinting with a new brightness. 'You're saying, with an incentive like that, we could speed up their talk?'

'Yes, and you have to make it fun, like Valentine's Day. Put up stickers – with pictures of Florida beaches – in the halls and inside the toilet. Beam America groups are named after basketball teams, right? Have scores ticking on a white board like a live match. Motivate them to keep talking at all times.'

Akriti was energized by the light in Sashwath's eyes. It was a kindly light, the light of someone beholden forever. It was time to remind him about her cabin.

'It's a thought, Akriti,' said Sashwath. 'I'll ask the Operations Manager to think along those lines.'

'Also, Sashwath, can you call Varghese about my cabin? He hasn't done anything yet.'

'Will call him right away. Chap needs prodding now and then.'

Though her boss hadn't done the test, Akriti bounced out with her spirits intact. Crisis or otherwise, she stayed responsive and empathetic. What would Sashwath have done without her radiant presence?

Three nights later, office cubicles hummed with an everyday tedium. The storm had subsided, Callus had survived. There was a party the previous night to celebrate the client's compliments on their disaster management capabilities. She had forgotten about the CEO's personality test when his secretary called. 'Boss wants to see you at once.'

'Akriti, I did your test before the party. You won't believe the results,' said Sashwath, grinning widely.

'Let me guess, you're a FIRE?'

'No, guess again.'

'SUN?'

'No.' The CEO's eyes twinkled.

'STAR?'

Sashwath laughed, swivelled his wheeled chair forward. 'An ICE, I-C-E. Varghese is right, the test is bogus. The questions are insane. Let's ditch this crap and get down to real issues behind agent attrition. If you don't have any ideas, ask Varghese. The fellow has horse-sense, he'll know why people quit. By the way, I've heard one of our strong trainers has quit.'

'Strong trainer?' Akriti was the centre's best trainer, everyone knew that, but Sashwath rarely acknowledged her worth.

'Yvette's quitting,' he said, with an inexplicable sadness.

'Yvette?' said Akriti, clutching the visitor's chair.

'I used to think she was dull. But of late, I've heard other reports. Many agents acknowledge her advice has helped them in many ways.'

'Where's she going?'

'That's the funny part. Apparently not to Bodmas. She wants to study something.' He walked towards his French window and sighed. 'This is the trickiest part of running such a business – retaining your best people.'

Akriti did not follow him into the terrace garden. Back at her cubicle, she thought back on her encounters with the CEO. Why hadn't she seen it earlier, the stubborn sticking to old ways, the impulsiveness to do this, then that, the unwillingness to chart new objectives or give up on a dying vision? The man was selfish and obstinate, obsessed with himself. She could see it in his room, walls prettified by non-achievements. Where did he do his MBA again? Why flaunt the certificate like a small-town dentist? And why those photographs? Especially family ones, considering he spent no time with them? How could she think he liked her? Despite rumours in the office, there was *nothing* between them. She was merely a 'human resource' to be milked for profit. She rescued him from the hurricane's surge, yet how quickly he dismissed her help. He hadn't acknowledged her contribution to others, hadn't thanked her even. What was that about Yvette being a *strong trainer*? Had Sashwath witnessed her weird outbursts? Did he know how confused she was at all times?

Just then, Varghese leaned over. Chap was so short, he stood on his chair. 'I have news for you, Akriti. Boss shot down your cabin request.'

The counsellor did not look up from the plastic rolodex where she could have sworn she had filed the recruiter's number. Nothing in this company bothered her anymore, not even Varghese. For a brief second, she turned her face to him and smiled. She had no idea what Callus attrition would be in six months, but she knew where she'd be: most definitely at Bodmas. Where had she filed the recruiter's number? Did the name start with K or J?

Deliver Us From Evil

Bitty thought of it as a tumour, safer out than in. She looked at her watch, strapped to her wrist a few inches below the IV needle, and computed the time left. The cleanup, they said, would take thirty minutes. They promised she'd be discharged by sundown, hours before the office van scooped her up from her doorstep. She hadn't applied for sick leave. She wondered if Callus colleagues would sense a difference, nose out a sticky placenta or dried-up blood, vile pink tissue dangling between her legs when she thought it was scrubbed out, totally purged.

She turned in her bed. The clinic had hard mattresses and stiff pillows. Was this a special bed, reserved for people like her, wicked women punished for their sins? The clinic, the best given her constraints, was not spotless: there were brown stains on the walls, dark lines on the mosaic floor. At least the smell was antiseptic, unlike her father's Ayurvedic clinic that reeked of his tonics. She turned to her left and stared at the wall – a framed poster of a sallow Jesus smeared with vermilion, garlanded with blue plastic flowers. On hand for a final expiation?

Outside the room, nurses shuffled inside starched saris. Were they ready to wheel her in, the third operation that morning? An ovarian cyst, a puffy uterus and then her *thing*, a mass of sprouting cells. In the distance she heard a newborn wailing and the exuberant cheers of a waiting family. She wished she had her Callus headset to muffle the sounds. A nurse entered the room and gathered the green bedcover from the second bed. She fluffed up the pillow which seemed, from across the room, squishy and pliable, unlike her stiff rubber pillow. The second nurse followed, propping another patient up with her arm, a woman with a bulging stomach.

Bitty was hoping to be alone inside the double room. And a pregnant woman was the last person she wanted around. Both nurses waited by the side of the woman's bed and hoisted her up with a solicitude reserved for life-givers. Bitty walked in alone, heaved herself onto an unprepared bed.

'Careful, ma, careful,' said a nurse, tugging a white sheet across the woman's swollen torso. 'Just relax okay, only few hours.'

'How much more time?' asked Bitty of the nurse who was dragging an IV machine closer to the woman. 'What time, my procedure?'

'Deliveries first,' snapped the nurse, patting the woman's belly. The same nurse who thrust the IV into Bitty with a fierce jab slid the point into the woman's plump vein with a painless nudge. 'Just a small poke, ma, close your eyes, will be over in few seconds. There, finished. Did it hurt?' To Bitty it was: 'Show me your arm, don't move. What did I say? Keep it still.'

'Did you have anything to eat this morning?' asked the second nurse, her hospital checklist clipped on an exam board. 'Nothing? That's good. I think you know all the rules, only little bit juice is allowed.' To Bitty, she'd snarled: 'I hope you've come on empty stomach otherwise we have to give enema.' The last word spat out as if ejecting the *real* stuff was disgusting enough so why deal with her crap as well.

'Can I have some juice?' asked Bitty.

'Now?' said the nurse, twirling on her flat heels. 'Now too late.' She turned back to the other woman, stroked her hair. 'Do you want, ma?' she asked.

Shortly, the nurses left the room and Bitty shut her eyes. 'Is this your first one?' asked the other woman.

'Hmm,' said Bitty, opening her eyes very slightly to take in as little as possible of the irksome face across the room. Long hair tightly twisted, large red bindi, kohl-lined eyes, a middle-class daughter-in-law, mother of one, second on its way, corked up inside a poky apartment with meddlesome in-laws. Bitty could run through her life with no effort. The husband, a featureless, briefcase-toting office-goer, submissive to his mother, indifferent to his wife, the household spite worn down by everyday routines into a humdrum civility. The kind of life Bitty's parents imagined would be hers until she started working at Callus. They didn't know, of course, about the object in her stomach. They could take her sullen withdrawals, her late-night outings, her shopping sprees but they couldn't take this: the permanent 'spoiling' of an only daughter.

'Are you excited?' asked the woman.

'Hmm,' said Bitty.

'Do you know if it's a boy or a girl?'

Bitty grunted. The woman didn't get it, did she? Indians were so unabashedly inquisitive. Yanks at the call centre never intruded like this.

'These days, they don't tell, no? Is your husband here?'

Bitty turned to face Jesus, his kindly eyes taking her in with a stolid evenness. She examined the turmeric and vermilion smears that turned him into a deity like those on her mother's puja shelf. Her flesh felt dense, impervious to the barrage of nosy questions from the other bed.

'Are your parents here? Your in-laws? Do you live with your in-laws?'

Bitty imagined it was an overhead voice like a railway announcement about trains on other platforms, sounds removed from the scope of her attention.

After a few minutes, the woman sighed and picked up a magazine. Bitty, who still faced the wall, her spine stiffly resolute, heard paper crackling. *Do you live with your in-laws?* The agent smiled when she thought of The Dude – a metal man not conceived in flesh – so rugged he must have been born that way. He couldn't have been at any point a bawling infant, a frightened child, not the kind to have parents ever.

She wished she had a book herself, a distraction from her anxious thoughts, something spiritual to allay her fears of wretched after-effects.

At first, she had worried about her virginity. She thought the tear showed in an altered gait, in a ripened body, in the way her jeans rested below her hips, glaring signs to those who could discern such things. Difficult to disguise because she didn't know the giveaway signs. It was a friend at the call centre who had convinced her – before she did it – that guys can tell the lax from the unyielding. 'We can tell if a chick has done it,' he said.

'How do you know?' asked Bitty who was at that point generally puzzled, not personally bothered. 'Difficult to explain but we can tell.' An elusive quality like the judgment people possessed about real versus fake jewellery.

The first night at work, she was wary; watchful of wisecracks that could allude to the slight soreness and impurities inside. At the Ladies she lingered in her stall, expecting the defilement to leak into the commode like her monthly period.

A few nights later, Bitty was less concerned. The Dude by then had hooked up with a trainee chick on another shift. He wasn't the enduring kind. Bitty wasn't despondent or heartbroken; she'd known from the first night that her fling was a short pretence, a freak fantasy like the Universal Studio pics of her aunt and uncle in Schwarzenegger bodies. The dumping inevitable yet the mercurial switch from Bitty-Betty to Janaki-Jane briefly startling.

It was the night work, calls in the centre, screeching customers, dissatisfied bill-payers that had a numbing effect, the event receding from a lasting violation to a foggy slip-up. 'Just a little bit of fun,' as The Dude described it.

She was late by forty-five days, hardly aware her periods had stopped. She wasn't the kind to tabulate dates or note how soggy her pads were. There had been other times, when her monthlies tripped on the 30-day cycle, prompting her father – quietly tipped off by her mother – to prescribe a slew of tonics to restore her balance. So glad her dissipation hadn't been caught out, not by her parents, not by all-seeing Callus boys, she was inattentive to her spotless underwear at the Ladies.

Even the nausea, her queasy stomach after dinner at the cafeteria, hadn't alarmed her. For two nights, she thought it was the food: the dosas newly oily, the rotis too thick. She picked up a food survey from the HR Department and flogged the cooks for 'carelessness'. 'Dosas are yuck, my stomach feels sick after eating in this cafeteria,' she wrote. The third night, she brought dinner from home, curd-rice with lime-pickle to settle her juices. A large brown tablet as well, doled out by her doctor father. But the acids welled up and the revulsion surged into her throat, a loathing so sour she could hardly pacify customers. She'd abandoned four calls mid-sentence to puke in the loo: a vile yellow liquid and her entire tiffin-box of stomach-appeasing home-food.

Bitty had heard of morning sickness but the night-sickness stayed unconnected, in her mind, to that one-time trespass. It was some Yank on the phone who set her thinking. 'I haven't paid my bill because I've been busy with doctor visits. I'm expecting another baby. I'm so excited but the nausea's terrible. And I get it in the evenings too.' Between her 'Yes, ma'am's and 'I understand, ma'am's there were bells ringing in Bitty's head. By the end of the call, by which time the customer had laid out all her symptoms, the clanging was fierce. Bitty ran into the Ladies, her tangled headset cast off, to retch out goopy bile and noxious thoughts slamming her brain.

The next night, she was at it again, keeling over inside the loo till every sliver of her daytime meals tumbled out in foul heaps, trickling along the sides of the commode in curdled red, green, yellowish-pink: curly tomato peels, spinach, gobs and gobs of rice, whole, unbroken. She knew, as she flushed coloured specks off the white toilet bowl, that a test was needed, a urine test of some sort; she'd heard her father prescribe it to patients.

The home toilet was unthinkable for trials of any kind. So she brought a vial to work, a glass bottle stolen from her father's storeroom. It was ghastly to trap her liquid and seal it inside a Tommy Hilfiger handbag. But the next day, docking the bottle into a pharmacy lab was easier than she imagined. She expected a zillion questions: 'When did you last have your period?' 'What is your husband's name?' 'When were you married?' She had the answers ready in case there was an official grilling.

The lab lady behind the window, stout inside her white coat, was incurious; the slight awkwardness at the clinic window prompted by Bitty's fumbling about the test's intent. Reluctant to say 'pregnancy test' she said, 'Can you test for *it*?'

'For what?' snapped the woman, her ballpoint roving impatiently over a preprinted form. 'Do you have doctor prescription?'

'No,' said Bitty. 'Can you test for *anything* inside?'

'For what?' asked the woman, turning to the man behind Bitty. 'Sir, what do you need?'

'Can you test for a foetus?' said Bitty finally.

'Foetus?' said the woman as if that wasn't something she'd heard before. 'You mean baby? Do you need pregnancy test?'

'Yes,' said Bitty.

'Why can't you tell properly? 300 rupees, results after 24 hours.'

Bitty hoped for a negative or inconclusive result. But the report was emphatic: 'HCG level positive.' At first Bitty thought it was something else – a terseness like HIV – Human Chronic Galactosemia responsible for her everyday sickness. She asked the lab woman, who handed the paper without comment. 'What is HCG?'

'Hah? Why you want to know all that? You want baby, you have baby,' she said.

'Does HCG indicate a foetus?' persisted Bitty.

'I'm telling you have baby, what more you want?'

'Nothing, nothing,' whispered Bitty, drawing out the paid receipt while her eyes misted over with unstoppable tears.

'So happy, she's crying,' the lab lady mumbled to the cashier.

At first Bitty imagined the 'cure' might rest on her father's storeroom shelves, in the rows and rows of greasy black bottles she'd detested since childhood. She walked past his doctor's office – below their upstairs medicine kitchen – past Godrej bureaus full of bills and papers, into the storeroom dingy with shuttered windows. 'Sunlight will spoil medicines,' her father said. Even at

244

noon, the steel shelves were cloaked in evening shadows. Wandering among the viscous, tart odours, she scanned labels written in her father's unreadable Malayalam. Surely there was something potent enough to expunge the HCG-something? If she quaffed a whole bottle or two – something bitter, something heat-producing – the thing should wash out. For the first time in her life, she rued her Malayalam illiteracy. So many summers, whenever her father offered to teach her the basics, she'd brushed him aside with this or that excuse.

She led her mother into discreet discussions on tonics good for expectant women. 'Did Achan give you special medicines before I was born?' she asked.

'Yes, you know your father never stops treating. Why?'

'Did he give you special medicines when you had me inside?'

'Yes,' said her mother. 'Why you are suddenly asking?'

'A friend's aunt is pregnant, she wants advice.'

'Friend, which friend?'

'You don't know her, ma, she works at Callus.'

'If she wants proper advice, tell her to come for treatment.'

'She was checking if there was anything *not* to be eaten?'

'Many things, papaya, pineapple, coffee. Better she consults with Achan.'

'What does papaya do?' asked Bitty.

'Miscarriage.'

Bitty, after seven days, had eaten two dozen papayas and yet the spotty evidence of a discharge was still missing. Her mother looked puzzled by her daughter's sudden interest in household foods; she wasn't the kind who shopped for fruit. 'Again you bought papayas?' Amma asked on the third morning. 'We haven't finished yesterday's?' And then, 'You're eating only papaya for breakfast? Why?' 'For lunch also papaya? Bitty, what's wrong with you?'

'Pimples,' said Bitty. 'My friend said papayas are good for pimples.'

'Which friend? Same one with pregnant aunt?' asked her mother.

'Yes,' said Bitty. 'Same friend.'

She bought women's magazines with articles for expectant mothers. She scanned Do Not lists for tips. 'Do not carry heavy weights,' said a doctor 'not even older children. This is a great opportunity to involve your spouse in household activities.' Bitty, for several days, surprised her parents with a bustling exertion they hadn't witnessed in 23 years. Flopping into bed at night, she overheard late-night discussions about the 'drowsy night worker'.

'What's wrong with Bitty?' Achan asked. Were there new imbalances in his sluggish daughter, suddenly zealous about cleaning counters and wiping tables? She hoisted grocery bags – several at a time, laden with two kilos of tomatoes, one week's load of onions – carried cartons of newly-shipped medicines from the storeroom to the clinic, climbed on ladders with several bottles in hand to reorganize shelves, lifted the old grinding stone to clean the mouldy underside.

'Mild exercises like yoga and swimming can be good for your body,' another doctor proclaimed. She

246

signed up for cardio-aerobics at a neighbourhood gym. The movements so vigorous, the sweat so profuse, she expected it to trickle out in the midst of the prancing exercisers.

The admission was a last resort. A few weeks spent screening clinics for remoteness from known people: her parents, relatives, her father's Ayurvedic patients – a gossipy lot, avoidable at best – Callus colleagues, anyone else who might tell anyone else. Then there were other factors – safety, hygiene, cost – the operation would take a large chunk of her monthly take-home pay. The small-time Jayanagar clinic, a charitable outlet setup by Bodmas, offered subsidized treatments. Four bus transfers from her Shivajinagar world, the place seemed a reasonable pick. Uncertain about dodging her family, flung unlike her father's patients across the city, she was surprised to bump into the Callus van-driver when she emerged from the scan room.

It took her several minutes to make out who he was, in his casual clothes and outside the van. At first she thought he'd followed her, dispatched by the company to keep a watch. She should have been scared, but she was angry, angry at Callus for invading her life in every way, at all times. She was about to shout at him when she noticed someone shuffling behind his shoulder, a lady with a bulge.

She realized then he wasn't looking at her, not directly at least. His sideways glances were shy and fearful. Like Bitty, the driver too had a secret. He wasn't here on an official mission. Perhaps the lady behind him wasn't his wife? Or he was here for some fertility treatment?

Whatever it was, Bitty was relieved. She smiled at him before a nurse escorted her to the double room.

Inside the white room, Bitty worried about the van driver. Would he greet her on the van, would he talk at Callus? Would he talk to her father, while waiting for Bitty: 'I saw madam in clinic waiting for pregnancy scan'?

Bitty turned to face the woman who rapidly dropped her magazine – a *Women's Era* – and greeted her like a prodigal daughter. 'You are awake? So long, no, this waiting?'

'Yes,' said Bitty.

'Is this your first?' she asked again, encouraged by Bitty's response.

Bitty pouted at the *Women's Era* cover story, 'Mrs India: Married and Beautiful'.

'For me, this is not my first, this is my third. First one, I was very nervous. Just like you, couldn't talk. But after operation, everything's fine. You don't even feel it.'

The nurses walked in to fetch the other woman. Bitty was taken aback when they lifted her – the rubber sheet crackling while they kept the IV intact – into a wheeled stretcher. Hadn't they said 'deliveries first'? No 'careful, ma', no 'look where you're stepping', but Bitty was pleased to overtake the delivery. Halfway across the white corridor, she asked: 'You said deliveries first?'

'Deliveries finished,' said the first nurse.

'The woman in my room?'

'She's not here for delivery,' said the nurse chuckling. 'Same as you, abortion.'

'Third abortion?' asked Bitty as the stretcher rocked past several patient rooms, into a glass door with a red sign that said 'Operation Theatre: Entry Restricted'.

The nurses mumbled but Bitty didn't hear them. They were changing her IV, filling her with a sweet blankness. Along with everything else inside the OT, their grim faces dissolved inside dark shafts.

The whiteness seeped into her eyes, clutched at her throat. What was she doing here, pinned to a rubber-sheet bed in this horrid green gown? What were these tubes tied to her hand? She rubbed her free hand across her belly – no stitches there – where did they cut her? A D&C, they said, no incisions unless required. Were they done? Had they removed it? She hadn't expected it to end so quickly or had it? What was the time? Four o'clock already? Four hours blacked out from her life? A nurse walked in and smiled at Bitty. Why was she smiling now? Because it was gone?

'Would you like some juice?' she asked.

'Yes,' nodded Bitty. Her lips were parched, it was impossible to speak. Was Jesus still there? Yes, he was – the same room, the same vermilion smears on his forgiving smile, *Deliver Us From Evil* printed under his thin face. He was not angry with her, was he? Not that she believed in Jesus, but who knew what was right and wrong? What if she became Christian now? Would He deliver her or had He already? Could she spill her confessions in exchange for release? She envied Christians their easy getaways and more than anything else the anonymous someone they could talk to behind a square box.

So many days, carrying her sprouting secret, Bitty wanted to talk it over, squash her uncertainty in another's solace. Her Callus colleagues were not to be trusted – too talkative – many knew where she lived as well. What if they bumped into her parents? Her relatives were unthinkable; they'd smirk and preen about their own kids, not 'spoiled like Bitty, the loose night-shift woman'. She hadn't intended to gush on the phones but perhaps the signs at the centre – 'Focus on I' – and the trainer's advice: 'Use personal stories to build relationships, customers like to hear about you, especially chatty ones' had goaded her outpouring.

She was used to hearing discharges on divorces or breakups, to effusive sorts who spilled everything but hardly stopped for an agent's problems. Fussy, high-pitched voices that screeched about 'fucked-up lives and now this fucked-up bill'. She was quick at sorting customers as the trainer had taught them into 'yappy', 'picky', 'flashy' or 'snappy' ones. This voice was different – grandmotherly, patient. The call, when it landed on her wires at 2:14 a.m. started out friendly:

'Did you say your name was Betty? I had a friend called Betty, she died last month. I'm so glad to talk to another Betty.'

'I'm sorry to hear that, ma'am. What did your friend die of?'

'Oh, a liver collapse or something. Doctors are so fuzzy these days.'

'Yes, ma'am. How can I help you today, ma'am?'

'Oh, you know, I just wanted to check if my bills are all

250

paid – I have this auto-something with the bank but you never know if things work the way they're supposed to.'

'Yes, ma'am. If you can hold on for two minutes, I will check your account right away.' Ah, thought Bitty, a lonely woman. Calling for no reason, no late notice, no termination warning. The account, as Bitty expected, was all paid up.

'I'm very glad to inform you that everything's paid up, ma'am, no pending bills.'

'Thank you so much, Betty. You've been very kind and courteous. Which state are you in?'

'Illinois, ma'am, close to Chicago.'

'Oh, I've always wanted to visit Chicago. My ex-husband went to high school there. I'm married to someone else now but I sometimes wonder what Chicago would be like.'

'Yes, ma'am, my boyfriend went to high school here. I grew up in Minnesota, moved here for work. And now, I have this operation coming up, I'm *so* glad I'm away from my parents. They're not the sort to approve.'

'Approve of what, dearie?'

'My abortion.'

'Abortion you said?'

'Yes, ma'am, I'm having one next month.'

And suddenly the grandmotherly voice became frantic and shrill: 'They're right, your parents are right. Abortion is a sin. I wouldn't do it if I were you. It's murder, it's stifling God's impulse – dear, I hope you've spoken to a therapist, you must at all costs bring that baby to life.'

There were other frenzied questions slamming Bitty's wires: 'Do you belong to a church? Have you spoken to your priest? You do realize it's illegal?' but Bitty flung the headset off, rushed into the Ladies to heave the raving woman along with yesterday's dinner and today's lunch inside a churning toilet.

Bitty was woken by a squeaking bed. They were wheeling her in, the other woman. Did the nurses say she'd done *it* three times? Or was it a blurred anaesthesia dream? It was Bitty who was now bristling with questions while the woman was savagely silent, knocked out by the operation.

'Still sleeping?' asked Bitty and there was no response, no foot stirring, no murmurs from the other bed.

Bitty asked the nurse to hand her the *Women's Era*, discarded on the floor.

After forty minutes, she heard a rustling, a shifting across the rubber sheet. 'Are you awake?' asked Bitty.

'Hmm?' said the woman.

'Are you in pain?'

'Hah? No, no pain. What time is it?'

'Five-thirty,' said Bitty. 'I have to get out soon, go to work tonight.'

'To work? After delivery? For three months you should rest.'

'Mine wasn't a delivery.'

'No? Then?'

'Just like yours, D&C.'

'Abortion?'

'Yes,' said Bitty. 'First time.'

'How come? Problem with baby?'

'Not married.'

'Oh?'

'What about you? Why did you do it?'

'I have to,' she said. 'In my work, can't carry babies around.'

'Where do you work?'

'I work for a magician.'

'Really? That's wild! I never thought, I mean, what do you do for him?'

'I'm one of his girls – used to be main one – now putting on weight so can't do tricks.'

Bitty remembered her last magic show. After her B.Com finals, the doctor had announced he had tickets.

'At this age, a magic show, how silly! I'm not a kid.'

'This man is a world-class magician,' said Achan. 'And a Malayali,' he added as if that confirmed the showman's supremacy. She reluctantly tagged along, determined to mock his tricks. She rolled her eyes when the Great Wall of China twisted before the Bangalore audience like a braided mountain: 'Now you will meet the famous Confucius and his Chinese parrot.'

Bitty stayed staunchly unmoved, revealing the magician's ploys. Achan disliked her exposés: 'You don't know everything, Bitty, the world is not what you think it is.' When she insisted the woman in the hoop, hypnotized to 'sleep on air', was held by glass wires, Achan refused to bend down and spot the see-through strands. 'Don't spoil the show, why can't you simply enjoy?'

Even Bitty had to admit the Flying Raja, where the turbaned Malayali sprang a few inches off the ground with his fierce smile intact, was fantastic. She searched in vain for glass threads or ceiling magnets clutching him but nothing was visible, not from Bitty's seat. 'How does he do that? Can you see glass wires?' 'Ssshhhh, some people have Siddha powers,' said Achan. 'You won't understand.'

'So you get sawed up on a table?' asked Bitty.

'Used to, now different girl. I help backstage with his costume changes.'

'You must tell me this, how do they levitate? You know the trick where the magician rises a few feet into the air? I can't figure that out?'

'You *think* he rises,' said the woman. 'You see what he wants you to.'

'What do you mean? Mass hypnotism?'

'No, normal vision. We think we see but our sights are limited. If he could levitate, would he *pay* to make my baby disappear?'

'Hmm,' said Bitty. 'How do you feel after this operation? Does it hurt? Does it affect you afterwards?'

'No. No difference.'

'Do you feel guilty?'

'About what?'

'About ejecting this thing?'

'Why should I worry? It's not mine, nothing's mine, not even this body.'

Bitty looked at Jesus again, at the luminous eyes, the unflappable smile. She turned again to face the woman. 'Why don't you run away?'

'I have my plans. Twenty-five years the man's lived in this state, doesn't speak one word of Kannada. A UP man, he made us learn Hindi instead. When it's my turn in his bed, I curse, the worst Kannada curses wrapped in soothing murmurs; he thinks I'm grateful, fond of him even. We plot our revenge, me and the other girls, in his

254

presence. If only he'll bother to learn our language, he'll know we steal his money, spit in his drinks.'

A nurse interrupted them, handed over Bitty's discharge papers. 'You can change your clothes. Billing is downstairs.'

'Before you go,' said the woman, when Bitty emerged in her black Levi's and Alligator T-shirt, 'can you give me 50 rupees? He pays for the operation, nothing else. The corner store sells paani puri and pineapple juice.'

'Betty Adam?' snarled the woman, behind the billing counter. She looked at Bitty in disbelief. 'You arrre Betty Adam?'

'Yes,' said Bitty, in her curliest Midwestern accent. 'On holiday from Minnesota.' She needn't have bothered because the billing woman paid no attention.

When Bitty stepped out of the clinic, a blushing sky scattered reds and crimsons on granite heaps. She walked to the bus, a little unsteady. When she stepped in, she stood near the swaying door without clutching the steel bar, resting against the cushioning back of a double-seat. As usual, many eyes were on her – the jeans-wearing rider – black dots boring into her chest, the tight grip of her jeans. Bitty stared back, unblinking. A man drooling red juice thrust his hips a little too close, almost rubbing her back while his hands slid down the steel column, his fingers an inch above her heaving breasts. Lech. A few weeks ago, she might have prodded him with a safety pin or a decisive blow in the right place. Today she didn't care, nothing felt ominous anymore. She stared back, her lips upturned in a friendly smile, her disposition sunny like her nightly voice on the phone.

Back at work, Bitty expected to feel guilty or relieved. Instead there was a numbness, the taut discomfort of something held inside.

On the phones, her performance was better than ever, she was charming with customers, she intoned perfectly in American-speak, empathized with cranks, coaxed the angry ones. She was held up by the Team Leader as a Callus role model. 'Try to be like Bitty,' he said. Earlier she might have been jubilant at her ascent but not anymore.

At home, where Bitty used to let off her office stress, scream at the coffee not being hot enough, snap at her mother's questions: 'Is that Lata girl married yet?' 'How much was the auto fare?' snort at her father's injunctions: 'Don't eat pineapple with orange, both acidic, not suitable for your constitution,' 'Drink hot water, not cold water,' she was strangely unexcitable, uncomplaining to an extent that her parents worried. She heard her father twisting on his cotton mattress: 'What's wrong with Bitty?' He thought the hormonal imbalances he'd predicted had kicked in suddenly.

At the centre one night, Bitty got a woman on the phone. The first three minutes, the call was uneventful. Till Bitty refused to refund the customer's 'extra charges'.

'Our records show you've used the service, ma'am. I can send you proof of downloads if you need confirmation.'

'I haven't used it. Are you saying I'm lying?'

'Absolutely not, ma'am, I'm just saying I cannot refund your charges. Is there anyone else in your house who might have used the service?'

'In my house? Why do you need to know that? It's none of your business.'

'Was just wondering, ma'am, if someone else has used the service?'

'Hey, by the way, are you Indian?' she asked, despite Bitty putting on her best Midwestern voice.

'Yes,' said Bitty, dropping her accent. Why bother when she knew anyway? She was distracted as well by a spasm, a cramp in her stomach that signalled her monthlies.

'So what's your real name? It can't be Betty Adams?' she said, her voice crusted with contempt.

'It's Bitty Menon.' She pronounced it like Achan did, her n's emphatically nasal.

'Goddamned Indians don't understand a shit. I don't want to talk to a fucking Indian.'

Bitty thought of shabby velvet curtains unspooling on the stage where she watched her last magic show. And the magician surrounded by sequinned assistants, their bodies darting like silver fish. They were packing props into large wooden crates and he was oblivious to the sting in their voices in the general clatter.

'You know something, mahdum,' said Bitty, switching to her nasal Malayali-English. 'I don't want to speak in a fuhking accent eidherrrr. I guess we zimmbbbleee don't have a choice, do we?' Her parents, if they'd been listening, would have understood her headphone speak, the only time in a billion calls. Usually they found her words perplexing.

'I don't get what you're saying,' the customer said.

The phone clicked off at that point. Bitty should have been nervous after a response like that. If Quality Monitors rummaged her records, she'd be promptly discharged. Vernacular Englishes were discouraged on the floor, banned on live calls. Bitty wasn't sure when she left the centre that night if it was a hormonal shift or something else, but she was awash in relief. When she got home, she buried herself in her mother's soft sari: 'Love you, Amma,' she said, snug and fearless, a warmth spreading inside her for the first time in many months.

Durga and Kali

The driver was set to take his wife to the clinic. Everything was fixed. He had spoken to a lab boy, agreed on a rate. He called the contractor, asked for 'early release'. He arranged with three other drivers to ferry his agents. The scan time, after conferring with his mother on Rahu Kala timings, was set for 7:00 a.m. The lab boy said early morning or late night was best, before doctors arrived, before colluding nurses departed. And then at 4:30 a.m., just when Panduranga planned to switch off his engine and leave his parked van, he heard the plodding of Varghese sir's shoes. The Admin Manager rarely visited the basement unless there was big trouble. Last time it had been an accident.

This time he walked to Panduranga's van with a packet. 'Driver, drop this package off. And listen, don't hand this to anyone else. Do it yourself.'

Varghese sir always called him 'driver'. Panduranga was used to that, but tonight it rankled. If he needed just a 'driver', why him? There were five other rogues loitering in the basement, none with scan appointments fixed. Hadn't Nanjundappa agreed to an early release? Before Panduranga could gather his English words, before he could interject with 'No, sir, I not give. I leaving early,' the manager's pyramid shape was swallowed by the basement lift.

The driver called Nanjundappa: 'I won't give the packet,' he hollered, his Reliance mobile quivering in his ear. 'I'm leaving early, I've told you already.'

'What packet?' asked the contractor, sunk in his full-whisky sleep.

'Varghese sir's packet.'

'Then tell Varghese sir. Why call me?' he asked with his blistered tongue. Why did he get commissions then, if he could not intercede on Panduranga's behalf? The no-good blighter couldn't tell pedal from brake, couldn't change punctured tyres and he ran a *transport* service?

'Varghese sir has gone,' said Panduranga. He wouldn't be cowed down by the contractor. Panduranga knew how many 'wives' he had: one wife, one daughter, nestled in a large house, with marble steps, an inside fountain, outside garden, servants' quarters; other wives, strewn around town, no fountains, no gardens, no servants' quarters; he knew them all. If he was a little braver, he'd yank the contractor's safari-suit collar to his dirty hideouts. Yes, he knew how Nanjundappa acted fully decent in the Callus office while his life was filthy like his betel-stained mouth.

'You want to give, you give; otherwise you tell Varghese

you're not giving. This is not my job.' Bastard knew Panduranga could not defy Varghese sir. The contractor swallowed full commissions but at crucial times, dodged duties.

'Then I need overtime,' said the driver, his voice firm.

'From my side, no extra payment,' he said. The mobile clicked off.

If Panduranga had a backup job, at a lower salary even, his arm would stretch out to fling the packet at that manager's face: 'I no dropping, sir, you ask other driver.' Not now; with his wife pregnant, he couldn't afford to cast off secured wages. But what about the clinic? The appointment was not easy. Several weeks, he approached large hospitals, medical centres, private clinics; all said no, no gender tests. The Jayanagar lab boy was a chance find, a neighbour's relative. And the time fixed after many long distance calls to his mother's village on good days, bad days, good times, bad times as if the scan itself could change everything. 'Scan like inside photo,' he told his mother. All interventions, she insisted, should be at auspicious times.

Any other time, Panduranga might have boasted about being singled out by Varghese sir. The manager didn't know his name, but he trusted him more than other drivers. Or was it Nanjundappa who recommended him? Double-faced blighter acted like it was not his duty. The driver restarted his engine. Not glancing at the green packet till his van swerved up the basement ramp, Panduranga was livid, brakes jammed, gears wrenched when he read the Malayali's rounded letters: *Opposite Petrol Bunk, Jayanagar.*

Jayanagar? That was seven one-ways and two unfinished flyovers away. Overtime was not enough, he deserved double overtime for the detour tonight. On the night he asked for early release, other drivers reached home two hours earlier. And why run errands for the same Varghese sir who spat on his honour in his showdown with the Rakshasa? Just when the van swung outside the campus gates onto the main Whitefield road, his mind braked with a squeal. Foolish driver, his hands fixed on the gear box, his eyes shining on the ramp, had forgotten the clinic's address was two bus stops away from the packet's destination. Only ten minutes in the Matador van.

Parking his van on a side road, by a video store shuttered and a drunk crumpled on the pavement, he called the general store opposite his house. In a few minutes, his wife arrived, panting. 'I'm taking you in the office van, be ready,' he told her.

Panduranga knew the rules, no taking office vans for personal trips. The last idiot who drove the van all the way to his village was carted away by the police. Panduranga wouldn't engage in such outings without reason. Tonight was special, the photo of his first son. In any case, Jayanagar was safe, far from Callus people.

Besides, why care about office rogues who did not grant him paid leave for the Sabarimala journey? That Nanjundappa rascal cut his salary when he missed three weeks' duty. In the Bodmas company, Sabarimala climbers were given five weeks without pay-cuts. Even on that mountain, watching for Ayyappan visions in scrubby bushes and sun-heated steps, he saw Nanjundappa and Varghese, hairy spectres shimmering in the hot air, cutting through his faith with disbelieving tongues: 'No special leaves for Sabarimala or any mala. For extra leave, full pay-cut.' At least Varghese sir, being full Christian, Panduranga could pardon for spurning his gods, but not Nanjundappa, godless devil, no belief in anything but his vile self and his loathsome money-making.

Panduranga had another thought: for the first time in his married life, he would travel with his wife inside a maximum chill A/C van without other public. Not only that, he would drive in fancy clothes, not in the Callus uniform. He reinserted his Yesudas CD, unused in the van for six months. The pitch rose – *Saranam Ayyappa. Swamiye. Saranam Ayyappa. Harihara sudhane. Saranam Ayyappa* – but didn't induce the right thrill. Tonight he was feeling reckless like his lorry days. There was no one else around, not even his wife. He stopped the chants, ejected the disc. Back rows were empty, front rows too. Even for the god-fearing, no harm in occasional thrills. He inserted the Rakshasa's CD. Rest of the way, till he reached home, the van jiggled and throbbed. Inside his neighbourhood he honked twice, then alighted from the van, face flushed.

Panduranga had visited the Jayanagar clinic twice without his wife. He was ushered to the backyard, where oval dishes and surgical instruments clattered inside a steaming pot. The lab boy, taller than the driver inside his blue-grey uniform, brimmed with a doctor's authority. Flicking his film-star hair, gloved hands in coat pockets, he explained the process. The scan, he said, will be treated like a regular pregnancy checkup. And the child's gender communicated verbally. The clinic couldn't have its medical license revoked for a measly 5,000 rupees. There were people, he said, who had paid lakhs for the same information. He almost acted like a higher fee would grant a positive response, a confirmation of a masculine presence. Any subsequent abortion would not be covered by the low scanning fee. 'Eksstra,' he hissed when the driver did not even want to conceive of such a scenario. Would he pay 5,000 if all signs did not point to a tadpole-sized Harihara-putra swimming in his wife's fluid?

That morning, the clinic's parking lot was almost deserted. Only two cycles and a beat-up Fiat car. The Callus van, with signs painted on all four sides – *Callus Inc., Callus Inc.,* – loomed over the lot. Fortunately he was many kilometres away from Varghese Sir and Nanjundappa, and from anyone else who could report to authorities about office vans used for family purposes. He hoped the lab boy peered from the reception window, noted the size of his vehicle. Before he alighted, his fingers squeezed the horn. When he led his wife to the clinic entrance, he felt like a Big Boss.

The clinic, built by the generous Bodmas company, was meant for ordinary folks. The red-yellow brick walls could not compare with the glittery glass of the IT Valley. At the reception area, the floor tiles were foot worn and dusty. Not the kind of clinic Callus folks would visit, certainly not those ferried in vans. So it took him several minutes, while waiting for the lab boy on the reception bench, for his mind to connect the blue lips walking towards the billing counter with the blue-lips Madam in his van. It came to him suddenly: third row, second seat. A tremor passed through him. The skin on his face prickled, a hot wave washed over his neck. His wife jabbered loudly about some vegetable she'd eaten and whether that would affect the scan's results. What bothered him most was the van parked so prominently. Blue lips hadn't seen him yet but she'd spot the van. They'd get him now, Varghese sir and the contractor, haul him behind bars. The lab boy approached, his chappals slapping the floor.

'Ten more minutes your scan,' the boy said. 'Advance in billing counter.'

There was nothing Panduranga could do to avoid the woman who dawdled by the billing window. With the same reckless courage that let him slam his lorry through Bihari borders, he rose, fearless.

Did she spot him from the corner of her vision? Did she recognize him? Did she mistake him in his striped terrycot shirt, light blue terrycot pants for someone else? When he turned his neck a little bit sideways her mouth split into a half smile. She'd never smiled at him before, never acknowledged his presence inside the van.

Panduranga reddened because he'd never been greeted in public by a woman who looked like that. His wife shuffled a few feet behind him, did not notice anything. But the lab boy who led them to the billing window watched with new eyes. Did he think Panduranga bartered all kinds of services? Before he reached the billing counter the woman moved away, escorted by a nurse. Fortunately she didn't turn to the parking lot or she'd have spotted the Callus van, impossible to miss the black-orange *Callus–Callus* towering over the Hero cycle. The billing man tapped the window. The driver counted out his carefully sealed 5,000 rupees. At least blue lips did not stay to talk, did not say 'Hi Paan-doo-raangah' in front of his wife.

When the driver handed the advance-paid receipt to the lab boy, the rogue's eyes twitched, as if he had a thousand questions, as if he intended to raise the price.

Panduranga's mind was still on blue lips while his wife hoisted herself on a green-sheeted bed. He turned his head away when the nurse loosened her petticoat strings. 'Lie here,' the nurse said, a Malayali as imperious as Varghese sir. She rubbed gel on his wife's protruding belly. Panduranga had never seen, not in such clarity, the pot shape of her stomach. He hadn't realized this time her belly was larger. Previous pregnancies, she hadn't bloated as much. It must be a boy. And a big boy at that, he thought proudly. When the nurse ran a white instrument on his wife's belly, when some bell-shaped watery image filled out on the black screen, his mind wandered to blue lips. What was she doing here, the Callus agent?

'This is embryo,' the nurse said, running her fingers on a swimming whiteness. Waves broke inside his wife's belly. A curved fish gleamed into view then flashed again from another side. 'Twins,' said the nurse, her many teeth gleaming like a witch. '*Eradu hudagi*,' said the lab boy, whispering the words into Panduranga's ear, as if his wife needed protection from the impending confusion. Not one girl but two. Dark waters pounded the screen broken by white flashes. Panduranga felt like he was sinking inside a cavern. This couldn't be right. Ayyappan would not clown around like this, not after the Sabarimala climb, not after sanctioning the test in company transport.

266

The next week, blue lips climbed into the van like nothing was amiss. She beamed at Panduranga and walked towards the back rows with a new spring in her step. He couldn't tell what it was, but there was something different about her. He watched through the rear-view mirror: she changed her seat, sat two rows behind her usual third-row and chatted gaily with a new boy agent across the aisle. Four stops later the Rakshasa entered. He had a new consort, a feckless creature who boarded with him.

And then at the Trinity Circle junction, where the driver could focus on the back row, he spotted blue lips rising from her seat. Many weeks she had not spoken to the Rakshasa. So Panduranga wondered why she was walking all the way on pointy heels to the last row, where the Rakshasa flopped inside his headsets, eyes closed.

He did not see her. She treaded, despite her needle shoes, with a stealthy silence till she was blocking the villain from Panduranga's mirror. If the driver had not turned his head for a direct view, he might have missed the scissors in her hand, the large kind used by barbers. He heard something snap and because he couldn't see clearly with one eye on the steering wheel, he thought she'd chopped off his ear. But it wasn't that, it was the plastic wire that strung his headset. Cushioned pads slid off the Rakshasa's ears, his eyeballs whirled in all directions. The driver slowed down, crawling in first gear, his focus on the back-row action. Madam lifted the CD player, dangling between surprised fingers, and smashed it on a steel headrest. Panduranga clapped at the TV drama acted out in his rear-view mirror. She wasn't done. She lifted her heel and carefully ground the spike into his exposed big toe.

'Whaa...' said the Rakshasa. 'Bl...oody shit, whaat the bloo... Whaaat are you up to?'

Blue lips said nothing; spun on her heel and returned to her seat.

'Sheett, bloody sheett,' barked the Rakshasa, his toe swollen and purple, his CD player and headphones and conceit all cracked. The driver delighted at the colours washing into his face, at his imbecilic sputtering and baby noises, at the pain streaking from his toe to his shaking limbs. He drove faster into the road's largest crevices, across the bumpiest centre of a mountainous speed bump, his short feet energized by back-row screeches: Aaiiah, aaiiah, aaiiah. Easy to jerk the van and rattle his rider.

By the next signal, the villain was hunched, squealing like a school boy, crumpled without his escort, his new woman scooting to a safer middle row. Blue lips stayed tight-lipped in her seat. They were almost at Whitefield when the driver surged with new courage. He ejected the Rakshasa's CD and reinserted Yesudas. The voice leapt from all four speakers like a rope, willing to strangle back-seat objectors.

When Panduranga reached the basement, all the agents alighted. The Rakshasa hobbled out, muttering under his foul breath. Before he limped to the lifts, the driver had a job to finish; he lifted the Rakshasa's CD from below the dashboard, and placed it like an Ayudha Puja lemon under the rear-wheel tyre. It took him only a few seconds to restart the engine, shift into reverse gear and shatter, like the ugly big toe, the vulgar plastic into a million dots. The hulk did not turn back but his shoulders flinched when the disc cracked.

Next morning when Panduranga got home, his wife showed a new mood, a coy mood he hadn't seen since the last pregnancy. She touched him shyly. Fully tired tonight, the driver patted her belly, shaped like a drum, pounded by small fists and baby kicks. He placed against her bulgy stomach his trembling ears, listened to waters quivering like a fish-filled tank.

She said a Shivajinagar clinic was willing to perform the abortion for 8,000 rupees.

'No abortion,' said Panduranga, who was listening for lusty kicks. He wondered which one it would be – a blue-lipped Kali or high-heeled Durga who would redeem his honour.

Badmash

Shot himself. Basu. Just like that. With a pistol, a Beretta 92FS. Two days after Sashwath had met him. It was Jags who broke the news, 2:00 a.m. India time.

'Bugger have you heard?'

'Bloody 2:00 a.m. here. Heard what?'

'Basu yaar, killed himself. Gunshot. To the head.'

'You've lost it man, really lost it. I met the fellow two days ago, he was fine. Cheerful as ever.'

'Sashwath, I want you to go to his place. Now. His wife called me. She doesn't know anyone else from the old crowd.'

'Wait a minute, can't be Basu. Chap's in some meditation retreat.'

'Listen, bugger, he didn't go to the retreat. Checked into some hotel in this godforsaken place – what was it, some Khandwa on his way to Omka-something – rented a room, shot himself.'

'Fuck.'

'Exactly.'

'Can't believe this.'

'Now move your arse. That woman needs help. And anything I can do, call me.'

The body was covered with wreaths and bouquets before Sashwath arrived. A quiet crowd had gathered in the living room. The CEO looked around and wondered who they all were: employees, relatives, schoolmates, neighbours? It was only 4:30 a.m., but people trickled in, took off their footwear outside the front porch and pressed against the room's white walls. The silence was taut, unbroken. It was not the kind of death that allowed for muted conversations, for murmured remembrances of the person who recently was.

Hunched on a chair, the wife, a thin, drooping woman, held her face in her hands. Some uncle or older relative kept his hands on her shoulders; beside her, two children – much younger than Sashwath's teenage son – stood quietly, too shell-shocked to weep. An old lady, who must have been his mother, clung to his white, wrapped feet. Every now and then, she scolded him in Bengali, with a cry more angry than sorrowful. Sashwath didn't know her language but he understood her scolding tone. Why this impulsive departure, she seemed to ask. Why the hurry? Why swindle me of a peaceful earlier exit? The last time she scolded him like that must have been many years ago, when Basu was a truant schoolboy.

271

Sashwath knew he ought to move forward, speak to the wife. He felt stifled in the small passageway that lead from a shoe rack to the wife's chair. He wondered how he should introduce himself: 'I used to know him at college...' 'I was with him at IIT...' 'I met him two days ago...' He ought to say something reassuring and supportive, but for once, he was at a loss for words. His wife would know exactly what to say at a moment like this.

He looked sidelong at the house: aggravatingly spartan, like the car the man drove. Even with the furniture pushed against the walls, the living room was smallish, unfit for a person of his position. Sashwath might have been relieved by shocking lushness, private excesses that explained this impetuous end. But there was nothing here, no fancy artwork on the walls, just tacky wall hangings that could have been bought from any handicrafts shop. No liquor cabinet, no wooden bar unit, no secret high life tucked into an old part of the city. If this was his house, these unpretentious people his family, then why the distress?

A new bunch of people arrived and moved towards the coffin. Propelled by their sense of knowing-what-to-do, Sashwath moved with them. He inched closer to the head, he peered at his friend's face from above the fibre-glass casing. A loud motor rumbled in the background, an ice-machine to keep the stiffness from decaying. A large part of the face was bandaged in white, several layers to keep the wound from showing. The doctors, nurses, undertakers, had been careful; because below the nose, only half-visible under white bandages, the lips were curved into the same beatific smile Basu always had. As if they'd asked him what expression he'd like to wear for his last engagement with the world.

This time Sashwath studied the smile more closely. There was a cost, he thought, to smiling like this, to hiding real emotions under a surface cheer. He examined the lips carefully, the folds on the double-chin, nostrils stuffed with cotton; somewhere in that neat arrangement had lain an anguish, a despair he hadn't seen. He wondered now, if he had really known him at IIT. Was everything an act? Did his exaggerated modesty and take-it-easy demeanour shroud a self-loathing more treacherous than a simple hankering for money and fame? What did he really want from life? Where did it begin, why did it end? Surely it wasn't the Wall Street collapse? Or was it? Was he unwilling to lay people off, to face weepy, betrayed employees? Too mushy for the ruthless motions of capitalist machinery? Sashwath would never get the answers. He should have spent more time with him at the last conference, looked at his face more deeply, offered help with whatever it was. He looked at the lips again; it was a smile all right, but not anything like his real smile anymore. The lips were pinched together and pasted into an arc, a falseness that Sashwath spotted on Callus agents when he entered the call floor.

He turned back to the crowd, still gathering, trickling into the small room a few at a time, and spotted old faces, shadows from his IIT days. It felt strange standing in this room, all the furniture moved aside and covered with white sheets, to encounter old friends as if the present had merged into the past, as if they were all together again, back-slapping and teasing, audacious about their futures as only the young could be. He wondered what memories Basu had of college. Was he really immune to the taunting and ragging, to being bounced around like a beach ball, not belonging to any group? He must have known he was popular, grudgingly admired for everything he was and everything he wasn't. Surely he'd have enjoyed meeting these people, been charged to realize he had that kind of impact. Sashwath wished he could relay this to his friend, tell him who was here, tell him what they were saying, invite him out for puff pastries and coffee.

Shortly, when light started streaking into the room, two priests arrived. With cream cloth draped over bare chests, threads flopping on heaving bellies, they scattered copper plates, brass pots, dry grass, packets of sandalwood powder, saffron, turmeric. Watching all this, the wife broke down, collapsed into the arms of another relative. Carefully, the feet were unwrapped but the face remained as it was, half visible. Small sprigs of tulasi leaves with dabs of sandalwood paste were placed on the mouth and throat while from an inside room, a brother emerged, a brother who looked startlingly like Basu. Sashwath hadn't noticed him earlier, among the press of mourners. He was shorter perhaps, less stout, but had the same creaseless face. Shorn of all expression, his bare chest draped with a white shawl, he repeated the priest's chants. Numb-faced but with trembling hands, he sprinkled Gangajal on his brother's smiling lips.

Outside, a black van was parked at the gate. Sashwath planned to accompany the body to the electric crematorium. He hadn't spoken to the wife yet, but it seemed pointless now, the woman inconsolable as the body edged towards the door, heaved by four male

relatives. Sashwath cleared the way for them, urged the
crowd to part, led Basu on his last journey out of the
gate. It was a long black gate with a wire mesh at the
bottom, a mesh that scratched the concrete driveway
when dragged open. Beside the van, a dark, leafless tree
was tangled in cable and telephone wires.

Sashwath didn't spot them at first, not while the body
was hoisted into the van's dark cavity; he was about to
climb in, when they accosted him suddenly, the gaggle
of reporters and TV cameras, waiting behind the van.
'Sir, how are you related to Mr Basu...' 'Sir, can you tell
us what transpired...' 'Is this the impact of the global
recession...' 'Was it the Lehman Brothers collapse...'
They were clicking already, a tumult of blue and white
flashes, microphones thrust on his chest, wires wound
around his feet. Sashwath blocked off his face with his
hands, palms turned towards them, like a convicted
criminal. 'Nothing to say,' he said, 'no comments.'

The next week, there was a curious buzz in the market.
Sashwath received another call from the American client:
'We received a tipoff about Mr Basu. Glad we didn't sign
up with him,' the Beam America VP said. Sashwath did
not respond. Americans, he thought, lacked propriety.
It seemed distasteful to talk like that when the chap was
dead, ashes scattered on a river.

As usual, the PR chaps were the last to hear it.
Sashwath heard of it on TV, from one of those shrill news
channels. He was flipping through the nightly roundups
when his friend's face – its crystal smile intact – wafted

into the right-hand corner of the screen. He was seized momentarily by the irrational fear of a ghostly visitation. But the anchor was muttering something about 'Mr Basu Chatterjee's benami shares', something about Basu buying up Bodmas shares through benami brokers. And planning to rig his stock price with acquisition rumours. 'Expecting the stock to rise immensely in the near future, he had borrowed from black-market lenders,' the anchor said. 'But the Wall Street collapse changed everything. With the stock market tanking, there was no way he could repay his lenders. Not even by disposing of his eight hundred acres.'

Eight hundred acres? Basu? What was that unpretentious house all about? Was it like his peaceful, childlike face, another front? For whom, for what? Had Mr Saintly-don't-care-about-the-material-world secretly tucked away grandiose mansions and plusher futures? Why did he project this uncaring, other-worldly image? Did he carry those contradictions inside himself? And was he, at the end, torn apart by opposing selves? Or simply scared of facing his lenders?

Sashwath muted the TV and called Jagdish. 'Listen, where are you?'

'Prague. Why?'

'Have you heard?'

'What now?'

'Basu.'

'What about Basu? Memorial event?'

'Yaar, log on to the net. All these years he's conned us.'

'Basu?'

'Basu was a badmash. Chap bought benami shares,

rigged his stock price, borrowed from the black market.'

'Sashwath, you're kidding. There's no way, I mean Basu, yaar, how can you believe this?'

'It's all over the news now, some broker must have squealed.'

'Shit.'

'Worse than that.'

'Fuck.'

'Exactly.'

The PR agency called on Monday. 'Sir, you do realize you're all over the papers. They're citing your relationship with Mr Basu Chatterjee at IIT. Overall, sir, I would say in your case, there is opportunity for positive coverage. You see, it's very difficult for a slow-growth company to get such media attention.'

'Listen, this wasn't the manner in which... Never mind, let's not talk about this.' He clapped the phone down. Were the PR blokes just half-wits or goddamn cheeky? What did they mean by 'slow growth'? Callus's growth hadn't been slow by any measure. He may not have conned the world like Basu, but he wasn't a low-lier either.

And did they know the American client had called back this weekend? That despite his team mishandling the excess calls they were being awarded more business? And there were new leads popping in as well? Many to do with mortgage-related calls that American banks couldn't handle anymore? The world in a slump and Callus on a fast-track. Of course, everyone wanted everything at the lowest possible cost, so he'd have to prune operating expenses. Perhaps the PR fees should be knocked off straightaway?

Blokes called back. 'Sir, we have several requests from newspapers and TV channels for personal interviews. All the big names, everyone's keen. Would you be interested?'

'About Basu? No, I mean what will I say? Tell them, I have no comments.' A few minutes later, he called back from his BlackBerry. 'Who were the big names? Okay, be selective, line up a few one-on-ones, yes, only foreign TV channels, or wait a minute, maybe high-profile national ones, yes, schedule it with my secretary.'

There was a crew of cameras this time. Many mics thrust into his face. Sashwath was framed by his terrace garden, the purple-pink orchids and golf-course grasses a fabulous backdrop. The movement of his office into the space occupied by the Callus kitchen was abandoned in the light of recent developments.

'Sir, can you tell us what Mr Basu Chatterjee's motivations might have been? Since you knew him personally...'

'That,' said Sashwath, who had filled many post-its with anticipated questions and carefully worded responses, 'is a very good question. It's clearly a manifestation of greed.' That was a good word: *manifestation*. And he pronounced it carefully so they didn't miss it. 'I think Mr Basu unfortunately became a victim of his own hype.

He was desperate to prove himself to the world at large, desperate for any kind of publicity. Now Callus on the other hand, our emphasis from day one, has been on corporate governance. On ethical growth. On moral profits. I've told my investors – I don't mind forsaking higher revenues, larger profits – for manicured growth.' *Manicured*, the word came to him in a flash.

'How do you define manicured growth? Are you saying companies should grow organically?'

'No, no, not organically. Forests are wild, untamed territories, quite different from a garden. Look around here at the terrace garden I've created. Do you know the effort that went into creating this artificial shade, to picking the right plants, here, look here, you can direct your camera on this patch, yes, yes, here, how many people have rock gardens on their terrace?'

'Can you tell us how this affects your business?'

'Yes, I run my business in the same manner. Carefully pruning weeds, picking plants with the right roots. Every day we prune, nip, cut; every week, we change soil, spray pesticides; every month, we reassess the plant mix, light and shade, temperature and humidity, everything changes based on seasonal factors; and it's the same thing in any business, isn't it, controlling every input to create a harmonious entity?'

'An interesting analogy, sir, but how is it different from other businesses?'

'What I'm trying to say is no impulsive acquisitions, no quick-fire tactics to inflate revenues or raise stock prices. There's no point pursuing growth as an end in itself if the growth is not aesthetic...'

'Can you tell us more about Mr Basu's college days?'

'I will get to that later. I would like to expand on how Callus is different from the typical high-growth company...'

An hour later, the cameramen and jabbering journos scattered from the shaded terrace. Sashwath, for the first time, was pleased with the press. They were not too bad if you knew how to handle them. He fondly touched his favourite orchid and thought of Akriti. Maybe he should give in to her cabin request, counselling was critical in stressful times. Basu himself could have done with a counsellor. Just then Jags called. 'Hey, I was just thinking of you,' said Sashwath. 'You know, yaar, I'm so exhausted, I think I need a vacation. Why don't we meet up somewhere, wives and kids, some Swiss chalet or French cottage? Can you get a week off?'

'Let's talk about that later. I'm calling about something else. I don't want to sound like a vulture, but you must know Bodmas is up for sale. Dirt cheap apparently. If you're interested I can organize funds. There's this fund in Hong Kong...'

'Of course I'm interested. They have big-league clients. Their process expertise will be a great fit for Callus.'

'You'll have to do a due diligence first. I mean, if he lied about shares and stuff, you have to be sure about the rest...'

'Yes, of course. But you know this will be fantastic for us. When can I talk to the fund? Who are the chaps anyway?'

'Hey, don't rush into it. We don't want to be impulsive.'

'Of course not. Manicured growth, that's what I believe

in. I'll talk to your people tomorrow. And I'll send a team on Monday to nose things out.'

He walked into his office, to the Jack Welch book that lay on his coffee table. He straightened it to align the horizontal edge with the table's edge. Maybe that's what it was, all this hoo-ha about passion. Staying on track, keeping at it, despite setbacks or hiccups. As he sank into his leather couch, it struck him suddenly, his overarching life goal, his quest for the future. He'd like *his books* scattered around the best business schools and Fortune 500 offices, Sashwath Tejpal's thoughts preserved in hardbacks. He must remember, first thing tomorrow morning, to call the PR blokes and devise a strategy. They might help with a ghostwriter. He buzzed his secretary. Before she responded, an investor messaged him: '*Wld lke to discuss interest costs for nxt 9 months.*' It was never easy, a CEO's life.

Cultural Labour

Yvette and Jimi were seated on high steel chairs in an empty cafeteria. It was 1:00 a.m., past the agents' midnight 'lunch'. The terrace cafeteria overlooked a jumble of steel-glass towers; behind the slender minarets of an ancient mosque protruded iron rods of structures to come; every few yards, construction cranes, silhouetted in dim street lights, lifted dark scraps with slow, pendular movements.

The trainer shifted her attention to the agent seated across the table and drew a questionnaire from her jute bag. She had consciously discarded her leather handbag after embarking on her sociology studies.

'Can we start?' asked Yvette. 'This won't take long.'

'Hang on, give me a few minutes,' he said. 'Need a fag.'

She remembered this boy from her early training days: his wilful stoop, his sullen shuffling through sessions.

Four years at Callus, he hadn't changed. He still wore his wiry Afro, and the stony impenetrability of a know-it-all or don't-give-a-damn. And still an agent? Why hadn't he sought other jobs?

'You work here, right? I've seen you before?' he said, flicking his ash into a Styrofoam plate.

'I was your trainer,' said Yvette, stifling the annoyance in her voice. She couldn't imagine he'd forgotten his two-week training, his first two weeks on the job, in such aggravating entirety. Her sessions were fleeting, all right, but her face and what she did – was that so easy to forget?

'Trainer?' he said, the blank look persisting. 'Oh, yes, I remember now, all that culture history crap. What's your trip now? Why these questions?'

'I quit Callus to do a Master's in Sociology. My thesis is on cultural changes in Indian call centres. I'm going to run through these questions and I want you to give me honest answers. Except for three questions on counselling services, this information won't be fed back to the company.'

'Master's? Where?'

'At the Sociological Research Centre.'

'Never heard of that. Why would you do anything there?'

She had done fifteen interviews but so far there hadn't been anyone this scornful. There had been one who said: 'Sociology? Why don't you do an MBA instead?' and another who suggested she focus on Economics: 'With Economics, you get foreign bank jobs.' This guy's sneer nearly dripped into her already watery tea.

'Because it's the only centre of its kind in Bangalore.' She bit her lip, steadied a quivering hand; she hardly needed to defend her decision to this wild-haired squirt.

Still that disinterested, glassy look. Did nothing stir this guy? The spelling on his name badge, Yvette noted, was not Jimmy but Jimi and then an H., scratched out on the plastic with a sharp ball-point. H for what? Halloween, hell, happiness?

She reeled out the first page – *how many people in your family, how long have you worked here, why did you join this industry, how did you hear of Callus* – and the man responded with blunt 'three, four years, nothing else to do, friends'. Other agents had spilled life histories, frustrations, future plans and she realized guiltily how little she'd known of her one-time trainees. With this chap, this was it, no leeway for more questions.

'What music do you listen to?' she asked.

His eyes lit with a sudden intensity, he said, 'Rock. Only rock.'

'No Hindi music? Not the Bangalore FM channel.'

'I said rock. The rest is trash – not music.'

Of course, the H was for Hendrix. Jimi Hendrix, the rock star, the American icon… but she couldn't ask him about that, could she? She remembered her advisor's injunction: 'Stick to data, the macro-view. Don't dwell on individual stories.' Yes, of course, Dr M., it was unscientific to dawdle, to step outside her survey instrument. Maybe H was for *hogwash*, all the stuff Dr M. kept writing and never published.

❧

Two years ago, Yvette was fired up, inflamed with a passion akin to lust.

It started with an accidental encounter with a roadside vendor. It was a morning after a training session, a few days after Natalie's review. The book vendor had set up shop a few yards from her apartment. While he tried to entice her with magazines – old copies of *Ladies' Home Journal* and *House Beautiful* – Yvette picked up a red book with a large heart on it. She skimmed through the pages, fidgety after the night shift; a book on love, she thought, on healing broken hearts. If only it had tips on managing reviewers. A few pages later, she realized this wasn't a self-help book, no corny tips for friends and lovers; despite a cyclist whistling near her legs, a passerby brushing a lecherous paw against her hip, Yvette stayed riveted.

'Madam, I give you three magazines for twenty rupees,' the vendor said, jabbing her with callused hands and a twisted *House Beautiful*.

'I'll take this,' said Yvette. 'How much?'

Hunched among comics and tech manuals, insensible to the recycler's calls for 'paypaarr, paypaarr', Yvette started reading. This book, this amazing book that had dropped from the skies onto the pavement near her house, described her centre, her job, everything she'd been thinking about as if the author were speaking through her.

Weeks later, when she'd read the book over and over, googled the author, browsed sociology sites, she realized the disquiet she experienced as a trainer was a legitimate way of looking at the world, a way sociologists commonly employed. There were others like her on the planet, others who engaged intensely with crowds but lived on

285

the fringes, who belonged to nowhere in particular but the society of other sociologists. Moreover, their way of looking and thinking was endorsed by reputed institutes and academic departments. Yvette, with her Bachelor's in Education, school-teacher experience and training stint at the call centre, realized how ignorant she'd been of wide tracts of knowledge, of a vast field of study that she was infatuated with like a high-school crush. She visited every bookstore in the city to rifle through books in the field. Several afternoons she burrowed inside musty, windowless libraries. 'Do you have any studies on emotional labour?' she demanded of tight-lipped, shifty-eyed librarians who shrugged at rusty steel shelves: 'You can check yourself. No taking anything out. No, you cannot take notes here.' Rummaging among books published in the '50s, '60s, '70s and '80s, among volumes flecked with brown, she realized how patchy the city's progress was: on the one hand, a booming 'knowledge economy', on the other, paltry resources for other kinds of knowledge.

If rotting shelves and unobliging librarians hadn't quelled the tingling in her stomach, neither did her colleagues' indifference to her new obsession. It was around the time Callus had acquired Bodmas, a larger call centre with five offices in Bangalore, three in other metros. Newspapers hooted about 'small fish swallowing big fish' and the Bodmas 'bailout by Callus'. The board outside their office was replaced by a new one: 'Bodmas: A division of Callus Inc.' When other trainers discussed Sashwath's inflated position despite the worldwide slump, no one paid attention to her abstract musings on 'multiple selves and divided identities'.

Akriti, who had planned to quit Callus, decided to

hang on. 'Sashwath has vision,' she said. 'You know that Bodmas chap didn't have it.' She studied a picture of Sashwath on the People page of a business mag: 'I was horrified when I heard he'd shaved off his beard and stuff. But I think he looks cuter now, don't you?' Yvette didn't respond. She was preoccupied by other things, emotional and cultural effects in agent psyches, shifts too small, too subtle for journalists.

She knew she had stumbled upon something, something she needed to study, document, publish, announce to a larger public. For a few days she dithered: should she, like her agents, live a double life? A night-time trainer, a daytime student? She added up her savings. She could afford, even with tight weekly expenses, a few months off. It was a meeting with her supervisor that prompted her decision: 'I don't know what you're doing, Yvette, but you're sending many vernaculars to the floor. Ops team is pissed. Other trainers crack down on mother-tongues.' He thought Yvette's response – a quick resignation letter – was impetuous. A month later, she registered for her Master's at the Sociological Research Centre.

Her mother was aghast. Flustered already by her daytime browsing of sociology websites, the growing clutter of sociology books, heaps of photocopied articles bunching on her bed and dressing table and bathroom ledge, her decision to quit Callus was the last straw. Maureen let out a flood of abuse so vituperative that Yvette was impressed. 'Where did you learn such words, Ma?' The trainer's other shortcomings were listed: bad skin colour, clumsy makeup, poor dress-sense, failure with the opposite sex 'because there must be a reason for your not having attracted anyone'. Mrs Pereira tried reasoning with her 'insensible' girl: 'Why muddle your head with all these ideas? What will you do with a Sociology Master's?' More worryingly, for a few weeks she stopped remarking about dirt or germs, her attention suddenly seized by the clutter in her daughter's life.

An unfazed Yvette sunk into her courses. The Research Centre, scruffy in relation to other Bangalore buildings, was by IT Valley standards a demolition target: walls spotted with green-black mould, a purple roof with shingles missing, a drying garden, dim classrooms where toilet odours wafted through barred windows, desks scratched out with Sociology jokes – *Chick enters room, everyone watches chick, sociologist watches everyone.*

Eighteen months fled in a fevered haze. Before the last term, students were asked to submit thesis topics. Dr M., Head of the Sociology department and her thesis advisor, hadn't approved of Yvette's topic: *Cultural Labour in Call Centres.*

'Why study glass towers? That's not the real India, Whyvet. Why don't you pick something in a village?' Bald, thick-lipped, big-boned, Dr M. towered over his desk. From under shaggy eyebrows, his eyes wandered across Yvette, lingered on her flat chest.

'That's India too. Those jobs are aspirations for millions, the pinnacle of urban dreams, we have to examine them.'

He was surly about her obsession with a foreign author: 'Don't assume everything written there is relevant here.'

'But this is exactly what's happening and there's more. You must read this book.' That wasn't the right note to strike with her advisor. A classmate had warned her: 'Don't recommend books to him. Doesn't like it if we read stuff he hasn't.'

There wasn't any response, not even a cynical comeback. He turned his back, his bald head glinting at her face.

Four companies refused permission for Yvette's research, a fifth did not respond. Eventually she called Varghese, the Admin Manager at Callus. He agreed to meet her at 12:00 a.m. 'You know our timings, Eewet.'

She met him inside the large conference room. A sprightly man with everything about him blunted – rounded fingers, a stubby nose, a dome-head popping out of a fuzz of black hair – Varghese bounded in with his laptop. After Hurricane Ike, many things had changed at Callus. Not Varghese.

'You've put on weight,' he said, when he spotted her already seated. 'So, you're doing a sociology degree? Why? If you had a problem with night shifts, you could have tried other things. What are prospects for sociologists?'

Of late, Yvette had been crafting wild responses to Maureen's nightly assaults. To 'What will you do next?' she said, 'A Master's in Archaeology' or 'A B.Sc in Oceanography'. To 'What will you live on?' 'Drugs, Mother, just drugs.' In the oak-panelled room, inside the carpeted hush, acrylic lights directed yellow shafts at the table. She looked at Varghese with madcap eyes but her voice was measured and serious: 'In the Anglo-Indian community, sociology is the ticket to marriage. Doctors, engineers, they're all dying for sociologist wives.'

Stroking his chin, the Admin Manager studied her carefully: 'You have changed, Eewet, a sea change. You used to be quiet in Callus.' Propelling his leather-covered executive chair forward, he drew his laptop closer. 'Anyway, send me your project outline, I will review it and get back to you.'

'I mailed it last week,' she responded quickly.

'Oh, that's your outline? Can I see your questions?'

'I mailed those as well.'

'Okay, let me read it.' He peered at the laptop, forehead furrowed. 'Oh, this one, yes, yes, I remember. Lots of pointless questions, why do we need to know what music they listen to, Hindi Pop, English Pop, doesn't matter to us. And why do you want *their* opinions on the job? You see, this will put ideas into their heads. You must understand these are kids, just bachchas, and if you stimulate them too much, they become unmanageable. Ask about this, they talk about that. Won't stick to the point, you see what I mean? Anyway, what will Callus receive?'

'A summary on social and cultural side-effects.'

'Effects of this industry? You worked here for two years, why do you need a survey? We know they're spoilt. Too much money at a young age. Overpaid brats. You will be publishing this report? Where?'

'Maybe a sociology journal.'

'Do you know you're the only sociologist I've encountered in Bangalore? And *I* meet with hundreds of people every day.'

290

'I hadn't met any either, not until I bumped into this book. Of late, I've discovered these journals and hundreds of people who study fascinating things.'

'My point is, why waste time if no one's going to read your report?'

'There are people who will read this, people obsessed with such changes, the slow erosion of ancient cultures, the death of languages...'

'Do they pay a lot? These sociology journals?'

'I don't think they pay anything.'

And then suddenly there was an inexplicable change in the man's expression as if he'd received revelatory tidings on the laptop. 'Can you add few questions to your survey?'

'I don't see why not.'

'Can you ask agents about Callus counselling services? Specifically, how have they benefitted from counselling? Oh, and while we're at it, add one more question, do they think counselling is an essential service?'

'Only counselling? What about other aspects of the job? Like food, transport, the workplace, aren't those concerns as well?'

'See, look here, Eewet. Between you and me, you know how foolish CEOs are. I used to think he was bad earlier but after the recession he's worse. He asked me to cut costs in all areas: remove paper towels from toilets, switch off corridor lights, cut overtime for drivers, etc., etc. All this I've done, but when it comes to women, he loses it.' He lowered his voice. 'With all support functions pruning staff, I suggested to boss we eliminate counselling entirely. Why waste money when the bottomline is at stake? And you know what he said? Counselling is the most critical function at Callus, especially during a recession. He said employee lives might be in danger. That people must keep talking so they don't shoot themselves. Such a deep slump and he allowed her to recruit a team of *junior* counsellors – two morons to report to her. And asked me to build her a cabin with a terrace. And nominated her for Best Employee of the Year.'

'Her? Akriti?'

His eyes wandered to the glass door. 'Let's not use names. I have even seen them...'

'Seen what?'

'You're doing a PhD and you don't know the ABCs of life? You see social effects, cultural effects, all that is fine. What about the here-and-now effects of local menaces – aren't those more important to tackle?'

'All right, I can add three questions. I will inform agents these questions are being used by Callus. But you'll receive summary data without agent names.'

'Of course, that's understood. We're professionals here. By the way, don't leak questions out. Things get around in the office and they'll come in with prepared answers. You know the Indian mentality: don't enter the exam hall till you've seen last year's paper.'

While they scheduled her to-dos, Varghese was a different man: springy, light-hearted, pirouetting here and there inside the glass office, plying her with coffee and cookies and ginger biscuits as if she were a godly deliverer.

On a midnight trip to Callus to transcribe live agent conversations, Yvette waited to 'side-jack' into a live conversation. 'Only few minutes,' the Team Leader said, waving from his seat, till springy-haired Jimutha could plug in Yvette's ear.

The Team Leader was huddled with Quality Monitors in a far corner. When she walked towards him, he had his back turned and she overheard a QM report: 'Boss, this Soumya female is bad, really, really high MTI, I'm telling you, you have to give final warning. Just listen to this call and watch the screenshots, customer's asking for the bill amount, she hasn't budged from the address screen, meanwhile customer's jacking her on all fronts.'

'I want to give her a last chance,' said the Team Leader, turning to face Yvette. She knew him, this chap, one of her ex-trainees. 'Hello, Yvette,' he said. His name badge read: *Azeem Ashraf, Employee Number 2409-0434*. Of course, Azeem, she remembered him, a quiet boy on crutches. He was filled now with a hefty authority, his crutches displaced by an artificial leg. Even as a sceptical sociologist, she had to admit the industry's positive spinoffs. Azeem, a case in point: who would have guessed the tremulous agent would acquire this jaunty heft in his shoulders, this leader position?

'Okay, boss, up to you, it's your team, but I'm warning you, she's yanking down your score. Her communication sucks. No other word for it, female's a recruitment mistake.'

'Nice to see you again,' Azeem said turning to Yvette, jerking back long, rakish hair. 'You haven't started? I told Jimutha to let you listen in?'

'I don't think he knows I'm waiting. Can you alert him again? I need to listen to 50 calls today.'

'Sure, I'll tell him right away.' He turned again to the Quality Monitor. 'Don't send this report to the Process Manager, not yet, I want to talk to the girl first. Let's give her a chance, she may pick up.'

'Process Manager has the report. Anyway your call, boss, your group, your score.'

'Yes, I know.'

'High mother-tongue issues?' asked Yvette. 'Many vernaculars on the floor?'

'Yes, too many. Trainers are not doing their job.'

'After Jimutha, I'd like to listen to that high-MTI girl,' said Yvette. 'The person you were reviewing, Soumya.'

'Don't think you can. Varghese asked me to assign high performers for your study.'

'Did he? But I didn't ask for that, I asked for a random sample.'

'You'll have to ask Varghese, he's coordinating your study.'

He guided her back to Jimutha's cubicle. When the Team Leader tapped the agent's shoulder, Jimutha sullenly handed her a headset that plugged into his. Didn't ask her why she was listening in. Maybe he knew, or more likely, didn't care.

Lights flashed on his digital touchpad: a new caller.

'Good morning, Jimi here, how can I help you?'

'Oh my God, I'm so glad, I've reached an American. I'm sick of talking to dumb Indians.'

Yvette, who'd heard this before, who had earlier fuelled their acting, nonetheless sputtered into the headset. It always felt incredible when callers didn't realize they were talking to 'dumb Indians'.

'It's a relief to hear a white voice on the line. You know these people,' the man continued, 'they take all our jobs and don't even speak English. At least the black guy, the new Prez, he's keeping jobs here.'

'Yes, sir, I see what you mean. How can I help you today?' responded Jimi, unmoved by the customer's outpourings.

'Whyvet, if forty million Indians can learn to speak English, why can't two million learn an American accent? Our country's so vast, we can absorb any difference.' Dr M. peered at her from behind his desk. His whirling eyes scuttled across the staff room's clutter, alighting eventually on Yvette's chest.

'When you reduce it to numbers, it is insignificant, but don't you see it's more than that? The accent switch creates perceptions. We're favouring a form of speech that's an outcome of privilege. The industry hires agents with *neutral* accents. And there's nothing neutral about neutral accents. These are the accents of convent-educated, upper-middle-class Indians. What is the message about our local languages when we rein in their influence in agent speech? There must be psychological effects on high-MTI kids.'

'What's high-MTI?'

'High Mother-Tongue-Influenced agents, kids with strong vernacular accents.'

'How many so-called vernacular agents have you surveyed?'

'Uh... so far, none.'

'None? What are you talking about then? You can't have some vaporous hypothesis without data.'

'I haven't completed my Callus surveys yet.'

'You have to convince me about the ill-effects of cultural labour – so far, I can only imagine positive outcomes. These kids are gaining self-confidence, the ability to negotiate a global world, what are you raising a hue and cry about?'

'I don't know, I have a hunch such changes have hidden costs. Everyone's caught up with job losses in the US, job gains in India, no one's examining costs to Indian agents. Don't you see, Dr M., this is important?'

'Convince me, show me numbers.'

Another meeting with Varghese to clarify if agents had been assigned randomly and if so, why hadn't she encountered any high-MTI ones?

'Of course we've picked everyone at random. Why question that?' She hadn't spotted this at earlier meetings but Dr M. and Varghese were remarkably alike. Looked alike, sounded alike. Except M. was a bit taller. They both had about them an appalling quality that was – there was no other term for it – so very Varghese. And she could hardly, with her hysterical defence of vernacular accents, reform their 'Eewets' and 'Whyvets'. If the Admin Manager were not dressed in Allen Solly shirts and Dr M. in his khadi kurtas, they might have coalesced in her dreams into a single malicious force.

'The Team Leader refuted it. He said only high performers have been selected for the study.'

'Eewet, between us, you know how crazy this business is. Do you think we control anything? Besides, the centre has changed since you quit; we're much bigger now, we hire only high performers. Not like earlier, bad apples and rotten eggs. Tell me frankly, what is your impression on agent quality?'

'Your agents – the ones I've side-jacked so far – act out superbly on the phones, some so well, they mask their skin colour.'

'See, business has evolved. It's different now. We're a leading centre in India. Once the recession lifts, we're planning an IPO. Eewet, you made a big mistake. If you'd stayed back, you'd have made a decent sum.'

'Really?' said Yvette, who was thinking of everything else but the Callus stock. When she pleaded again his lips stayed pursed but the message was clear: *take it or leave it, this is all we'll give you.* If her charm wouldn't work, she'd resort to other means.

The Ops team promised her 60 calls tonight. She walked up to Jimutha's cubicle and tapped his wall.

The agent looked up between calls: 'Thought you're done with me?'

'Yes, yes, I'm done with you. Was wondering if you know someone called Sowmya.'

'Who?'

'I believe her name's Sowmya, I'm supposed to listen to her next.'

'Yvette, right? Listen, I don't know any females here. Why don't you check with someone else?'

297

'Oh, okay, I was just wondering.'

And just then, just when Jimutha rehooked his obnoxious head into his call stream, she spotted her, a woman right across Jimi's cubicle, his neighbour, how could he not know her? Yes, it was her, a 'Samantha – Sowmya' badge pinned loosely on her kurta; there were other giveaways, her expression for one, forlorn and downcast with none of the verve and self-love neutral-accented agents flaunted on the floor.

'Uh, excuse me, Sowmya?'

'Yes?' she said, startled by Yvette's voice. Did she think she was a Quality Monitor, dispatched by managers on some sneaky mission?

'I'm Yvette. I'm doing a study on the cultural effects of offshore call centres. Can I side-jack your calls for fifteen or twenty minutes? I will be a silent observer, will not disturb your work in anyway.'

'All right,' she said, eyes glazed in disbelief.

'This report won't go to anyone, not with your name at least.'

'Doesn't matter,' she said.

Her phone blinked, she pressed the flashing button. Her nervous, rabbity movements reminded Yvette of an ex-trainee, a Malayali woman, a Bitty something.

'Good morning, this is Samantha speaking, can I have your name and account number please?'

'Yes, Samantha, can you give me my monthly bill amount? My name is White, my account number is 34233.'

'Thank you, sir, your bill amount is $342.'

'Great. By the way, are you Indian?'

'Yes,' said Sowmya. Yvette perked up, her pencil poised to transcribe the fiendish abuse she had heard often.

'That's wonderful,' said White. 'I've been to Goa, fabulous place. Are you in Bangalore?'

'Yes, I'm in Bangalore.'

'Awesome. It's cool talking to an Indian. I have many Indian friends and I love your food, tandoori chicken, mmmmm.'

'Yes, sir,' said Sowmya.

'Thanks so much for your help. I really appreciate it.'

The fifth caller drew Yvette's pencil to taut attention.

'Yes, I have a fucking problem with my fucking bill and I have been waiting on your fucking line for fifteen fucking minutes and now I get a fucking Indian on the line?'

'I'm so sorry for that, sir, can I have your account number please?' Sowmya's American accent dropped entirely.

'Are you a fucking Indian? I don't want no goddamn Indian. I want to speak to a goddamn white fucking American. Not to some fucking nigger Indian, you hear me?'

'Sir, I understand, sir, yes, I am in India, but I can help you solve your problem.'

'Listen, you fucking bitch, I want to speak to no fucking Indian, you hear me.'

'Sir, sir,' sputtered Sowmya. 'Please don't ask me to transfer the call, sir, please I can help you with your problem?'

'You goddamn Indian, I don't want your goddamn fucking help.'

'Sir, sorry, sir, please I can help you, sir, please give me your account number.'

'My fucking account number is 4568. I have a fucking bill that was never delivered and now I have a bloody termination notice.'

'Your bill, sir, was delivered on September 4th. However, I will ask for one more bill to be sent to your account.'

'Yes, and can you cancel this fucking termination?'

'Yes, sir, I will extend your payment period by a week.'

'You know something, you're not so fucking bad in spite of being a goddamn Indian.'

'Thank you very much, sir. Have a nice day.'

An acquittal after all that? Yet the woman's hands quivered on her digital touchpad. Yvette was overcome by an emotion researchers were not expected to harbour, an almost maternal tenderness for this clear-skinned woman with sullen eyes and shivering lips. Suddenly her study seemed too detached, too academic to describe the abuse pouring down the lines. It wasn't just her 'goddamn, fucking' accent, it was her submissiveness. She'd seen it in her training classrooms as well: poorer kids didn't engage in 'call control' in the manner of middle and upper-class agents.

When she questioned Sowmya, she denied any strain begot by her acting on the phones. She loved her job, she said. Loved the salary, loved the van ride, loved talking on the phones. And no, she was not affected at all by abusive callers. And no, it was not an effort to speak like them. Yvette left the centre filled with a new disquiet. Had she overplayed the effects of 'cultural labour'? Was it less alienating than she imagined? If Sowmya claimed to cope, so could others. Eventually these agents acquired the mannerisms of the ruling classes. Did they leave these jobs more empowered to negotiate a global market? Were there individual gains and community losses? Should that be the thrust of her paper? It was trickier to quantify community losses. How would she project that to a numbers-driven Dr M.?

Eight weeks later, her 50-page thesis spilled from the department's laser printer, page by miraculous page. Every comma checked, every line justified, headers and footers carefully formatted. If she'd known two years earlier how perilous her journey would be, she might not have started; each time she planned to quit, she was arrested by time already sunk into the project. Now when it was finally done, she was filled with an indescribable lightness.

It was a surprise when two days later M. invited her for a final review. From behind a shroud of unread papers, he tapped his fingers on Yvette's submission. 'I want to make sure your paper will get through the committee,' he said. So far, he'd shown scant interest in her work. Why such sudden regard? There was something in his tone that day, a kind of goodwill that was different from earlier discussions.

'Whyvet, I have only few suggestions. I've marked them out in pencil. For example, you say, "*As American companies vied with each other to set up their back-office operations in Bangalore, the name of a city morphed into a verb.*" You must note that Bangalore itself has moved away from its Anglicized name. It's no longer Bangalore, it's Bengaluru.'

'That's a good point. I'll add that.'

'And just one more thing, on page 31 you say, *"When customers abuse agents for being Indian, for not resolving the problem, for long wait times, agents put callers on mute and curse in vernacular languages. One agent said: 'When I release pressure, I need to let go of English, I need to curse in my mother tongue.'"* Can you remove that?'

'But why?'

'Whyvet, this is an academic paper. We're not interested in anecdotes.'

'Okay,' said Yvette, resigned to agreeing with anything else he had to say. For the first time, Yvette noted, he wasn't leering at her. Perhaps he was not as dismissive as he appeared and wanted her to make it?

'I know you can do it, Miss Pereera. Next time, I look forward to meeting *a qualified* sociologist.'

'We did not expect a negative report,' said Varghese, tapping the conference table. 'You never warned us about this.'

'I don't think it's a negative report. There's nothing against Callus or any other company, I'm merely documenting the effects of a larger phenomenon.'

'Still, it's not correct on your part to say we are practising "cultural labour". Was that the term you used?'

'It's not about practising cultural labour. I'm identifying the effects on agents. You can use this report to sensitize HR departments.'

'Effects you're talking about are too abstract. In any case, does not matter. Where did you say this will be published?'

'In a sociology journal.'

'Ah, yes, in that case, we don't need to discuss this. No one reads those journals. But do you know, everyone's writing these days? CEO's on the lookout for a ghostwriter. For a book. Something about running businesses during recessions like watering terrace gardens during droughts.'

'Really? I guess the recession uncovers new yearnings.'

'What was your finding about our counselling services?'

'You'll find details in my report but overall, agents are satisfied. They think counselling is a critical service.'

'*Critical?* What sample size have you surveyed? Your finding is not accurate.' The manager's mobile vibrated on the table.

'Seriously? What? Terrorist threat? Extra calls where? Shit, we're screwed.' He turned to Yvette. 'I have to leave, there's a crisis.'

'A crisis?' asked Yvette. 'Where?'

'This has nothing to do with your study, does it? If you will excuse me, I need to attend to this at once.'

Yvette dawdled inside M.'s room. The staff room was deserted. She clutched a Thank You card for M. The committee had approved her paper with few changes. Suddenly she saw them: a pile of glossy journals, all brand new, not a speck of dust on them. Foreign journals? She hadn't seen them in the library ever. Did M. get a grant of some kind? How did he afford these sociology glossies? Her eyes ran through the stacked spines: all blue and maroon. All the same ones, the *Global Sociology Quarterly*. She lifted the first copy, flipped through the Contents page. She almost missed it, almost did not read the fourth line from the bottom: 'When the Mind Moves Offshore' by Dr. M.

On page 34, the lead announced in bold fonts: **It's the revival of the spice trade. This time, we're bartering cultures, exporting minds.**

It took all of Yvette's strength to pick herself up and rush her tear-streaked face into the toilet across the corridor, the Thank You card crumpled in the hallway.

A week later, the paperwork for Yvette's graduation was complete. As she emerged from the administrative block, the blue sky clouded over with puffy grey, her mind exploded with Dr M.'s late-life success in sociology circles. One article and he was invited to three conferences, offered two resident-scholar positions. It was no longer shock, or distress, but a self-loathing her Master's status could not mitigate. Her thesis, at the end of the day, felt like a void, a two-year effort thrown into a dim emptiness.

When she looked up, slivers of sunlight slid off billowy edges. There was more to all this than her 50-page thesis. Varghese was right, she was dealing in abstractions, stuff people couldn't relate with. She couldn't let this fizzle out, could she? Like the manager said, who reads sociology journals anyway? What was that article about Indian fiction writers burgeoning by the week?

When she walked towards the centre's gates, she pulsed with new resolve.

Bibliography

Hochschild, Arlie, *The Managed Heart*, University of California Press, Berkeley and Los Angeles, 2003

Khera P.N., *Armed Forces of the Indian Union – Operation Vijay: The Liberation of Goa and other Portuguese Colonies in India*, Ministry of Defence, Government of India, New Delhi, 1961

Acknowledgments

This book was inspired by *The Managed Heart*. So my thanks foremost to Arlie Hochschild for her seminal work and for encouraging this project from an early stage.

For cheerleading, for excellent edit suggestions: Katie Boyle, Shivmeet Deol, Ted Glasser, Sam Miller.

For sage advice, for believing it was possible, for assistance of all sorts: Smrithi, Nayana, Supriya, Theresa, Carolyn, Meeta, Rajiv, Atul, Percy, Naim, Sean, Md, Maneesh, Mishi, Beulah, Deepika, Samir, Divya, Sangeeta.

To the whole extended family for being the bulwark of support: Amma, Bhuvana, Aruna, Srivats, Revathy, Dash, Lavoo, Arjun, Vees, Deepa, Rahul. To the little spots of sunshine: Ananya, Dhruv, Tarika.

To the ones who bore the brunt of my being locked in for four years, for being the lights in my life: Sekhar, Nivrith, Rishika.